COURTING THE LION

THE TIMEKEEPER SERIES
BOOK TWO

S.E. REICHERT

5 PRINCE PUBLISHING
5PRINCEBOOKS.COM

Published by:

5 Prince Publishing and Books, LLC

DBA 5 Prince Publishing

PO Box 865

Arvada, Colorado 80001

This is a work of fiction. Names, characters, places, and incidents are the product of the author's imagination or are used fictitiously. Any resemblance to actual persons, living or dead, events, or locales is entirely coincidental.

Digital ISBN: 978-1-63112-428-0

Print ISBN: 978-1-63112-429-7

Cover design by Marianne Nowicki

Interior design by 5 Prince Publishing

First Edition

F11172025

For more information about this title, visit: www.5princebooks.com

To Love,
and to all of those who have suffered in denial of it.

ACKNOWLEDGMENTS

I first and foremost must thank my amazing sensitivity and beta readers who helped me write a book that was worthy of Richard and Thomas's love. Scott Coronet, Pascal Barrette L.T. Larson, Emily Braunberger, Misty Combs and Carissa Morris. This is a new adventure for me, but the minute I met Dr. Richard Shaw, I knew he needed a love worthy of his heart, thank you all for your help in writing this story.

I want to thank Bernadette Soehner and 5 Prince Publishing. This is not a safe world to express love in all its forms, and you gave me a place to hold a beautiful romance that deserves to be told. Thank you for taking this chance, on Thomas and Richard, and on me.

Thank you to Cate Byers... always, forever. But especially when you have to sort out whose penis is whose when only one pronoun is being used. A good editor is worth absolute gold. You are so gracious and patient with me and I learn more from you than from an MFA program.

Thank you to my daughters, Madelyn and Delaney. You are my moon and stars, my sunshine and rainbows. You are my purpose. You teach me how to be better. You teach me how to be brave.

Thank you to my friends and fellow writers at Writing Heights. The ones who read my books and the ones who just prod me to keep writing. Lauren, Lisa, Chris, Jorie, Bobbi, JC, and Amy. Also, to Nina (9-uh) who gives me hope when the world hurts my heart deepest, you are a kindred soul.

A huge thanks to Bonnie McKnight and Josh Palubicki who keep the business running so I can do this occasionally.

To Matt. Because every girl should have a poet as a best friend.

ALSO BY S.E. REICHERT

COURTING THE LION

THE FUTURE DUKE OF MARLBOROUGH

War was hell, and Thomas had his fill of it. He no longer had the stomach for the blood, the gore, or the death of humanity that fell with countless lives. While he was good at his job, a strong warrior and in defense of the King, he did not believe in the forcible overtaking of land in the name of anyone, God or man. He was weary. He longed for rest, for a quiet, fire-lit room away from the groans of the dying, the clashing of blade, and the iron smell of blood spilled.

He knew with certainty, the day he killed seven men within moments, between his blade and musket, that he needed to leave the front lines. But the only thing that awaited him at home was a title and the expectation of a wife and heirs to the family name. He trudged through the heaps of overturned soil and scattered bodies, seeking life.

Which was worse? he thought numbly. A life where he at least had some sense of freedom? The occasion to pursue some sort of career, the comradery of his unit, even with the strange and awkward times that his heart questioned where his loins lay? Or to be tethered to the 'fairer sex', most of whom he knew to be cold and calculating, eager to send him in to battle and a hopeful death? Children he did not mind. They were full of wonder and reminded him of the opportunities for wild and adventurous hours that he himself had tried to escape to. But a wife; the idea sat uneasy with him. He knelt beside the body of one of his young soldiers, and gently closed the man's eyes.

As he stood and looked out on the battlefield, where the smoke from cannons settled into the low valleys between, he thought back to when he was most happy. He wanted to be free. To paint, he thought as he flicked his saber and the red droplets hit the ground. He wanted to study the natural world, do something useful with his birthright. Travel, establish libraries, exercise the country's mind instead of its might. He wanted to find the company of a learned man with whom he could talk for hours. He wanted something more from such a man, something he feared. Eternal damnation nipped at his heels with such thoughts.

Love and solace were two things Thomas would never know.

So it was better to die in battle than to think of the rest of his life in lonely nights, tied to a title and lands that he did not want, wedded to a woman he could not love, and required to extend a family name, that served a crown above humanity. As he made his way through the wreckage of what he'd wrought, helping fellow soldiers up from the ground, gently covering the faces of those who would not ever rise again, he knew that his eternal resting place would be in the soil, next to his brothers. There was no other way.

THE LION OF THE LIBRARY

Doctor Richard Shaw was in his sanctuary, the library, listening to Taylor Swift's latest release through his AirPods. His only real place of comfort was settled in between his books, and sipping contentedly on his rose matcha, oat milk latte. Especially after the last three months. It had really begun with Lillian Byrne crying in his library. Which then led to her connection to the journal, left to him by his great-great-great grandmother. Which then led him to the discovery of time travel, via thin space or portals in the fabric of time. He had helped Lillian jump back in time to be with Matthew Blackwell, the doctor she'd fallen in love with during her first accidental trip to 1812. It was Matthew's journal that Richard had been left. But with the disappearance of Lillian at the base of the Westbury Manor stairs and the subsequent changes in the good doctor Matthew's journals, subtle shifts had become noticeable in his everyday. Shudders through the stacks of the library, strange dissonance in events he remembered from history and what was now found in the library. He thought often of Lillian and what wild and new timeline she and Matthew were instigating. Even knowing that there was adventure to be had, Richard told himself he wasn't ready for it. Yet he had dreams of Lillian disappearing into time. And he found himself researching similar incidents and any possible clues about the secret society of Timekeepers Lillian had spoken of, whose job it was to keep the timeline intact.

He told himself he did not want adventure, even when he travelled to Westbury and found, in its small and crumbling museum, a map that was said to belong to one Colonel Mayfield. He told himself that it wasn't really stealing, when he took the map from the unlocked plexiglass case. He told himself it was safer that he should have the map of portals, then it falling into the wrong hands.

Richard Shaw did not want adventure, but he still kept the map, always in his jacket pocket, close to his heart. He took it out at night and traced over the odd and mathematical lines drawn with starred points at certain intersections, which he assumed were portals to different times. No one should lay hands on it, maybe not even himself. But Richard had at least a mind to preserving time, to understanding the responsibility of wielding such a power. The historical implications could be disastrous if the map were to be used by someone with poor character.

As the months progressed, unease seemed to settle in Richard's world. Nothing he could directly put his finger on, but strange shifts in what he thought he once knew. He referred often to Matthew's journal. The lonely entries that had resided in them before Lillian had returned to Matthew were faded and gone. Lillian had erased Matthew's desperate past, and Richard couldn't help but wonder what new future they would write. What might that do to the timeline? Thoughts of this gave Richard some cause for concern. If the doctor had not gone on to Wales, and his practice of helping others, what possible implications would it leave in the present day?

Richard used his worried energy to start running again, and joined a gym to lift. His large frame transformed into something quite impressive. He hadn't spent that much time sweating since primary school, but now his hard work showed in his large and muscular physique. Doctor Travers stopped mocking him about his pastry intake. In fact, everyone looked at him with a sense of fear. Some of them with desire. He was no longer teased.

He truly had become the Lion of the Library. He kept his beard trimmed short, oiled and maintained, always covering his cheeks, particularly the left side. He didn't want to see what lay beneath it, let alone show it to anyone else. When he wasn't running down the road, listening to various historical podcasts, or slinging weights around like a goddamn barbarian, he was devoted to studying the history of England, anything that might tell him where Lillian ended up and if she'd survived.

If he did not see her in history, he hoped it was because they were keeping low profiles and trying not to muck anything up. Did they ever have children? Were their heirs somewhere in Great Britain today? Where in the hell was Lillian? He tried not to dwell too long on the great romance he had helped to save. He was lonely himself. The dating pool for a man of his intelligence and quiet life was shallow indeed. It did not help that he was painfully shy and did not prefer the crowded nightclubs or dating apps of the day. Impersonal and hook-up culture did not interest him.

He much preferred books to people. In the fervor of his renewed studies, he always seemed to come back to a singular fascinating figure from sometime after Lillian's era. Richard took the well-loved book out from his drawer, looked around for patrons who might interrupt, and delved into the pages like a starving man into pudding. He read and reread the same story, once and again, on repeat. Every time gleaning something new from the history of a man he so longed to meet.

His Grace Thomas Alexander, Duke of Marlborough, fifth in line for the throne of England and eldest son of Duchess Anna Roquet and Duke Alexander Marlborough. But it wasn't his born nobility that fascinated Richard. It was the undeniable progress the man had sparked in the era with his unfailing commitment to the education of Britain's poorest population, the advancement of the arts, and the establishment of the first library systems. Richard would be lying if he said he wasn't the slightest bit in love. The young duke never married, as he was a soldier and officer in the King's Royal Army, before settling into his role as duke sometime after the war. It was a faulty heart, historians speculated, that had ended his grand and illustrious career in the arts.

The story of adventure and romanticism told that after Thomas was injured in battle, and saved by a young doctor on the field, he devoted his recovering years to the intellectual advancement of the country. In doing so he established some of the greatest social systems that contributed to the academic and intellectual excellence of the current century. In a system of monarchies and colonialism the duke's greatest accomplishment was not in his rise in the army, or his bravery and strength in battle, but to build libraries and give funds to the arts. He fostered the poor houses of London that helped to alleviate the extreme poverty of the time.

Photos of the portraits of Thomas were dusty and faded. A strong jaw and boyish light in his eyes. Not so hardened from the battles he must have seen, but perhaps softened by them. Richard spent hours, staring into the blue of his eyes and wished that the man would have had a family. Someone of his line, that might be here in his time. Someone who might find him, a kindred soul in need of a lion. His loneliness roared somewhere in his chest.

It was no matter. The past was the past. Nothing could be done. Richard stopped when he felt the map in his jacket pocket. It felt warm. It tempted him with the possibility that the past actually *was* accessible. The junctures and stars, the lines of a map that he knew held meaning, could very well lead him to Thomas.

Richard shook his head. The past was not to be tampered with. He sighed and traced his finger over the man's jaw and the typeface of his name below the photo of the portrait that hung somewhere in some grand hall, in a manor belonging to someone who had no idea of the caliber of man Thomas Alexander had been. The page was becoming creased. He'd had this particular book on the history of England out on loan for months. More than just admiration, Thomas was someone that Richard looked to as an example. That he might one day become such a man. That one person could do so much for the fate of the world. For the future.

All he could do presently was keep the records organized, shush the students, and try to keep that pest Hoskins from stealing his best specimens through shady loans. Richard scowled over his glasses. Even if it was the best he could do in the present, he couldn't escape that he wanted more. Something else. He wanted adventure. He wanted to test his mettle. He wanted something deserving of his heart.

Richard's last two relationships had both been fleeting and shallow. Converging and careening paths that would not stay together. Such was the problem of dating within his professional pool. They were all busy with their own research, and publications, and climbing the academic ladder for future pedestals. Such ambitions all seemed like fading monuments to academia as far as Richard was concerned. He traced over the better man's face before closing the book. He put it carefully back in his desk drawer and switched off the light.

A strange rustling filtered through the empty library, from no source Richard could find. It was soft, at first, sifting from the back of the hall, rattling the oldest collections, up through the stacks and shelves, like a low whistling banshee that sent a shiver up Richard's back. It ruffled the posters on the wall and the small signs that hung by chains reminding students to be respectful and quiet. It danced through potted plants and rustled the draperies. Richard watched the minute movements and reached for the map in his jacket pocket without taking it out. It was warm, but that was of no consequence as it had been pressed against his chest all day.

He patted it softly before gathering his things and locking the doors on his way out. Richard took the tube to his apartment, a short walk from the station. He must have been tired or spent too long in the obsession of the past. Because everything seemed slower on his way home. The train seemed sluggish even as it made its way under the grit of the city. The streetlights' glow seemed duller. Even the wind shifted and felt confused as it ruffled his dark hair. If Richard believed in ghosts, which he absolutely did not, he would have thought there was a great haunting in the air. Like a shudder in the very fabric of the world.

When he'd eaten, brushed his teeth and crawled into his large, lonely bed by himself, he pulled the map off of his bedside table and opened it. He must be tired; the lines and points and strange symbols were blurred. He sighed, of course they were, he'd left his glasses in the bathroom.

No matter. He was sure with a good night's sleep it would all be better by the morning.

3

A BEAUTIFUL DAY TO DIE

Today was the day. Thomas was certain that the scouting party's information had been sound and the start of another bloody battle was on the dawn's horizon. He felt sick to his stomach. Though there were many things he had not yet done, there were also many he knew he could never do, no matter the length of his years. And if you could not live with your own heart, find solace and rest, and love, then what was the reason for existence? Better that he should die in battle on a quest to save any one of his men. Better he should do something brave as his last act on Earth. To be immortalized as a warrior.

He went about his normal duties. Washed his face with nearly clean water, and shaved. He abhorred a beard. He dressed and combed back his hair. Regiment men had longer hair but his was always maintained. His, a dark sandy blond, was thick with a slight curl, and in need of a good washing.

But no matter, they could wash his body when his soul was departed. He finished shaving his face with the sharp blade of his dagger and put on his red coat with its golden buttons. He did not wear armor, nothing to stop blade or bullet from finding him. And yet he hoped for not a quick death, shot to the head and done, but one where he could witness the life draining from him, and know in confidence that he would not survive. He wanted a chance to look once more upon the world, feel the dirt beneath his fingers, see the blue sky through the hazy cloud of gunpowder smoke. He only wished to meet his maker a better man than when he lived. He said his prayers, quietly, as he tied on his saber and cleaned his musket. He would be on the front lines today, with his men, not behind them. He prayed that God would help him to meet his destiny with honor. Thomas strode out of his tent, content with the last morning of his life.

Richard woke to strange and disturbing sounds. Sirens going off from different directions around his flat. When he looked out of his window, the sight of his street was unfamiliar. It was trashed, and the windows of the shops across the street were boarded up; some broken. Small fires in cans raged on side streets stretching out as far as he could see. It was gray and dismal and he counted seven different police vehicles moving with haste in the short time he stood at the window.

"What in God's name?" he whispered and turned on the telly to see what he'd missed in the scant few hours of sleep. The news was confusing. There were riots "again". Masses of humans were without food or medical care and were wandering the streets. Rioters were protesting the governmental shut down of schools yet again and Dictator Jensen was now demanding that any woman caught with a book be stoned to death.

"Bloody hell," Richard whispered and quickly ran for his clothes. If books were being banned and the government was dictating what knowledge was allowed, what in God's name had happened to the library? What about Oxford? Surely it was still safe? He took his coat and found the keys to his office. He pulled out the map. He briefly looked it over, but the lines and points that were there before were blurred, as if water had been spilled on them and he couldn't make out any of the portals that had been there just yesterday.

"What is going on?"

He hurried across town, not pausing to linger on the streets, and in awe of the propaganda and hateful posters on the walls of the tube. The cars were mismanaged, dirty and empty. Like no one in their right might would ride them. But Richard did not have a right mind now, he needed answers.

When he arrived at the university, he found it fenced off and had to climb over the brick wall to get in. There were only a few people in the halls and they shied into their offices when they saw him coming. He didn't recognize any of them.

When he came to the doors of the library, he was confused to find them boarded closed. He employed an iron crowbar, discarded in the rubble by the door, and beat against the boards, shuddering through the large muscles of his back, arms, and legs until he broke through it. Inside it was dark and smelled like ash. And burning. And sorrow. Richard yelled and covered his mouth as the echo of his despair rattled through the nearly empty shelves. Only charred piles remained. Only the tattered and burnt edges of a few tomes fluttered in the air let in with his arrival.

"No! What is this? No!" He ran to the vault, unlocked the door with his key and tore down the stairs. The sanctuary had not been found but only a few books remained. Richard closed his eyes and took a deep breath.

Something had happened to history.

Something had changed overnight.

Frantically, Richard searched the piles that felt familiar only in the way having déjà vu might. He'd been thrust, overnight into a different timeline. Which meant...He scrambled back upstairs to his desk and found the one lavender journal of Matthew

Blackwell. Richard grabbed it and flipped through it quickly. Every page was full, but not of the story Richard already knew. The adventures of Lillian and Matthew spanned their entire lives in this journal. He flipped to today's date. Lillian and Matthew had planned a nice holiday on the western coast. It was rumored that the British and French were at war to the south. Though Lillian had suggested they could help with the wounded, Matthew was determined to keep her safely away from the danger of battle. Richard shivered, placed his finger over the date. Something inside of him drove him back down to the stack of books.

Near the back of the vault, in a box labeled 'important', Richard found his volumes of the History of Great Britain. He checked the quiet doorway before, locking himself in the vault with the remaining books and opened the first volume, searching quickly for what had changed. What had happened so long ago to send the country on a tailspin of ruin?

All seemed to be going along as he remembered. Up until 1815. He read the chapter over and over again, sure that he must be mistaken. Sir Thomas Alexander had died in the battle of Manchester. He was stabbed through the heart by a French general's bayonet. In the service of his friends and fellow soldiers, he had a brave death.

But it was not the death he was meant to have. It happened years before he should have died. He should have been saved in this battle from his injuries. Thomas Alexander had taken his second chance at life to do something good for his country. An early death meant that the work that he had done after the war to help strengthen the social and educational systems of the country, had never transpired.

"Why was he not saved?" Richard closed the book, closed his eyes. Thomas was attended to by a doctor after the battle of Manchester. A young doctor who had devoted himself to the war. That doctor had helped Thomas with insight to see the importance of rebuilding Britain as an educated and egalitarian society. The doctor had a vision of the future, and in turn had influenced Thomas Alexander.

The young doctor.

Richard opened his eyes and they landed on the journal. The violet journal filled with new adventures and travels of Lillian Byrne and Doctor Matthew Blackwood. A doctor who, until his love returned to him in a new timeline, had spent his lonely days without her, wandering the country, spreading socialist ideas and saving handsome future dukes on the battlefield.

"Fuck me," Richard breathed. This was all the fault of love. Matthew never saved Thomas on the battlefield. Thomas had died far earlier than he should have. Richard took in a deep breath, and pulled out the map. He was the only one who knew what happened, and how the world was supposed to be. He alone knew how the events had collided and misfired to lead them to this hell. He opened the trifolded paper map that felt thin and brittle in his large hands.

"Show me. Please show me where I need to go." The lines and dots blurred and shifted, Richard let his eyes unfocus and blur with them. "Please." When he focused again, a spiked star appeared on a small outcropping, twenty miles west of Oxford, on the edge of a field now overtaken by a shopping mall. It glittered, shimmered and faded. Richard didn't know if he had time, or even if this portal would be the right one. He only had to believe that the timeline didn't want to be on this course and if he asked it for help in correcting it, that it would oblige.

Richard packed up the journal, the volume accounting Thomas's untimely demise, and anything he could find of use in the back office. There were some old costumes from a probably now non-existent theater department. He put the simple breeches and flowy white shirt in his bag. This was surely suicide. But what other choice did he have? If the map was indeed trying to help him, it would put him in the path of

Matthew and Lillian and they could formulate a plot to help find the battle and save the duke so he could go on to then save the country.

It was the stupidest, worst thought-out plan he'd ever created. But it was the only one he had.

4

PLANS ARE HATCHED AND FOILED

The intensity of this battle was unlike any Thomas had fought in. The French were destructive and fighting against moral code. They'd destroyed one of the only roads out, so supplies and further aid would be nearly impossible to reach. They fought as desperate men, with nothing left to lose. But Thomas was desperate too. He'd cut his way through the middle, fought alongside two of his most trusted soldiers. They were more than just that. They were friends. Friends that had families to go home to. Thomas only had them and his deep desire to never go back to a world where he could not be himself.

The minutes felt like hours as they tore through smoke and bodies, laying waste to enemy soldiers by any means necessary. Thomas was brutal and felt pieces of his soul cleaved away with every life he took. He could not survive this battle. He only hoped that God would forgive him and tally the losses up against the gains of saving his friends and fellow soldiers. He would make his death glorious.

∼

Richard made his way through the city as inconspicuously as possible, utilizing abandoned streets and back alleyways. The portal was in a field just beyond a dilapidated shopping center. Richard caught a train to the closest depot. Riding it, his heart was heavy and sad at the state of the poor; the women, the children, the lost-eyed men on board. Each looked as though they would rather die than continue on in this life.

What would a life without books be? Without knowledge? Without free thought? Tears came to his eyes. He had to find Matthew and Lillian. He didn't care what it cost him or if he got lost in time trying. It was imperative, he thought, looking into a young girl's soft eyes and picturing a world where she could read. About science and dragons, grand adventures, and the nature of leaves. About anything she wanted. To be anything she wanted. He sniffed and smiled at her before looking out the window.

There were few things Richard would die for, but the written word, and people's right to knowledge were at least two of them. He arrived at the closest stop and disembarked. Not surprisingly, his phone was not working and had odd settings, that only allowed him to use some search engines, and only specific topics. Nothing allowed about history or past battles and, it seemed, what he could find was seriously edited, and retold in a way that made the current administration look like the natural and most evolved version of the country that they could hope for. *Typical*, he huffed and entered the back gates of the shopping center.

Not sure what exactly he'd do next, he ducked into the bushes to change in the cold and foggy morning. *Blast it*, who could survive in these itchy and ridiculous clothes? The breeches were tight on his legs, and the shirt had a tie close at the top that did nothing to hide his broad chest. Dark hair peeked out from the gap and he sighed. Maybe looking like a damn Shakespearian actor would make him seem trustworthy?

"Ugh," he whispered and did his best to tie the shirt closed. He took a deep breath and began to trace the boundaries of the parking lot, and through the chain link fence. He took the map out once more. The spot it had shown him flashed and he looked ahead to find a small well. It was overgrown with vines and covered in leaves, and its wooden top was all but rotted through.

"You can't be serious," he whispered. Was he supposed to just jump into it? He couldn't see the bottom. He tossed a pebble in and did not hear it hit water or ground. "Fuck me." He shook his head and looked up to the clouded smog settling into fields, the distant sound of sirens, air raid warnings. The little girl's eyes from the train sought out his conscience.

"There's nothing to be done about it, but this," Richard said softly to no one. He grabbed his one bag of possessions, including the map, and took a deep breath as he sat on the edge of the stone well. "You wanted adventure, Shaw. Saint's then, let's not dawdle." Richard released his breath, and jumped.

Thomas had been prepared to die and when he found himself surrounded, he knew that today it would end. His suffering and his obligation would also. He would be free. He had fought bravely. He had saved some lives and taken more. When he saw the opposing general sifting through the clamor, bloody sword in hand, he knew that here was an honorable death, come to meet him. He threw down his dying opponent and tore open his own shirt to expose his heart. If this be the day, the hour of his eternal reckoning, he would meet it standing, in bravery.

Richard didn't land at the bottom of the well, or even on his feet for that matter. He landed in the middle of the clatter and chaos of a field ripe with blood, smoke and the yells of men. His head felt like it had come out of a horrible vice and the world spun. He threw up ingloriously and staggered through the smoke-filled air. It took him a matter of seconds to realize that something had gone horribly wrong. He was not on the peaceful coast of western Wales, where surely Doctor Blackwell and his wife were on holiday. When he heard a bullet whiz by his ear he dropped quickly back to the ground.

Had he come to inner city London? Was this a riot? His fingers dug into the soft ground of a field. The green grass was splattered with gunpowder and blood. His heart rate rose as he saw the bodies, blood red coats and blue, all fallen together. The French. The British. 1815. This was the Battle of Manchester. Nowhere near Oxford, Westbury, or wherever the hell Lillian was now. The map must have shown him the portal that would not just take him to the right time, but also to the right space. The southernmost tip of Wales. Richard sat up and tried to wrap his head around the knowledge even as he dodged away from skirmishes happening in every direction. The smell gagged him. Blood, and guts spilled; fire and filth. He staggered to his feet but stayed low and tried to get out of the fray as quickly as possible, even as he came to the horrifying realization that the portal had landed him directly into the battle where Thomas Alexander would be killed.

As he neared the edge of the field, the smoke cleared enough that his burning eyes could make out singular figures. He saw two men, still standing. From their uniforms, he could see that they were higher up in the ranks and on opposing sides. His eyes fell to the man in red, his coat torn open revealing his smooth and pale chest. The look on his face of resolution to die was apparent. His face. The face Richard had burned into his memory, a thousand times more beautiful than the portrait could ever do justice to, looked accepting of his impending death at the tip of the other man's sword.

Thomas Alexander, future Duke of Marlborough did not

intend to survive this battle. And it would be the undoing of the collective future of Britain itself.

The well had not sent him back to get the doctor. Time sent him to intervene directly. Richard didn't have to think; there was no moment of question.

The pained expression, split second on the man's face, as if he were already accepting his death, drove Richard to run, an epic battle cry springing from his lips, as he moved to intercept. If Thomas died, so many others would follow. So much knowledge, the future of their country, the health and safety of its people all hung in the balance. Through cannon fire and bloody bodies, screams of dying men and the shouts of the still fighting, Richard pushed his massive body through the staggering crowd, a train on a singular track.

He'd asked to save the world. Time had given him one chance. He would not falter.

Within feet, he held out his hands to protect the precious soul now exposed to die. "My lord!" he yelled and pushed the man in red to the side as the blade narrowly missed its intended target and sunk into Richard's chest, a hair's breadth from his heart.

Everything epic and grand happens at once in slow motion, and too quickly to feel. Richard tumbled into Thomas, the knife broke off against the bulk of his shoulder girdle and Thomas fell to the ground. Richard turned, adrenaline and shock, coupled with the insanity to protect the future, pumping in his blood.

He thought he would have died in that first bold move, so to find himself still standing and the future of his country still alive, his body rushed with a renewed sense of strength. The blade was still in his shoulder, but Richard could feel little else but rage as he saw the bright blue of Thomas's eyes flash up at him in shock. Richard picked up a club, fallen in battle next to its owner and swung it into the side of the opposing general's face, spraying blood and teeth into the battle ground and crushing the man's skull.

As he fell to the ground, another came to replace him. Richard met the next attacker with the same intense drive. Swinging the club in a large arc, he killed three more French soldiers, a semicircle around Thomas who had gotten to his feet to put his back to Richard's and faced the battle with a strange air of someone who had been given a second life—confused, unsure on how to proceed, but not about to stand idle while someone else fought so intensely.

As reinforcements piled into the fray and word spread on the opposing side that their general had fallen, the French began to retreat. The soldiers in the English regiment gathered and cleaned up the remaining enemies with swift precision, leaving no man on the ground alive that was not their own. Richard felt his limbs go heavy at the sight of the soldiers coming to their aid. The British soldiers stared at him with some trepidation, but that Thomas was back-to-back with him, seemed to reassure them that he was on their side, although not in uniform.

Richard was bleeding and he reached up to touch it, oddly rubbing the sticky iron between his fingers. Was it all his? It seemed like too much. He looked back at Thomas, who was stabbing his saber through a fallen man to ensure he would not rise again. Thomas's eyes came back to Richard's. A spark, a falling, a strange desire to spend more time gazing into those eyes hit Richard and he was lost in them. Richard was also incredibly dizzy. He stumbled, weak with the sky's light seeming to fade, even in the brightness of the morning. Thomas dropped his weapon and caught Richard by the shoulders.

"My lord," Richard whispered, at ease that he had done what he could to save the future. More at ease that his last vision, last thought, would be of the future duke's angelic face, still alive and looking at him with such remorse and care. "You are beautiful," he said softly and touched Thomas's chin, smearing blood against the sharp line of his jaw. "You must live," he whispered as his weight resigned to Thomas's arms and the world fell into darkness.

5

AN UNEXPECTED ALLY

Thomas had not expected to see the next sun rise. He assumed he would be gone, his soul departed with the day, carried away to a place more peaceful. He had not expected the giant to come out of the smoke and fire, like some old-world God, barely wearing enough clothes to cover his body ... his magnificent body. Thomas tried to stay focused but the man's shirt stained with blood and delicately hanging from the imposing chest of his savior was distracting. When the man had shoved Thomas to the ground, the first feeling was anger at his audacity.

But watching him move, hearing his battle cry, the sheer curiosity in his manner of fighting was beautiful and terrifying. Where had he learned to fight? Some backwoods brawling outside of pubs and in streets, no doubt. Surely not in the King's service. He was a brute and Thomas ached looking at the spear's tip, broken inside the man's shoulder, seeping blood out. That could have been his death.

This strange, beautiful creature had come out of nowhere and saved him. Taking the pain and the blade into his own body. Poetry and confusion filled Thomas's heart and he tried to remain stoic. The man had wielded the heavy club as if it were nothing, and the quick and intelligent maneuvers were well-planned, as he'd focused holding off the soldiers until Thomas could get to his feet.

Thomas was no longer as angry at missing the opportunity for death. He was intrigued and reinvigorated. When he'd fought next to the man, he vowed that he would survive at least long enough to learn his savior's name. To thank him and ensure that he was lifted from his obvious lowly position to ranks in the regiment, or at least in society. He should want for nothing for his brave and selfless act.

When Thomas felt the weight of the man's body sink into his arms, worry and heat filled his chest. Then his words. *My lord.* Shivers. *You are beautiful.* Heart catching. *You must live.* The oddity of such a beast speaking poetry on the verge of his own death upended him. Thomas lowered the man to the ground. He inspected the wound, saw the metal sticking out and noted its proximity to the man's heart. He must be moved carefully and they must see to extracting the blade immediately. The fact that the man had fought on, with the sharp and deadly weapon lodged so precariously inside of him, as if it were merely a scratch, sent an odd thrill up Thomas's spine. This man was more than just a shield; he was a warrior. A great lion of a man for whom it would require several of Thomas's men if he were to be carried towards safety.

Thomas stared down at the man, even as he signaled to his seconds to assist him. The battle wound down and those that hadn't retreated or surrendered were laid to rest in the piles of bodies from both sides. He couldn't be certain, but this man might have turned the tide of the battle and the very war itself.

Thomas placed his fingers on the man's thick neck and found a flutter of a pulse, though he remained unconscious. There was hope, to repay such a debt.

"We must save this man," Thomas said as he helped lift the massive weight of the stranger back towards the safety of the camp. "Mind his shoulder, he's a blade in him." They did their best to keep him immobile as they traversed the uneven ground.

"My lord, who is he? He is not dressed in colors, for either side." One soldier groaned under the weight and they all stared down at his too-tight breeches and his fine woven shirt. The material was strange and much softer than Thomas had seen. Even in the finest shops in London. Perhaps he was foreign, from some exotic land where they used spun silk regularly.

"I do not know, he seemed to simply appear from the smoke. I have never seen him before, but he saved my life. Several times over. That blade was intended for me."

"Then he must be protected," Andrew, Thomas's second in command and closest friend agreed. All together they took him to Thomas's tent and laid him on the soft bedding where Thomas had woken that very morning, thinking he had nothing else to live for, but now he felt the fluttering of purpose in his heart.

6

RICHARD FEELS LIKE HE HAS BEEN STABBED

Richard was certain he was in hell. His body burned with fever, and rather than being left to fade away into the oblivion of the life after, he was continually roused to drink water, to be moved, to roll over. Fingers prodding and poking and hushed voices. Just when he was certain he was going to die, he'd open his eyes, see the angelic face of the man he'd crossed time for. Through the pain, his mind was still too fuzzy to be sure that he had saved him. Richard might have died three hundred yards away from Thomas, running into battle. For all Richard knew, he might have tripped over a mound of peat and hit his head. The pain assured him that he must still be alive. That, or he was in hell. But angels shouldn't exist in hell, so as long as when he opened his eyes and saw the concerned look of the angel floating above him, he must be fighting towards life.

He didn't know how long he was unconscious, but he did know that he started to come to when the pain in his shoulder became excruciating. Someone told him to drink something. His parched mouth complied, only when it was too late, realizing that 'something' was a burning and horrid liquor. It made him cough and wheeze and then the ache in his arm burned as they poured the same mixture over the wound.

"Steady now, lion," he heard a voice whisper and turned his head to see Thomas Alexander, son of the Duke of Marlborough place one hand on the bruised and tense muscle of his shoulder. "You must lay still," he said softly, and Richard's eyes drifted closed.

"Anything, my lord," he whispered, and felt like the angel was requesting to take him to the afterlife. He would gladly comply. Thomas's hand tightened on his shoulder and a great burning pain seared through Richard. He sat up and roared, the blood from the wound spurted and seeped. Before him stood Thomas, eyes wide, the broken spear in his hand, the other palm out in a sign of surrender. Both covered in blood.

"You asshole," Richard breathed, before promptly passing out.

Thomas tried to not look at the man. But there was nothing else that held his interest so acutely. He took up all of his sleeping blankets and there was little room for much else. The French invaders who had breached the southernmost tip of Wales had met their untimely end and the remaining soldiers had turned tail to run. The King's navy had assembled in pursuit. The battle on land was done, at least for now. Messengers from the top generals had given orders to bury the dead and return home to their families for a much-deserved rest.

Thomas did not want to think about returning home to his overbearing father and his power-hungry brothers. He did miss his younger sister and he'd heard that her upcoming nuptials would be the event of the summer. Nuptials gave way to the maelstrom of the expectations that waited for him the moment he walked through his family's prestigious gates. He didn't want to think about those obligations right now.

He just wanted to be here, staying still and watching the strange and weakened man, thrash and burn in his bed.

Andrew cleared his throat at the opening of the tent. "My lord, the orders were to pack up camp."

Thomas sat, hand propped on his knee as he studied the bearded face, still covered in so much blood. The battlefield didn't lend much in the way of cleanliness. Who knew what disease and filth was on that blade? They'd cleaned the wound as best as possible and were now at the mercy of the man's will, determination to live, and constitution. Thomas sighed.

"I do not know if moving him would be in his best interest."

"Thomas, we do not even know his name. He is mortally wounded."

"So you would have me leave him? The man who saved my life? The man who saved all of our lives? He killed the general! He should be lauded—"

"Of course! I meant no harm in suggesting. It's just that it would be difficult to move him as he's—" Andrew paused and they looked the man over, both trying to calculate the possibility of transporting him.

"Built like a damn fortress?" Thomas said softly, eyebrow arched.

"A beast to be sure. What if he's a spy?"

Thomas scoffed at Andrew. "A spy would not risk his life, and kill a high-ranking soldier. For what purpose? To gain my trust? I'm not the power behind the crown, Andrew. I feel like he knows me. He was specific in his purpose to save me. I want to know what that purpose is."

"Of course, Thomas."

"Send word to my mother, tell her I'm requesting a carriage at Bristol. As soon as possible."

Andrew nodded. "Capital idea, sir."

"If we can get to it before he dies, it will be," Thomas smiled and Andrew left on the task. Boiling water over his outside campfire, Thomas washed strips of cloth. He cleaned them as best as he could, letting them stay in the hot pot as long as possible. When he returned to his tent, he had to let them cool enough to be of comfort but not burning. Then, with utmost care, he sat beside the bed and began to tend to the wall of a man.

First, he began with his face. The smell of blood and dirt wafted up from the warm and wet cloths. The man moaned and turned into the attention. Thomas felt his body respond. It wasn't the first time he'd had such a response. It seemed to boil up inside of him, despite everything he'd been taught and told in his life. Still, it was private here, much of the regiment was moving on and Andrew would be busy with the request.

The sunlight streamed through the tent walls as the start of its setting began. It lent a soft and orange glow and Thomas took a deep breath and continued to wash the man's face, forehead, down the length of his nose, and through his thick beard. Never had he seen a beard so well maintained. In the camps, men did not have beards, it was considered barbaric and unsanitary. He thought briefly of shaving it off while the man slept, to give him the air of someone born to higher esteem. But Thomas also liked it. It was soft beneath the pads of his fingers. Thick and dark, like the man's brows.

He did not look of this time. He looked like someone from a legend, coming out of the smoke, wielding a club like a brute. Yet now, how complacent he rested in his bed, at Thomas's mercy. Thomas felt heat rise from between his thighs and cleared his throat. This man saved his life, he owed him in kind. To entertain any of the unbidden thoughts in his head would be irreverent. So he moved on, changing the dressing around the wound and washing the length of the man's arm, his thick forearm, his broad expanse of chest.

Thomas stopped to examine the stitches he'd sewn himself, tight and small to limit the scar and hopefully not create immobility in the man's shoulder. Wouldn't want him not being able to swing a club after all, Thomas smiled and looked around the stitches for signs of red and rot. He poured whisky on the cloth and cleaned it once more. The man twinged and took in a breath, his hand came up quickly to grasp Thomas's wrist. His eyes opened, glazed and dark.

"Ouch," the man said, and Thomas froze.

"Apologies," he whispered. The man's gaze fell to his lips, strange and dreamy they stared at each other for a full minute before the man fell back to sleep. Thomas moved on to his other arm, covering and uncovering only one part at a time, to protect both of their modesties. When he got to his trunk-like legs, Thomas sighed and shook his head. What kind of work instilled this sort of musculature. Marching? Running? Lifting giant boulders for fun?

He doused and redoused the cloths in his effort to clean the man, from his thick thighs to his feet. Thomas stopped, gently massaging the soft soles, a strange place for a man to be soft, he thought as his fingers pressed into the arch and the man moaned. Thomas looked up and saw that the man was gripping the bedsheets beneath him. But beneath the sheet on top of him, a very large bulge had risen. Thomas's body reacted with heat and sweat. His mouth watered.

Heavens, he was in trouble. His only hope was that the man was a spy, or a right ass, or something terrible to withstand, so this strange and powerful desire would subside. He covered the man's feet and took the bowl of dirty cloths outside quickly, trying to cool his own reaction. He stood outside in the chilled air for a long while, disposing of the bloodied rags in the fire, and warming broth with meat and potatoes in a small kettle. Andrew arrived just as the simple soup was getting done.

"My lord, the carriage has been ordered, though it may take a couple of days, so you will have time to make the crossing. How does he fare?"

"He's not yet lucid. But the wound is not infected. If we can strengthen him enough to walk by tomorrow, then we might arrive in conjunction with the carriage. I cannot ask you to stay with me, Andrew. I know that you have family waiting for you and they will be anxious to know that you are well."

His friend looked at him with a smile. "I do not mind a few days, and I would not abandon you to this man until I know what his intentions are."

"You are a true friend."

"Always, Thomas. I am concerned for you."

"I am well."

"Are you? I could have sworn I saw you charging into the blade that that man took for you, from across the field."

Thomas hung his head to his friend's astute observation. Before he could answer, a grunting came from the tent; strange words in a string of profanities.

"What the bloody fuck?" drifted between the two soldiers.

Andrew cocked his head and his eyebrows rose. "Seems the brute is rising." Thomas did not allow his mind to wander to all the ways that magnificent man had risen.

7

THE LION MEETS A DUKE

Richard was having the worst dream of his life. Or the best. It began with fire and heat, burning in an inferno, weak and unable to move his limbs or even to cry out. His shoulder hurt. His whole body hurt, the muscles in his back, his torso, everything. He kept seeing a man with a broken and bloody blade and on its tip was his impaled heart. He pictured laying in a soft bed of grass, dying, while an angel, blue eyes and soft brown curls tied at the nape of his thick neck, washed away the blood. Warm cloths, the smell of lavender and whisky. He felt the man touch his cheek, gently soothe his brow. Exploratory, and reverent, and curious.

Until the angel had stuck his finger into the wound and Richard roused to grab the warm and sinewy forearm.

"Ouch," he'd said and met the eyes of Thomas Alexander, the future duke he'd meant to save. He'd fucking died. He must have. Because now Thomas was studying his mouth and apologizing and Richard was naked but for the thin blankets and as he succumb to the dizziness in his head, he felt the wandering hands wash him, touch him, in ways more intimate than any partner he'd had. There was no world wherein this would be a reality.

By the time the angel reached his feet a different sort of fever began to burn through Richard's veins. Though he was weak and had suffered a loss of blood he felt his body react to the caresses that had become less about cleaning and more about enjoying. The man's fingers into the arches of his feet made Richard's toes curl and he was suddenly hard and erect. His hips tightened and he wondered if the bathing would continue below the sheets. Delirious and hopeful, he fell off the edge of consciousness once more when the man's hands left his body.

When he woke, sometime later to the smell of something cooking and the cold shivers in his body, he was hopeful he'd dreamed it. Otherwise the poor soldier, or even worse, possibly the future duke, who had bathed him must have been disgusted. This was not an era that promoted free love and experimentation. He wondered if he'd be stoned the minute he came out of the tent.

He put his useable hand to his aching head and wondered, since he was alive, what would become of him now? Had he changed the future? He'd killed people. Maybe ones that were not meant to die. Richard's stomach tumbled, not so much in the act of murder itself, but the idea that those were people who might have made an impact in time. What in the hell had he done? He sat up and searched for his belongings. The map! The journal. Where were they?

"What the bloody fuck?" he grumbled as he found himself stripped bare and the place he'd been stabbed stitched up. It burned and ached and he couldn't raise his left arm.

He looked at the tent walls, now showing shadows of a campfire outside and the silhouettes of two men talking. He didn't hear the rumble of a busy camp and wondered how long he'd been out. Was he going to die of some horrible infection?

"Saints what have I done?" he whispered.

"Saved my friend's life, and possibly the fate of The Crown," came a voice and the man, unfamiliar to Richard, stepped through the tent opening. Richard pulled the covers up over his chest, embarrassed at his size and the dark hair that covered the broad expanse.

He cleared his throat. How did people talk in this era? He tried to recall Jane Austen. She was not his favorite author. He thought of Lillian with an air of sadness and suddenly wondered where she was in time, and if he'd ever see her again.

"Pray tell, good sir, where are my clothes?"

The man smiled "They were, ruined in the battle I'm afraid. We had to dispose of them. I did retrieve your satchel." The man nodded to the corner of the tent, where his blood splattered bag sat. "Interesting map you have in there. It does not seem to have much information on it," the man's brow rose with the question.

Richard's face flushed under his beard. "It—it is an older map, my lord. Gifted to me by my father. I was using it to get home. Do you not have spare clothing I may borrow?" he said, trying to distract away from the map, that he hoped was still working.

"All in good time, but for now, there's no need to be bashful. We're all of the same design here. We'll find you something," he studied Richard's body and shook his head. "With any luck, that fits."

"I would be grateful," Richard said and tried to not meet his eyes. Of the same design or not, Richard was never proud of his body and it was far worse to him to think he would be so bare in front of the future duke. As though his thoughts had summoned the devil, a cool wind blew into the tent and Thomas stepped in. He looked pained, or angry. Richard couldn't tell which.

"How is he?" Sharp, clipped. Very business-like and not a shade of the man who had bathed him so tenderly an hour ago. Richard sunk into his embarrassment. It had been him. He'd been so excited, even in his weakened state, that it must have disgusted him. He berated himself and tried to return the man's coldness.

"*He* is fine," he answered, royally.

Thomas's head inclined towards Richard and he nodded to the other man. "Andrew, give us a moment."

"Of course, my lord. I'll see to the dinner."

"We'll be out presently," Thomas kept his eyes on Richard, a cold stare that felt like the beginning of an interrogation.

Fuck, Richard thought. *How will I explain myself?*

Thomas's mouth watered when he saw the man sitting up, clutching the blankets to his chest. Heard his rich voice, the strange intonations, the odd accent that was … British, but not. His fiery brown eyes sparkled in the dim light as he watched Thomas pace the small length of the tent.

"Who are you?"

"Richard Shaw. Doctor Richard Shaw."

"You're a doctor?"

"Not a medical doctor."

"What other kind of doctor is there?" Thomas crossed his arms over his chest and stared at him, sharp eyes piercing.

"I am a doctor of literature." Thomas stopped pacing and glared at him.

"A doctor of books? Do you repair them?"

"No," Richard sighed and Thomas heard his voice become deeper and commanding. "Well, sometimes. But, mostly I study them. I study stories and writing. I oversee the housing of them in the library at Oxford."

"A librarian," Thomas scoffed. "So, to be sure an intellectual. Still, you do not look like an intellectual."

Richard scowled at him and stood, wobbly at first, dropping the sheet lower to his waist. Thomas's eyes fell to his naked torso. He studied the perfect V of hair descending below the blanket. felt his cheeks grow warm, and his hands tighten at his sides. Richard stepped closer and Thomas leaned away.

"Where I am from, they give out honorary degrees called doctorates to those who devote their time to specific fields of study."

"And you—" Thomas tripped on his words and he swallowed. "You study books?"

"Literature."

"But you're built like a blacksmith."

"I cannot help my genetics."

"Your what?" Thomas chuckled. Richard rolled his eyes.

"Who my parents were, and what they gave me."

Thomas's eyes fell to study his body. Thank God for what his parents gave him, Thomas thought and ached to clear the world of anyone but Richard Shaw. Doctor of Books.

"Why did you save me, Doctor Shaw?"

This seemed to trip the doctor up. He looked down at the ground, frustrated.

"Need I an explanation for saving a man's life? Is it not the right course of action?" Richard tied the sheet around his waist more securely. Thomas sighed, part in relief but also part in disappointment.

"I merely wish to know where you came from." Thomas's voice was leveling. Richard kept his distance. Both knew that Andrew stood on the outside of the tent, listening to every word.

"A nearby field." Richard said. Thomas scowled at the dodge of truth. "I heard the battle cries, saw the man coming for you. I made a decision."

"Are you in habit of risking your life for strangers?" Thomas asked.

"Only for—" Richard's voice fell away. Thomas could see him struggle with his next words. "Only in the service of the Crown" he finished. Thomas's expression fell, as if he'd hoped Richard would have said only for him.

"Of course."

Richard stayed still and looked down at his bare feet.

Thomas's eyes fell there too. Remembered how soft and well-kept they were. How much he'd enjoyed his exploration of Richard's body, and how now the large man seemed to be shrinking under some kind of shyness. Thomas did not want him to close down.

"You said you are in residency at Oxford. Do you do anything else there? Beyond being a doctor of books?"

Richard looked up. "I maintain the collection. Occasionally I teach classes."

"Teach classes?"

"Uh, tutor? Instruct?" Richard fumbled for the right word. A smile tugged at the corners of Thomas's mouth, thinking of Richard teaching club-wielding classes to a classroom of startled students.

"Is that so?"

"Yes, my lord," Richard nodded.

"Then perhaps you could instruct me someday." Thomas's eyebrows lifted and his eyes lingered a little too long on Richard's chest before he turned away. How he wished he could be instructed by Richard. He needed to put space and decorum between them. He cleared his throat. "We'll find you more acceptable clothing. Though I do not know if you'd fit in the typical uniform." He watched Richard cling to the sheet tighter and wished he would not have to put clothes on the man. The thought shook through him with guilt soon following. He turned away. "Andrew will bring you supper," he said and left quickly.

It was as though a wall had come down between them. Richard felt dazed, drunk, too weak to stand. He fumbled back to the bed and did as he was told. He wondered how much blood he'd lost. He also wondered if he'd ever get home again.

The stew was paltry but it tasted better than anything Richard had eaten in a long while. He felt a drowsy ache fill his bones. His stomach was at least somewhat full and his blood was starting to rebuild its resources. His forehead seemed warm and he wondered if he would die before he had time to formulate a plan to return home. What would his mother say? His brothers? No one would believe that the mild-mannered librarian would have rushed into battle. Richard scarcely believed it himself. He finished his portion and closed his eyes.

Is this how Lillian felt? Scared, lost in a strange land that she hadn't even been born in? Worse, in a country she was unfamiliar in, where she held no power and was promised to marry a violent and horrid man? At least Richard had the privilege of being white and male. And the savior of a powerful man in the King's service. He felt nauseous. What had he done? His forehead swam with heat and he felt fever shiver through his body. Andrew stepped back into the tent.

"I regret that we are currently without a doctor on the field," he said and took Richard's empty bowl. "I had hoped that our reinforcements would have reached us by now. They are but ten leagues away."

"Leagues, are you a navy man?" Richard asked. Andrew's keen eyes leveled on him.

"I was. I found I preferred the land, and to be closer to my children." Richard looked up at him and nodded.

"Understandable. How many?"

"Three, a fourth on the way."

Richard's eyes went soft. "I'm glad you survived the battle then, I'm sure they are missing you."

"Have you any children?"

"No, my lord," he said softly and shook his head, wiping the beading sweat away.

"A man like you? No woman has cornered and trapped into loving matrimony?" Andrew laughed. Richard shook his head with an eyebrow raised.

"I have not been so lucky as you, my lord. Someday," he paused and thought about the very real possibility that he might never return home, and all that meant for his ability to lead a different life. "Someday I hope to be married with children." Thomas came in with relatively clean clothing that he'd found in an abandoned tent. A shirt, vest, brown scratchy coat and breeches. They'd salvaged his strange shoes and Thomas laid the clothing atop the boots.

"And you, my lord? Do you have a family?" Richard asked. Thomas stood still for a moment.

"Not presently but I'm sure my mother will make quick work of that when I return." He didn't sound happy about it.

"It is a blessing!" Andrew teased him. "To have a woman warm your hearth and home. To bring you little darlings into the world, fill your bed—"

"Enough," Thomas held out his hand with a laugh. "One man's heaven is another man's hell."

"Love does not make a prison of your life, my lord. It frees you!" Andrew laughed back.

"The man in prison argues with affection for his chains," Thomas said and went quiet. "Please take my portion." He handed his bowl over to Richard.

"My lord, I would not."

"I know you would not, which is why I command it. You've lost much blood, at my expense."

"But you—"

"Must survive, I know. So you have said. We'll all be getting more than we can stand soon enough and I need you strong enough to walk in the morning." Thomas commanded. Richard took the bowl from him, their fingers gently grazing as he passed the bowl.

"Have you sent word to your family, Andrew?"

"Yes, my lord, when I made the request for the carriage in Cardiff."

"Good, and will they be meeting you?"

"Jane's condition requires that she stay at home." Andrew's eyes fell to his feet, where he sat beside Richard who delicately sipped at the soup.

"Then why are you traveling with us east, when your destination is north?" Thomas interjected.

"My lord, you need assistance getting to Cardiff," Andrew looked at Richard.

"Do you fear that this man would hurt me?" Thomas turned his head to eye him also.

"No, my lord, but should he collapse along the way. I fear you could not lift him yourself."

"How long until the arrival of your child?" Richard asked.

"Weeks to days."

"I will be quite well." Richard spoke firmly. "There is no need to worry for me and I do not have to accompany you, if the trip will be made easier by my absence."

"You will absolutely accompany me," Thomas returned.

"But, my lord—"

"The future duke cannot go on his own," Andrew argued alongside Thomas.

"But I am an invalid and would slow his progress to home and the impending matchmaking of his mother." Richard said. Thomas glared at him.

"You felled seven men with a blade sitting kin to your heart. You are not an invalid. And while I do not need anyone's protection, I would be remiss if I did not see to it that you were well taken care of and honored. Unless you have a family to go back to?" Thomas's perfect brow arched at him.

"He has no family," Andrew said, happy that the conversation was back to keeping Thomas safe. "And it would ensure that you did not run from these upcoming matchmaking schemes if your mother was expecting to meet your savior, which she is, because I told her so in the letter."

"Bloody hell," Richard groaned and buried his head in his hand. Thomas did too.

"What?"

"Well, I told her that a man had rushed into battle and saved your life, and that you were bringing him home to honor his sacrifice. Knowing your mother, I'm sure she's planning an entire event to welcome you both. She probably wishes she had another daughter to marry him!"

"Fuck," Richard breathed under his breath. Both Andrew and Thomas's heads swung his way with smiles that only soldiers would don in the presence of such a word. The rules of propriety were different on the battle field.

Richard could not do this. The longer he stayed with the future duke, away from his time, the more dangerous he became. The more people he talked to, interacted with, touched, the more likely he would affect the future. This was a horrible idea. He could, under no circumstances, accompany Thomas home.

"Pardon me, my lords," he cleared his throat. "Though I appreciate your kind words and the honor of your family, I really should return to my work—"

"Oh? Are the books missing you?" Thomas teased.

Richard glared up at him through his heavy brow but Thomas did not cower.

"No, my Lord, I've no one to miss me, but I do have work to do."

"Then you may get back to it as soon as you've met my family, I suppose."

"My Lord, I beg of you," Richard sighed, closing his eyes.

"I insist. And I rarely use my position to ask for anything."

"That is true," Andrew agreed.

"I will not be at ease if I do not see to your full recovery. You are fine for now, but the wound is deep and I would have a more skilled doctor—not of books—to see to it that you regain full use of your arm."

Richard and Thomas locked gazes, challenging one another.

"It is simply best to just concede, my friend. He never gives up when he wants something." Andrew whispered to Richard. He was tired, his shoulder hurt like hell and they had effectively reached an impasse. They would not allow him to leave.

"I'm tired, I should like to rest before our journey," he said softly, and Andrew took the empty bowl from him.

"As you like it. Andrew, accompany me, we'll prepare camp for an early departure. You will head north and Doctor Shaw will accompany me to meet the transport to Marlborough."

"Yes, my lord, thank you." Andrew turned to Richard. "Truly, friend, thank you for seeing to his safety so that I may be with my family."

"Of course, Andrew. I wish your wife an easy birth and a healthy addition to your family." Richard nodded. His head felt heavy. He felt his body giving up the fight as he sunk down on the cold ground, made better by Thomas's bedding. He caught the scent of the man as he adjusted the small blankets. The fever was shaking his body. He felt delirious. How would he manage this? A journey was hard enough, but a trip home with a man he'd only meant to save and then disappear from seemed impossible. When they'd both gone to sleep, Richard would rouse himself, and return to the well. He hoped that it would get him home to the correct timeline. And the nearest hospital.

8

AN ESCAPE PLAN FOILED

Thomas worked out the details of Andrew's trip, packed up supplies and whatever he could to ensure a safe and comfortable journey back to the northern township where his wife and family anxiously awaited his return. Andrew went to his own tent that evening, but turned at the opening.

"Where will you rest, Thomas? You are welcome here."

"I think I shall finish readying for our trip and find a corner to sleep. I'd like to keep an eye on him. I worry his fever is returning."

"He seems a quiet and stubborn man. A brood if I've ever known one."

"There is, indeed, something broken and sad about that man." Thomas shook his head. "What vexes a man to be, at once, a reluctant warrior and yet so good at it?"

"I think he has fought battles we know not of, sir. Perhaps ones not on a field, but of the heart. Watching him move, was more like watching a man driven by love, not duty, to defend something he held most dear. It was not perfect technique, but when you have little else to live for, one does not need years of training," Andrew said softly. "I believe in the goodness of his heart. I fear he has been alone for a long time. No family, nothing to tie him to this land. Be careful, Thomas. With him and yourself." The warm and caring words made tears threaten behind Thomas's eyes. He sniffed. There was something broken about them all. War was hell. Even he woke in the night with the terrors of it.

"I can't explain it, but somehow I feel better going home with him at my side." Thomas confessed. Andrew nodded with a smile.

"Strange as he is, he seems to want to protect you with his life. I'm sure that won't change either on the battlefield or in the ballroom. Good night, my lord. Rest well." Andrew retired to his tent.

Thomas sat beside the fire and thought about anything that didn't entail what would happen when he reached the gates of his father's manor. Even with his sister's wedding coming nearer every day, even with the fact that he would be alive to see it, even to have the comfort of hearth and home drown out memories of freezing nights in tents and the blood of battle, he was still edgy in the gut to return.

He would have his strange and stoic new companion. At least until the wedding. Then, he supposed, they would part ways and he'd be alone again to navigate the world of becoming a duke, and all the chains that came with it. Thomas didn't know how long he stayed that way, staring into the fire. But as he was getting ready to retire, Richard came out of the tent, fully dressed and not at all subtle. He looked like he meant to run away. He had on his jacket, his shoes, a canteen of water. He flinched at every movement, obviously still suffering from the wound. Thomas stood.

"And where are you going?"

Richard swayed on the spot and sighed in frustration. "Damn it. I had to relieve myself," he lied and swallowed.

"Is that so? Well. Go on then." Thomas said and nodded to the nearby bushes.

"Well, I—" Richard supposed he could pee if he had to. Though he wasn't sure when the last time he drank water was. No wonder he was dizzy.

"Unless you really meant to run away to avoid meeting my family. To which I would respond, let us do it together." Thomas said, face serious. Richard's nervousness fell. Thomas seemed to fear his family more than death in battle. Maybe that's why he'd been rushing into it so fervently. Richard threw the canteen back into the tent with a scowl and walked over to the bushes. Untying his breeches, he took a deep breath and tried to not make it weird that he had to pee in front of the man. He heard Thomas shifting behind him.

"You do not like your family then, my lord?" Richard said over his shoulder while he tried to focus on relieving himself. Men talked to each other when they peed, right? This did not have to be an ordeal.

Until Thomas stepped up beside him and undid his own trousers. Richard tried to keep his eyes on the dark leaves in front of them, the stars in the sky above them, anywhere but down. When he glanced over, Thomas took a quick look down at Richard's groin and emitted a small sigh. Richard couldn't help himself; he glanced down too.

Fuck. He looked quickly away. Jesus, the man was … well endowed.

"They have expectations. Expectations I'm in no mind to live up to." Thomas said, giving a small grunt as he finished and secured himself. Richard wondered if it hadn't been on purpose, his coming over during the delicate moment. Him looking when it was universally known, different timeline or not, that you simply did not look. He finished, tucked away his partially hard member and all the erotic thoughts that seemed to swarm his blood-deprived brain. This was a horrible idea. This whole thing was a bloody mess.

"Surely, you are looking forward to a family. A wife." Hadn't the duke had a wife? Richard could not remember. He felt dizzy.

"Surely, I am not. Come, to bed with you." Thomas nodded to the tent flap he held open. Richard glared. "We have a long journey tomorrow and we both need rest."

Without making a huge deal of it, Richard laid back down and Thomas lay beside him, not touching. Richard threw the blanket over him and settled into the sleeping mat. He was tired, it was probably stupid to run into the dark night in search of a hole in the ground to God knew what timeline. Richard listened to Thomas breathe, deep and even. The man had large and healthy lungs to match every other large and healthy part of him. Richard gave a little groan of frustration at his own stupidity before he fell fast asleep.

Thomas turned his head to watch Richard's profile. Sleep eluded him. Richard did not want to stay with him. And who could blame him? It wasn't like he'd made the journey home seem a happy event. Had he been too forward? Had he scared the man?

He was merely curious. Not that it mattered, or it that it was any of his business. Thomas felt his face grow warm. He'd never met a man like Richard. The beard, the intelligent eyes, that brute-like body. He was an enigma that made him curious. He itched to touch the lion. His hand came up and he quickly pulled away.

Ridiculous! This was a mistake. This was a horrible and ill-thought plan. But it was the only one Thomas had. He thought he would sleep very poorly but after only a few minutes of watching Richard's face, by the dying candlelight, ease into peace and hear him softly snoring, Thomas's eyes felt heavy. For the first time in months, he felt … safe. He fell into a dreamless sleep, half of his body warm from Richard's feverish skin.

9

RICHARD IS NOT DOROTHY, THIS IS NO PLACE LIKE HOME

When Richard woke, he was certain that he would open his eyes to the view of his ceiling fan, in his apartment, in his king bed, with its soft Egyptian cotton sheets, down duvet and adjustable mattress, his ergonomic pillows, with stacks of books beside his bed, and the softly glowing light from outside his third floor apartment windows.

He'd make a cup of tea, eat the biscuits that he'd gotten from the new French Boulangerie near his flat. He'd take a leisurely stroll through the markets and pick out something for dinner. He would continue on through the park, read in the sunlight, come home and cook. The world would be right once again, because the past twenty-four hours had been nothing short of an extraordinary dream.

Richard felt the sunlight warming his face, he kept his eyes closed, willing his vision to be true. He heard birds chirping, but smelled the faint odor of smoke. Blood. His own sweat. He groaned, his whole body hurt, but nothing as much as his shoulder, which felt like a low dull thudding echoing through his torso as if the blade was still lodged inside. He shifted uncomfortably and his mouth felt dry and disgusting. He moaned and curled away from the sun. The longer he was conscious the more real the nightmare became. Richard squeezed his eyes shut.

"Are you in much pain?" came the deep voice. Richard rolled back over, the sharp stabbing pain from moving his shoulder caused him to cry out angrily. He opened his eyes to see Thomas standing at the tent's opening. The man who had stopped him from running away. Kept him from his warm bed and the convenience of running water and penicillin. The spoiled nobleman was even kidnapping him away to his family, no doubt full of pretentious jackasses like himself, to avoid confronting them by himself. Richard's head ached. He could be in the hospital right now. He could be getting better. But he wasn't. He threw off the covers in anger. He also wasn't going to give the man the satisfaction of seeing him weak. He stood quickly.

"I am fine." Richard lied, through his clenched teeth. Ignoring the way his body wanted to faint. Ignoring the decidedly horrible need for a cup of tea. Mornings could sod off. Mornings with a fresh-faced Thomas, who seemed more apt to ruin history than save it, were even worse.

"Are you?" Thomas's eyes narrowed. Richard huffed and moved past him to go relieve himself in the bushes. Thomas did not follow him this time. When he'd finished, and wished he had even a wipe or hand sanitizer, he turned back to the fire pit where the future duke was crouching low over a boiling pot.

"Come and sit," Thomas said, tersely and motioned to a log beside the ring.

"Shouldn't we be leaving?"

"We should, but not before we see to the wound and you get something in you besides blatant rage."

Richard stopped up short. "Something in me?" What the actual fuck did he mean by that? Thomas cleared the fire and he saw a pan of eggs and bread sizzling and a kettle, with tea brewing.

"It isn't much, but you can't possibly expect to stay on the horse with all the blood you lost."

Richard wanted to cry. "Where did you come by eggs?"

"Andrew left them from the stores, he knew you'd probably be hungry when you woke."

"Andrew is a saint," Richard breathed.

"Well, I cooked them," Thomas said and Richard's head swung to watch him. Was he … jealous? What a prat. "Sit." Thomas commanded. Richard thought to defy him just on principle but the eggs and bread started to emit a lovely aroma. He closed his eyes. "Now, Doctor." The deep impatience. The angry scowl on those pretty blue eyes made Richard hesitantly sit on the log. "Take off your shirt."

"I'm a grown man, I can tend to my—"

"Now!"

"Fine. Fuck." Richard said, completely forgetting his manners. "You demanding and spoiled little shit." He tore his shirt off, with little care for the state of his body. The shoulder that had taken the blade was bruised deeply, purple and blue. It ached and he had a hard time raising the arm at all. The shirt hung from the injured arm lamely. The fire warmed his toes and Richard stared anywhere but at Thomas who came to kneel before him with clean cloths from one of the pots boiling on the fire.

"I am sorry," Thomas said softly, not meeting Richard's eyes. "I am not accustomed to people saying no to me. I forget that you are not one of my soldiers."

Richard watched the concern etched in Thomas's features as he studied the wound and gently started to wash away the blood and ooze that had accumulated in the night. A captain, a future duke, on his knees in front of a lame little librarian. Offering apologies.

"I am the one who begs pardon," Richard said, low and purring. Thomas's eyes rose to meet his. "I—I am disagreeable in the morning and in pain, and I should not have called you—a little shit. You have offered me much kindness, and I do not deserve your—"

"You do," Thomas interrupted softly. He looked back down at the wound, keeping his eyes from Richard's. "You're within your rights and I know that waking up this morning must have felt like a bad dream." Thomas's hands were steady and warm as he gently rotated Richard's shoulder backwards and forwards. First, Richard had to grit his teeth to stop from crying out, but the movement helped to loosen some of the stiffness and after a few minutes of his massaging and coercing the muscle, the pain eased. He supposed when you were in battle and short of medical personnel, you had to learn things yourself.

"Thank you, my lord," Richard sighed. Thomas's fingers lingered on his shoulder and he stared at them; Richard watched his face, and genuinely questioned if the future duke was indeed going to marry a woman.

"You ought to call me Thomas, while we are alone."

"You ought to call me Richard," he returned softly. Thomas's hands fell and he looked up, from his knees into Richard's face. The morning was warm, and soft, and they were alone. Richard wanted to tilt Thomas's strong chin up, get lost in his eyes.

"Right," Thomas sighed and rose, quickly. He busied himself with breakfast. "We should get on the road while we have daylight. Cardiff is a long day's ride, if you think you can endure it."

"I can," Richard said and looked down to the clean and changed bandages. He put the shirt back on but did not fasten it as he only had the use of his one hand. He'd have to show up to the town looking like a half-wild beast on the heels of the nobleman. What a fucking mess.

Taking down camp was slow with only three arms between them, but the last thing Richard wanted to be was a burden. Plus the quicker they left, the sooner they'd be around other people and the sooner he could forget about how distracting Thomas was and the inappropriate feelings that seemed to rise up between them. Certainly, it was just a lonely spell, and when Thomas was again in the company of women, he would remember how enticed he was by the 'fairer' sex. Richard took a moment, while Thomas was smothering the fire, to look at the map.

There was a door near Cardiff. A portal. It wasn't glowing, but what did it matter? Richard knew that the more jumps he chanced, the more risk he took. Lillian had only briefly told him about the secret society of Timekeepers, how her father worked for them, and how they were supposed to have agents in the field handling these kinds of mishaps. Richard worried that the Timekeepers would discover what he'd done and come after him. He needed to get home as soon as history was assured to be set right. He was surprised that they hadn't fixed things themselves, as that was their whole job. But it was no matter. He'd used the map and a portal, it had taken him exactly where he was meant to go. He'd changed history back. They ought to be grateful. Right? Richard reasoned to himself while he folded up the map and turned to watch Thomas.

Richard watched the muscles of Thomas's legs, without his coat on to hide the curve of his backside. Fuck. This was just … Richard sighed … intolerable. Some Timekeeper was probably having a jolly old laugh at his expense. He would try for the door in Cardiff. Thomas would return home, meet his destined wife, and all would be right with the world again. With any luck, Richard would be sleeping in his own bed tonight.

They packed up the horses with the salvageable gear, Thomas tied back his hair in a neat knot at the nape of his neck. With the remaining water, he frothed up a foam from a small cake in a tin. He lathered his face, and put a small mirror on top of a stump. So practiced and precise in his movements that Richard guessed he was used to his battlefield barbering. Thomas leaned over the mirror to shave.

"I do not understand why you are bothering," Richard said, cinching the bags tight to the horse. He hoped they were walking alongside them because he had no expertise nor inclination to ride.

"Some propriety must be maintained. After all, we are not barbarians." Thomas said simply, then took in a sharp inhale as he nicked the line of his jaw.

"Here," Richard rushed over to take the mirror. He snatched it quickly from the stump and Thomas sat up with a scowl.

"How dare you—"

"Do not be an idiot," Richard interrupted and used the cuff of his shirt to wipe the blood that had sprung up from Thomas's jawline. That strong and beautiful jawline. "I didn't take a bayonet to the heart to have you slit your own throat."

Thomas stared at him for a long minute, a sadness, a question in his eyes. Richard nodded in understanding. There was a time, in his own youth, when the world had been unkind to boys who preferred boys, that he carried the weight of that same look in his eyes. He softened his features and gently dabbed at the blood once more.

"Allow me to assist you." Richard held the mirror and Thomas resumed the task, upright and with better light. Richard tried not to watch how steady and smooth his hands were around the blade, or how the barely present blond stubble seemed to come off like a fine layer of butter with every scratching stroke. Thomas looked up to see Richard watching. He looked away quickly to the road, the horizon, anything but Thomas.

"Someday you'll allow me to assist you," Thomas said, standing straight and gently touching the tip of his blade to Richard's dark and soft beard. He resisted the urge to flinch away. Instead he met Thomas's eyes without fear.

"My beard stays."

Thomas leaned back, looked down his nose haughtily at him and arched a brow. "We shall see." He rinsed his face with water from his canteen, wiped the hair from his blade, and sheathed it at a holster on his back before donning his bright red, regiment coat.

"Mount up, Doctor of books."

"I prefer to walk."

"I beg your pardon?" Thomas's hand paused on the stirrup and he glared at him over the rump of Richard's horse. "We will not make it in a day if we do not ride. Have you something against horses?"

Richard had everything against horses. They were large, they were too smart, they were large. They smelled, they were unpredictable, they were large.

"No, sir, but my shoulder," he paused, "will make it hard to mount." Thomas came over to him, a strange and tight smile on his face.

"Really?" Thomas was close now. Too close for comfort, he smiled. "It's never stopped me before." Suddenly the future duke was leaning against Richard, offering his knee and a hand to get up onto the probably fiercely unpredictable beast. *Fuck*, Richard thought.

How did they do it in the movies? Richard thought back to every western he'd ever seen. He'd just pretend they were on set and he was an old pro at this. He used his good arm and stepped as gingerly as possible onto Thomas's knee, swinging his other leg over so enthusiastically that he almost fell off the horse on the other side. The beast shied and pranced beneath him and Richard let out a girlish squeal before regaining his composure and his bowels. He took a deep breath, sat up, with the reins in hand as though it might bolt off at any second. When he looked down Thomas was chuckling.

"So, you are not fond of horses then?"

"There are a great many things I'm not fond of," Richard barked.

"Right. Mornings, pain, horses, and … what was it you said? Spoiled little shit dukes?" Thomas ticked off things on his fingers.

"The list just keeps growing." Richard growled back and stared ahead while Thomas, still smiling, mounted his own horse with grace and ease.

This was going to be a long fucking ride. How in the hell had Lillian managed to only screw up the little and isolated time she was there? He was about to doom the entire country; he was almost certain of it.

10

DOCTOR SHAW HATES HORSES

Richard felt like a damn bushel of potatoes. Jostled in every bone and joint, and every muscle irate, every footfall of the horse brought more jarring pain to the injuries he'd sustained in battle and the continual soreness of sleeping on the ground and without proper ergonomic support for the last two days. More than the atrocious discomfort, he worried that an impending infection would mean certain death. He supposed it might serve him right for ever trying to interfere with history.

Thomas was silent for the trip, and Richard wondered if he was frustrated with their pace. Surely he was not riding as quickly as he could have if he were by himself.

"My lord, you should go on without me. I am a hindrance and you will miss your carriage."

"Nonsense," Thomas replied, not looking at him. "There is pleasure to be found in the journey. I am not rushed to return to life." The quiet tone, the deliberate way he spoke, gave no cause for Richard to believe he was lying to make him feel better.

"Might I inquire as to why, my lord? Surely yours is a life of great ease and comfort. I'm sure you are weary of battle."

Thomas was silent and Richard feared he'd gone too far in his assumptions. He watched Thomas's hands tighten around the reins before they loosened and he closed his eyes with a sigh.

"I *am* weary of battle," he said softly. "But, my family is a different sort of war." He sat taller. "Forgive me. That must seem very ungrateful. Spoiled even?" he tossed a smile over his shoulder at Richard. But Richard did not smile in return.

"I know of this kind of battle myself, my lord." He took a chance, opening some of his own vulnerability. Perhaps if he could discover why the future duke wanted to end his life and help him find peace, then the effects of his survival would be more lasting. Maybe that's even why he'd been thwarted in returning home. Perhaps the timeline knew his job was not done. Saving Thomas once, did not guarantee that he would evoke great change. It only gave him more time. Thomas had to *want* to accomplish those things.

"Oh? You have an overbearing father and a romantically driven mother? A vivacious younger sister and glaringly perfect brothers who constantly tell you how to run your life?" All of it deluged out and Thomas hung his head.

"I have an overbearing mother to be sure. She's very opinionated on how I should … conduct myself. What jobs I should take, what I should wear. Whom I should see."

"See?"

"Court?"

"Oh," Thomas breathed. "Yes. They do seem to want to put their fingers in as many pies as they can, do they not?" He paused to scoff, "Even what you wear?" Thomas eyed Richard disbelieving. "Given what we found you in, she was not doing a very good job, if you would not fault me for saying."

Richard laughed at this and the horse perked its ears to the sound and trotted a bit faster, catching up with Thomas. Their legs brushed. "She would be appalled at my current state, it is true."

"My mother has grand plans as well, especially since my sister became betrothed. Seems she doesn't want one of us marrying too far ahead of the other and I have been putting it off as long as possible."

"If I may say, that seems a pity."

"A pity?" Thomas's eyebrow arched seductively. Richard swallowed.

"That some young and well-bred lady should not have caught your eye?"

Thomas's eyes went to the road ahead which had begun to broaden. "I'm sure I've caught the eye of some, but most are only interested in my position, my estate, and the esteem of being the future duchess."

"Do you think yourself unlovable?"

"What is there to love of me? When they discover that I'm a battle-worn man who prefers art to company and quiet evenings under the stars alone to grand balls and dancing? When I couldn't care less what their dress is made of, or who was proposed to? When I'd much rather draw up battle plans and strategy than accompany them hat shopping? I am quite unlovable."

Maybe this man was not gay, Richard looked to the road again. Then again, being conditioned to like certain things was a sign of the time. When you weren't given a choice otherwise you found solace in the things you could.

"And what of children?" Richard asked. Thomas pulled in his reins and stopped beside Richard.

"First, you tell me something. Why are you not wed? Why do you rush into battle instead of having dozens of babes to bounce on your knee? Surely a man as virile and handsome as you are must have caught the eyes of many a young lady."

Richard quirked his head at him with a glare. Did he just call him handsome? "I've been too busy in school to think of starting a family or finding a ... a suitable partner."

"But there have been women?"

Richard swallowed. "I have loved few." It was not a lie. He loved his mother, and friends, and had formed a quick affection for Lillian during their brief time together.

"And what of your father?"

Richard looked away, angry and started the bobbing, hobbling pace again. Thomas had to catch up.

"Oh, and is it a sorer spot than all before?" Thomas asked.

"What of children?" Richard asked in return, desperate to not say any more about his father.

"Of course, I want children. I love them. Their authenticity, and joy, and free spirits. I would love to have children of my own. It's the only bright spot in thinking I must marry."

Richard's heart hurt. If Thomas was, in fact, not interested in women, there would be no other way, for him to have a family in this era without having to go against his own heart. What a painful burden.

"Your father?" Thomas questioned again.

Richard looked at him, he felt the burn of tears in his throat. "I have not spoken to him in years," he said softly. "The story of that is long and cutting." Thomas was silent as he watched Richard trying to pull his emotions in. "What of yours?"

Thomas shook his head. "We have a long journey before you'll ever have to meet the sorry old bastard. Let's save some of the revelations for the road ahead of us, shall we?"

They continued on in silence, at a steady and even pace and the road gave way to several side roads and more and more farms, and soon, houses. The congregation of people and buildings grew thicker as they approached Cardiff. The night was starting to replace the day and the dying light of dusk made it hard for Richard to see. He didn't have his damn glasses. He lost them somewhere on the battlefield, perhaps even when he fell. Being immobile, and relatively close to both Thomas and Andrew, he hadn't suffered much yet. But being particularly hard of sight at night certainly wouldn't help him steal away to the nearest portal while Thomas was otherwise distracted with sleep or the lasses in the tavern they would no doubt stop at.

Richard recalled from his studies that men in the British Army were often sought after by the fairer sex. Whether or not he was interested, Thomas was bound to have attention. Though most of the lower ranks were poor, officers were generally men of great wealth and power. They were known to be brave, smart, and best of all, lonely. Their bright red coats stood out in the era's more muted colors of brown, gray and blue. And so some young ladies honed in on them like bees to a garden.

They had not found Richard a regiment coat, which was fine by him. He wanted to blend in as much as possible. Richard watched where Thomas rode ahead of him, he didn't know his way through Cardiff, especially not the city as it stood in this era. He had been trying to plan out his next move and hadn't thought about where they were headed after, as he planned to be home before Thomas moved on.

He knew that there weren't going to be passenger railways for another decade or so. Which meant if he were to get trapped into riding with Thomas back to his home estate, they would do so by carriage and then a small ferry probably from Wales into Britain. He hated boats. He became sick quite easily. The fact of the matter was that Richard was good a great many things, but travel was not one of them. He'd even retched when he first jumped through the portal. While Thomas rode on, Richard pulled out the map. He swore there was one here when he'd looked that morning. But the map was bare of any points.

"What the bloody hell?" he growled and held it up to the fading light. "What the devil is this? What are you trying to show me?" The only discernable portal was on the water's edge where they would be crossing into England. Which meant—

"What is wrong with you now?" Thomas's voice roused Richard. He put the map away quickly.

It meant he was stuck with Thomas for at least another day.

"I'm weary of this horse," Richard did not lie. Thomas gave the 1800's British equivalent of an eye roll, scowling at him over his shoulder.

"Some soldier you are."

"I'm not a soldier, I told you." Richard snarked back.

"Right, I suppose being a medic to books doesn't allow for much time in the saddle."

"Ha ha," Richard grumbled back. "You are so witty, my lord." Thomas faced forward again, a smile on his face that irked Richard.

"I'll see to it that you get food, Little Lion, that will sort you out."

"I'm not little," Richard whispered beneath his breath and felt his stomach growl. He hadn't eaten since the eggs they'd had that morning. He was feeling weak, and tired, and put out of sorts. The babying remark made him mad and needled under his skin. "Don't we have a carriage to catch?" He grumbled and rode ahead, holding his body upright in a painful show of pride. Sweat began to bead on his forehead and he clenched his teeth. Thomas studied him from the side.

"Not until morning. A short ride to the ferry cross, and then another carriage will meet us on the other side of the inlet. We'll stay here tonight. Ale and food, and a decent bed will put you to rights again."

"A decent bed," Richard scoffed but his mouth watered. He looked over at Thomas who was still staring at him. Richard's eyes dropped to his mouth, the half-smile, the full bottom lip, the strong jaw now showing the stubble from just a day. He looked away quickly. A bed of his own meant time to plan his escape at the inlet crossing.

"Come on, Not-little Lion." Thomas joked and urged his horse to a canter, crossing the last few miles of their journey in haste. Richard had no choice but to follow, the seat of his ass bruised and sore. He fucking hated horses.

11

STORIES AND BATH TIME

They arrived at the inn and the keeper was most gracious, giving Thomas his best room available. Nothing but the finest for the son of the Duke of Marlborough.

"And my good man here will also need a room for the night." Thomas said and gently nudged Richard's sore shoulder.

"I apologize, my lord, but with the regiment in town and the Counselor's Fair we only have the one room."

"It is no matter. We share a battlefield; we can share a room."

"Surely he can sleep in the stables, my lord." The innkeeper looked at Richard who was dirty, and smelled and looked as though he might bite someone's head off at the slightest provocation. For someone who prided himself on his manscaping and grooming, Richard was surprised to find that it felt like he was the savage in this story.

"Not at all, this man saved my life and was gravely injured. I would have the town's finest physician come to our quarters as soon as we've settled." Thomas said, neither in anger nor in teasing. He did look seriously at the man, defending Richard in a way he needn't.

"Yes sir, of course. Right away."

"And hot baths for the both of us. It was a bloody battle."

"Yes, my lord. We'll have an extra tub taken to your room."

"Excellent," Thomas nodded, paid the man from a small leather pouch on his belt and turned to Richard. "One room it is."

"Fuck," Richard rolled his eyes until they closed.

"You do not wish to at least bathe? I wish you to if I'm to be stuck in a room with you for the night. You smell of blood and horse."

"Thank you, my lord. I'm aware." Richard said, annoyed, sore and hoping if he clicked his heels together, he would just be sent home. To his three-headed shower, and his silk pajamas, and all the CBD cream and paracetamol he could get.

"No matter, let's have a pint while the room is prepared." Thomas said. "And you're welcome by the way." He strode ahead to the pub beside the lodgings. Richard watched him go and felt horrible.

When he caught up to Thomas at a small table in the back, Richard folded his hands—bruised and cut knuckles from the fighting—in front of him and bowed his head.

"My lord, I did not mean to sound ungrateful. I'm merely tired. I am very thankful for the room, though it is not necessary. I can surely find other lodgings and you do not have to pay for my room."

"Where would you find lodgings, Doctor Shaw? The town is booked up. Sit down."

"My lord, I do not wish to be—"

"A burden? Then come sit beside me, Richard, and lighten my load." Thomas said, eyes deep and blue in the low light of the pub.

"Thomas, I—" Richard felt the blush spread up his neck to his cheeks, thank goodness most of it hidden by his beard. "I don't know how I could possibly help you."

"Tell me a story. You know books, you read, you are a learned man. Tell me your favorite story. Ah, here's the lass I want to see!" he said suddenly, and smiled with a perfectly dimpled chin to the young and busty woman who set down two tankards of ale and two bowls of stew before them. He winked, Richard watched and thanked the woman. She blushed and curtseyed to him.

"See? Not all women are terrible," Richard said, groaning as he sat on the hard wooden bench. It was still better than a damn saddle.

"I've nothing against them." Thomas said and his eyes quickly fell to the food and the drink. He looked more longingly at it, Richard liked to believe. The ale was dark with molasses and it felt round and beautiful against his tongue as Richard drank it down, almost with one swallow. Gods, beer was the last thing he thought he'd like. "That's right, man," Thomas smiled. "Another for my friend!"

"My lord," Richard burped into his hand. "I apologize, I was thirsty."

"Drink up my friend, a hot bath awaits you. But first my story."

"Yes, my lord. What shall it be? Adventure? Romance? Mystery?"

"I've no mind for romance. I'm trying to steer clear of it. How about adventure?"

"Fair. I just didn't know if you needed a respite from the fighting." Richard said softly, looking into the bottom of his empty tankard. He remembered, a flash of last night. Thomas had groaned in his sleep. He'd lashed out only to curl back over with a sob. He'd thought he'd dreamed it, but as he stared at the bottom of his glass, the memory clarified.

"I heard you in your sleep, Thomas. I know that battle sometimes stays in a man's minds, even when we try to put it aside." Thomas was silent, he took a long drink of his ale, closed his eyes and held the cup in both hands. Richard stayed silent beside him. Their knees touched beneath the table.

"There is no shame in it, my lord. We are not above the

horrors of war. We are not meant to live on the constant edge of death, witness to the worst of man, and survive it unscathed."

"What would you have me do?"

"You can talk about it. That often helps."

"What do you know of it?" Thomas's jaw clenched and Richard turned to him.

"You said I was a learned man, intelligent. I beg you listen to me. No human can carry the grief of taking lives and watching those they care for lose theirs. And the good heart is susceptible in worse ways, my lord. I believe you have a beautiful and good heart. Otherwise you would not suffer so."

The woman brought another round and a loaf of bread with fresh cream butter. Richard nodded his thanks and tore a piece off, putting it in front of Thomas. His hands were shaking. Richard gently reached out and put the tankard of ale in them.

"Let me tell you a story about a man who lives in the Americas and he has a traveling show. With wild beasts and indigenous men, and a woman who can shoot a musket from the back of a horse and hit a target at two hundred paces."

Thomas's eyes shot up, the tears they held reabsorbed and he smiled. "Yes, I'd like that very much."

They ate in leisure and drank in earnest. By the time Buffalo Bill Cody's story was finished, and jokes and barbs were thrown back and forth with gusto and good humor, slurring their words and throwing arms around one another, the innkeeper stopped by to give them the key to their accommodations.

"Thank you, my good man."

"Your baths are prepared and the doctor will meet you shortly after you've settled."

"You're a gentleman and a decent fellow, you are," Richard clapped the small man on the back, nearly sending him sprawling. Together he and Thomas trudged up the stairs to the top level of the inn, at the end of a long hall, and into the largest room, reserved for the most noble guests.

Inside, was one large bed, canopied with fine linens, a wash basin, a changing screen, a fireplace and two copper tubs filled with steaming water. Richard knew he would not all fit in it, but it was the sweetest sight he could have imagined. Thomas began to disrobe without pause. He hung his coat up and folded his shirt neatly, but when it came to his pants, he wobbled from the ale. Richard tried to look away. But the man was captivatingly strong and beautiful. He barely had any hair on him. His chest was muscled and defined, scarred with the wounds of many battles and his hips were narrow. Muscled lines traced down his flat stomach to a slight trail of hair below his belly button and Richard turned away.

"Do us a favor then?" Thomas chuckled, stumbling on one leg to get his pants off. Richard cleared his throat, put on his best sober impression and stood at his side, allowing Thomas to put his hand on his shoulder and hold on while he took his pants down. Richard stared at the ceiling, the rafters, anything but the naked and firm ass of the future duke, whose hand was now digging into his shoulder.

"My god, you're strong as an ox," Thomas was saying, now naked, hand still on Richard. He paused to knead into the taut muscles of his one good shoulder. He stopped moving. Richard chanced a look down to find Thomas staring at his shoulder, his neck, his face. "Watching you in battle was a sight to be seen, doctor of books," Thomas's voice was soft, his eyes fell to Richard's lips. Richard leaned closer, his eyes made the same mark.

"I do not wish to battle tonight," Richard whispered, the drink and the food and the comfort of the quiet room doing everything to conspire against his insistence that he would not fuck up history any further. He certainly wanted to fuck something up. Thomas gave his shoulder a squeeze.

"Then let us rest." He stepped into the hot bath with a groan and Richard waited until he'd sat back, eyes closed, sighing with the warmth and pleasure of it, before he undressed. Despite the long day, the lack of food, and the obvious loss of blood, his body had still responded and Richard did everything he could to rush from behind the changing screen to the tub without putting it all out for Thomas to see. When he hit the water he hissed and growled, it must have been just beneath boiling. It probably would cool quicker than he would like.

He sat back and closed his eyes. He heard the gentle sloshing next to him and felt his own hands go beneath the water. He was still hard, though as his body relaxed so did his muscles. Saints, was there anything better than a bath? The ache in his shoulder subsided and he fell into a relaxed state for the first time in days.

Thomas should not have drunk so much. He was open-hearted and foolish, and brazen. Though it should not be a matter of importance to disrobe in front of a fellow soldier, it felt different with Richard. Everything felt different with him. Being alone with Richard, the stalwart and quiet giant, made him feel somehow ... shy. He had to put on his best cavalier face to not seem strange when they'd gotten ready for their baths. His hand on Richard's strong and giant shoulder made Thomas wonder what other miraculous muscles the man had. He'd learned much of his body when he'd washed his torso, but that was a time of healing and worry. Confusion as to why someone would want to save him so badly that they'd take a blade into their own body had kept him fascinated with the man as a whole.

When he saw the way Richard was concentrating to look away, he started to wonder if it was his own shyness or something else. Though punishable by death or being locked away in an asylum for the insane, the feelings that rose up in him, didn't seem anything but a natural response. Richard was a beautiful man, an exemplary specimen. Strong but silent, intelligent but cautious.

He wanted to press his nose to Richard's neck. He felt his cock grow hard when he studied the pulse in Richard's throat. The curve of his lips beckoned and he smelled of dust, and blood, and sweat. A particular smell that drove something animalistic in Thomas. He wished he could share his bath with the man. Feel his skin on his, the warmth, the strength, the gripping hands ... He quickly jumped into the hot bath to keep his reaction to himself.

When Richard, large and imposing, stepped behind the screen to disrobe, like a blushing virgin, Thomas fought against the urge to make fun of him. He didn't want to embarrass either of them. They had a long way to go and he didn't want to risk Richard leaving. Still, he watched the silhouette of the man, and closed his eyes, his hands on his body, cradling the hard evidence that he was too long away from attention of any kind.

His eyes remained closed and he listened to Richard hiss and grunt when he entered the hot bath, water sloshing over the sides, not enough room for both it and the massive man. He couldn't help opening one eye to look over at the way his jaw went from clenched to soft. When Richard moaned, Thomas's hands tightened on his hard shaft and he nearly came. Gods but he was too lonely. Too far away from touch. And the touch he truly longed for filled him with confusion. Thomas shuddered in the tub and his hands fell away from his still aroused body.

Sitting up quickly, and trying to move past the feelings for this strange and large gentleman, Thomas began washing himself with the bar of soap provided. He took too long, perhaps, with his nether regions, but Richard was resting, eyes closed and he was caught up in how good it felt, watching him and touching himself. He would be discreet. Just as he got closer, closer to the edge, Richard opened his dark eyes and looked over at him. Thomas cleared his throat, frustrated and angry that he hadn't gotten to release the pressure, but almost relieved that he hadn't finished something so bold.

"Are you well, my lord?" Richard spoke softly, sat up and flinched as the stitches pulled. He looked down at the red and puckering wound.

"It is I that should be asking you," Thomas rinsed his hair and his body. He took some deep breaths and tucked away his desire with thoughts of the impending doom ahead of them. Nothing cooled one's desire like thinking of being with their overbearing father soon. What if the company set to greet him upon arriving home included possible marriage prospects? His stomach felt ill and he scowled. He handed Richard the soap, wet fingers touching. Before he could pull away, Richard took his wrist.

"I hate—" he dropped his eyes. Thomas's throat felt tight and stuck. Richard must have seen what he'd done, felt the desire he was radiating. What had he done? Surely he should hate him. Thomas would be ruined. His father would commit him. "Hate to beg of your help," Richard finished and closed his eyes before he leveled them on Thomas. Dark and lit by the firelight. Thomas was lost.

"Ask of me anything," he whispered back.

"I cannot reach, all of me, with my shoulder. You do not have to comply." Richard's face went red and he hung his head in shame. Thomas's eyes turned hard, even while the idea of touching him made his whole body alight. He clenched his jaw and nodded, stoically. *I must remain unfazed*, he thought. This was a battle of a different kind. A good man, a man who had saved his life, now asked for his help. Thomas could see Richard was ashamed. He hated being weak. He would not be weak if not for jumping in front of the blade intended for Thomas. *I will be honorable.*

"Of course. It won't do to be only half clean." Thomas rose from his bath, pink and glowing skin over his hard muscles and wrapped a bath sheet around his body. *With efficiency*, he thought.

I must do this in a non-caring manner. I must not enjoy this. I must not … appear to enjoy this.

When he knelt down beside the bath, Richard sat forward and Thomas began with the back of his thick neck, where hair was growing in, down his shoulder blades, a finger grazing the line of bone, his spine, the mountains of strength where his fibrous muscle attached. Thomas's hands remained resilient, digging into the muscles and the lines of Richard's back, slicked with soap. Richard groaned and his hands went below the water, between his legs before he quickly put them on the sides of the tub.

Thomas watched, his touch lightening. He gently raised both arms and scrubbed the hair beneath and down to the water line. He washed Richard's neck, his wound, his arm. He paused when he'd done all that was necessary, but not all of Richard's body.

"Shall I continue?" Thomas asked, voice heavy. Richard's skin was flushed and he shook his head.

"I believe I can manage the rest on my own." Thomas nodded and turned to leave but Richard grabbed his sheet, stopping him short. "Thank you, my lord. Truly." When the lion looked up at Thomas, there was more than gratitude. Thomas began to wonder if this wasn't all some elaborate trap. Who was this man, really? Why had he saved his life? Was this all some ruse to keep him alive to be married and carry on the family honor? Thomas scowled.

"I shall go and see if the doctor is ready," he said and stepped behind the screen to dress. Somber and sober, Thomas left the room without saying another word.

12
POPPY POWDER AND MUTUAL SUFFERING

"Fuck," Richard said, as he watched Thomas go. The man was going to kill him. Richard wasn't a virgin, and he wasn't an idiot. He'd known exactly how Thomas had felt when he'd leaned on him naked. But he'd also denied and shut down those feelings. Richard was an observer. He paid attention. He listened as Thomas's breath deepened and quickened, the gentle slap of the water against the copper basin when they'd sat beside each other.

Who was he to judge how a man needed to release pressure? But surely it would be something he'd do in private? Only when he'd glanced over, Thomas was looking at him. Then came the embarrassment. The piety, the withdrawal. Richard felt his groin pull. To live in this time, to want a man, to be denied or worse, killed or committed, where they'd scramble your brain and beat you into submitting?

"Fuck," Richard said again and sat forward to wash his straining body. His soapy hands traveled over his body, where Thomas had touched and all of the places Richard wished he had. He couldn't let him continue on this path. It would damn his soul and Richard would not be the one that drove the future duke into the next musket fire, out of guilt. Had Thomas had relations, before, with a man? Was he secretly taking lovers? Is that why he didn't want to go home to tie himself to a woman? Or is that why he wished to die in battle? Richard felt sad for the charismatic soldier who by all accounts was the epitome of manliness and strength. Any woman would be biting at the bit to tie him down. So was Richard.

"Stupid. You need to get home," he reminded himself and looked around at the room, the map, dangerously across the room in his dirty clothing. "Stop thinking with your dick and start using your brain," he reprimanded, got out of the tub, and wrapped the clean sheet around himself. He stood by the fire, towel at his waist and contemplating the map. The pinpoints of swirling blue light lit and extinguished as if the entire timeline was in flux. What the hell was he supposed to do now?

He wondered, then, if Lillian's father was still around. Was he in this timeline? Was Lillian? Could he find either of them? Thomas's father would know of many families, perhaps the Blackwells were well known. Maybe, if he started to screw things up badly enough, the Timekeepers would come and rescue him. Or kill him …

The door burst open and Richard fumbled with the map, tucking it back in his jacket as Thomas and a genteel-looking man with round spectacles came through the door.

"Is this the man?" his old voice was craggy. "Or did you have a fortress put into your room."

"This is the soldier, Dr. Worthington. I would be exceedingly grateful if you could inspect his stitches and see that he is healing properly."

"Ah, very well." The doctor turned to Richard again. "But you must sit down, because I have not a step ladder, and I shall never reach your high walls." He laughed and Richard couldn't help the smile that came to his face.

"Of course, Dr. Worthington. I appreciate you being here at such a late hour."

"Eh? Oh yes. The duke, Thomas's father, is a good friend of our family. Why, we were just discussing the trip to his estate to attend his sister's wedding. We may travel with you part of the way."

Richard's eyes darted to Thomas who was busying himself with anything other than looking at him. He had not known they would be there in time for the wedding. Only that he might have to suffer through a few awkward dinners. Perhaps meet his sister's fiancé. A wedding was a larger problem. Records might be made, journal entries written. The strange Doctor Shaw exposed to several people. Richard sat in the chair and allowed the doctor to look at his wound.

"Aren't we all lucky to be going to a wedding?" Richard said tensely, more to Thomas than to the doctor.

"That we are. A right joyous occasion! One I'm sure his mother hopes will be a double event."

"Let's not get into that, William," Thomas said and poured himself a glass of wine from the side table. "Not tonight, I've already seen enough battles for the week."

Richard leaned in towards the doctor. "I have told the future duke and I will tell you now, as a trusted friend of his, that I should not accompany him home, especially on the eve of such an event. It would not be polite of me to—"

"Eh? Nonsense!" The old man shouted and knocked Richard in the good shoulder with his cane. Richard yelped and both men looked at him. Thomas hid a smile behind his wine glass and turned away. "That boy needs all the allies he can get once he returns home."

"I am no ally, I—"

"Oh no? Did you not step in front of a blade for this man? Risk your own life?" Doctor Worthington leaned down, took out another set of spectacles to put on top of the ones he already wore and looked at the wound. Richard should ask him where he could obtain such glasswork, but the doctor shook his head.

"A gnat's breath closer and you would have been dead. You are quite lucky indeed." The doctor sat up, looked at both of them. "Lucky to have found each other, in the middle of battle. To have been there for one another." His eyes bored into Richard's. "You do not leave his side. Do you hear me? Or this wound was all for nought," his voice was quiet, away from Thomas's prying ears.

"What was that?" Thomas asked.

"I said you aren't to leave this man's side." The doctor directed the command to Thomas this time. "There may be complications. He will be quite weak. I will clean and dress it, properly this time, not some shoddy battlefield child's play, and you will keep him calm and comfortable. So that he may arrive at your family's estate in good health. Do you hear me, young Thomas?"

"Yes, old William, I hear you," Thomas said and sipped his wine, watching the process as the doctor went about treating Richard's shoulder. Richard wondered if he was trying to learn how to do it 'properly' for the next time in battle, or if he liked the way Richard squirmed and hissed when the doctor prodded, poked and restitched anything that had popped open in the course of their horrible ride in.

When he had finished, he gave Richard a glass of wine and poured a small glass jar of powder in it.

"What in the devil is that? I'm not drinking that."

"It is merely the dust of poppies. It will help you to rest and the pain to not be so intense. You have a long carriage ride tomorrow. We all do."

Richard eyed him suspiciously but took the wine. Thomas raised his twice-filled glass to his, in toast, and they drank.

"Goodnight, captain and soldier. Keep each other alive until morning, would you?" The old man waved as he left, closing the door behind him.

"Best field medic the King's service ever had. Probably the best England has known." Thomas said. Then he set aside his cup and stood. "Well?"

"What?" Richard said, already feeling drowsy and strange.

"Well, off to bed."

"I'm not sleeping in the bed! You're the duke, you sleep in the bed."

"Don't be ridiculous. I am not a duke yet, and you are injured."

"I don't matter," Richard barked suddenly. "It's you—" he paused, standing and woozy, feeling like the world was turning around him. "You must be kept safe. You must live. I'm just a librarian," he whispered, the last thing he saw, was Thomas rushing up to him. Then the world went black.

Didn't matter? Thomas thought as Richard fell into his arms. He carried him, as well as he could, to the large bed and flopped him into the soft comfort, adjusting his body to favor the injury. Thomas watched him for a while, the towel around his waist had come open and his thick legs were exposed. Blushing, Thomas closed the towel before Richard could shift again and show all of what he had to offer. Thomas already felt conflicted about the evening, and all of the desire that still pulsed in low waves through his body. Richard murmured in his sleep.

"I need to save him. The world. I want to go home ... I don't want to kill ..." Richard started to sob, incoherently into the bedding. Thomas watched, as Richard's teeth clenched and he clung to the pillow beneath him. His heart hurt. How many men had he seen, fallen in battle, mortally wounded, devoid of hope? How often had he, himself felt these things? He thought of Richard's words over their ale and food. They had lived through horrors untold, that often followed them off the field. Soldiers were often stuck in perpetual hell and there would never be peace. Not even in their dreams. Thomas sighed, removed his shoes and his shirt and crawled into bed beside Richard. He ran his calloused hand through Richard's thick hair and down his back. Meditative and sweet, the touch gave comfort to them both.

"Hush now, all will be well," he said softly. Richard's aching sobs grew quieter. "I am here now, and as you saved me, so shall I save you. From night terrors or real ones. I'll not leave your side." Thomas wasn't even conscious of the words; he was too caught up in the small curl behind Richard's ear. The strange contradiction of a man so large with so soft a heart. So little concern for himself, and so much drive to keep Thomas alive, despite his best efforts to end his own life. Thomas fell asleep, his hand across Richard's body, clinging to his hip. His dreams of war were quiet that night. He was in a soft field of grass, a steady heartbeat beneath his ears. The dark, his greatest friend. The quiet moment, theirs alone.

Richard had swirling dreams, falling through a dark tunnel into a battlefield, fire shooting through his body, screams and cries, his own included. Aching for normalcy, aching to be not so alone in this new and brutal world. Where his life was a secret and his future uncertain. He wept into the darkness, clinging to the soft covers around him until a hand came to soothe. Warm, rough calloused palms, heavy and strong against the trembling of his muscles. Soft words, fingers in his hair. Richard was soothed and his body relaxed for the first time in a very long time. He pressed into the touch. He wanted it to never end. His dreams settled and became soft. Richard rolled over and took a warm body in his hands and together, they kept the world and the darkness at bay.

When Richard awoke, he felt first the stirrings of his body, needing to pee. The unfortunate effect of that was his hard erection pressing into a very warm and firm cradle. It felt so delicious that he was sure he was still dreaming. Spooning a lover. A late Sunday morning, about to get up, make sweaty and slow love, and hit brunch and maybe the markets. He took in a deep breath, nuzzled into a neck, smelling of warm soap and traces of wine. His nose traced under and behind the man's ear and he moaned. His hands tightened around the broad and smooth chest. The muscled body moved deftly against him, sliding up and down slowly.

"My lord," Richard groaned and his hands tightened into flesh as he felt his body respond, throb, ache. The warmth and quiet of the bedroom filtered in slowly. Richard's brain told him that something was wrong, but his body wasn't listening.

Thomas shifted in his arms, his hand covering Richard's, tightening. Whether to stop him, or to encourage, he did not know. Richard held his breath in expectation of either route. Thomas sighed, groaned and then held still. Very still. Even his breath stopped, silent in his chest. Richard took his response to heart and pulled away quickly. He cleared his throat and swung his legs over the opposite side of the bed. "My lord—" he whispered, head hung.

"Richard," Thomas breathed out and moved to leave the opposite side of the bed.

"I apologize," Richard said quickly, and took the sheet where he'd become undressed in the motions of his sleep, to wrap it once more around his waist. Nothing could hide the bulge. Nothing could seem to make it go away. Thomas turned, his eyes fell to it, his breath quickened. Richard reached up to touch his pounding head. "I think whatever the doctor gave me—"

"Of course," Thomas said, a small break in his voice. "It's nothing of consequence. The body is a strange universe indeed and yours has been through much." He took his shirt from the edge of the bed and dressed, faced away from Richard. "I'll see you downstairs." He took most of his belongings, in haste and slammed the door behind him.

"Fuck." Richard growled and slumped back into the bed. There was nothing for it. He couldn't start the day this way and his sexual need was not going to help him or Thomas to get through the next few days. He lay in bed, took Thomas's pillow and pressed it to his face. Just for this moment, just for this time. So that he could focus ... he inhaled deeply, trying to recall every hard line, every smooth curve. His hands found his throbbing cock and he shook with anticipation, buried in the smell of Thomas, undulating into the sheets they shared, imagining it was his body he was with, the round and muscled backside, the hipbones, the flat chest to bite and lick, his thick neck and soft brown curls ...

Richard came hard and fast, into the sheets and called out to the gods to make this torture stop. He sobbed, he ached, he wished he'd never traveled through time. Surely the apocalypse wouldn't have been as bad as wanting a man he could never have? He waited for his breath to slow, cleaned himself up and got dressed. He was able to move his shoulder well enough to get his own clothes on. He should just leave. Sneak out the back door of the inn. But the doctor knew he was going and had told him to stay with Thomas. He had told them both that they needed each other.

Thomas didn't need him. He was a bonafide cad. Richard splashed water on his face and tried to get his heart and mind together, at least long enough to plan his escape to any other timeline than this one.

Thomas slumped against the closed door, with his ear pressed to the wood. He listened to Richard curse, shuffle, fall back into bed. He heard the bed frame hit the wall, he heard the desperate grunts and it drove his hands to his own body. The hall was deserted in the early hour and he knew it would not take long. Not for all the desire he'd woken with. He thought of Richard's hard cock pressed in the crease of his backside that morning, the strong grip across his chest, the beautiful noises the man made into his ear as his nose traced the lines of his jaw. The thought alone made the pressure build and swell ... gods, he wanted that man. Thomas used both hands, squeezing tight in long strokes until he heard Richard grunt and cry out before sighing into the bed. Only then did he let his own body give in. The climax rocked him hard against the wooden door frame and shot through his body, hot and desperate. Sweat formed on his brow and he looked down to the mess he'd made.

"Fuck," he reiterated the word Richard seemed so fond of and it felt like a release in itself. He cleaned himself with a kerchief and felt the weight of pressure relieved from his shoulders and hips. He wanted to go back in, to tackle him into the bed, and fall asleep in the warm morning light. He wanted so much to let Richard know his reaction and his need was not unfounded. But he had no idea if the man would survive the shame or even admit to his desire. Thomas knew he couldn't very well admit to his. Even though he'd always known.

Tears came to his eyes, he clenched his jaw and leaned against the wall, as the ache, the hurt, and the shame passed over him.

He willed himself to think of anything else, find a better purpose. He must go home, to see his family. To be with his sister. To spend whatever little amount of time he had left with Richard. Even if only as a trusted friend, he would take the time he gave him. Even if it was only given reluctantly. Thomas left the hall and went down to secure the carriage for the road back home.

When Richard finally made his way down the stairs of the inn, the lodgers were bustling about, in hallways, in the dining area, on staircases, all preparing for departure or checking in from long evenings on the road. Richard, a good six inches taller than most, stood out from the crowd and elicited stares. In his own time, he was only a bit above average. But here, probably due to the nutrition and just the steadily growing genetic pool, there were no overly large people. Even Thomas.

He was only a couple of inches shorter than Richard. Slighter in build but a body hard-earned on the battlefield. He had thick shoulders from fighting and swinging his saber, and narrow hips accustomed to marching and long hours in the saddle. Richard tried to turn his thoughts away from Thomas's riding skills. He closed his eyes and tucked away the feeling of Thomas's muscled ass against him. When he descended the last stair he saw Thomas, in uniform, fresh shaven and speaking with the doctor and a woman of equal age and stature, who was probably the doctor's wife. They looked like two little hobbits about to go for an adventure. Richard tried not to smirk.

He did like the old doctor, but he'd not allow him to put anything else in his drink. When he approached with his wife, Richard suddenly felt nervous. Meeting men in battle was a different sort of greeting. Women were astute, they understood body language and subtleties. You couldn't go balls out and yelling with a club. Richard took in a deep breath, put on his most genteel smile, even hoping one of his dimples would show beneath the beard, and stopped before the doctor and his wife.

"Doctor Worthington, and Mrs. Worthington I presume," he said softly and bowed, hands behind his back. "It is a pleasure to see you both this morning."

"My God the man's a bear!" Mrs. Worthington gasped and then covered her tiny mouth. "Forgive me, I am told I am too loud of mouth." Richard smiled down at the gray-haired sprite, now looking up at him with mischief. Richard took her hand in his and bowed to kiss it.

"Just as I prefer my women, Mrs. Worthington," he said and winked and she burst into laughing. When Richard unbent, Thomas caught his eyes with a curious scowl. Doctor Worthington smiled up at him and pinched his elbow.

"That's a right lad then, how are you feeling?"

"I am much improved," Richard paused to breath and gave a fleeting look at Thomas. "I was plagued with strange dreams but, slept better than I have in months." He looked back into Thomas's eyes before smiling at the doctor.

"That is good news. Yes, the poppies sometimes uncover all the things we bury, it is to be certain. But you must use caution, they can be highly addictive."

"Noted, good sir," Richard said. "I should not be needing more of it for a good long while."

"Not unless you plan on stepping in front of a bullet for this one next." Doctor Worthington poked Thomas with his cane and Thomas blushed. He did not smile. Richard looked at his downcast face.

"It would be a decision that would be easily made in defense of his life. We must keep the future duke safe." Richard said and nodded to the doctor and his wife. "If you'll please excuse me, I will retrieve my belongings and meet you at the livery." He did not look back to see the way Thomas watched him with intensity.

1 3

A MOST PRECIOUS GIFT

The carriage was grand by current time standards and Richard helped the doctor and his wife up into their seats. Thomas had disappeared after they had broken their fast, assuring them he would meet them at the carriage within the hour. The doctor and his wife sat beside each other, as was proper, and so he would have to sit next to Thomas. It wasn't a large seat but it was far superior to a saddle. He tried to stay on his side, even as they waited for Thomas to arrive. The couple talked of the weather and the journey ahead, all very innocuous until Mrs. Worthington began to talk of the latest gossip from Cardiff and Richard felt like it was becoming awkward. Where had the future duke gotten off to? Had he made a run for it? Richard felt a sweat break out on his neck just as Thomas tore open the door and startled them into a coordinated jump.

"Apologies," he breathed and stepped into the carriage. "I thought you could use these for the journey. I had to wait for the shop to open and had quite the time finding the exact things I wanted." He put a stack of packages, wrapped in plain brown paper on the seat next to Richard and knocked on the top of the carriage. "We can be off!"

The jolt caused them all to falter and correct their postures in their seats. Richard looked at the parcels. "What is it that you have purchased?"

"They are for you. For the journey. I knew you must miss them." Thomas said, rather indifferent, and then looked out the window. Richard looked down to the plainly wrapped rectangles.

"But my lord, you needn't have done anything."

"Nonsense. Do not be coy. They will serve no good purpose beneath the paper." Both the doctor and his wife watched with anticipation as Richard took the first parcel and slowly unwrapped the twine holding it. He gasped and his heart ticked up madly. Inside of each wrapping was a book. Beautiful, hand bound, printed books. His eyes filled with tears that he quickly brushed away. Poetry, social essay, literature, philosophy, something from every category the shop probably sold.

"I did not know your preferences," Thomas said, not looking at him. Richard wanted to pull him into his arms and smother him with kisses, and cuddles, and every hot and needy caress he felt thrumming inside of him.

"This is an exquisite selection, my lord, this is—" Richard sniffed and shook his head. Thomas looked from the outside passing of the town and into his face. His features softened. "This is far too generous," Richard said, shaking his head and biting his lip. Thomas watched his teeth play over it, and his eyes narrowed, darkened.

"Well, in any case, it might make the journey less torturous for you." He looked quickly back outside. Richard wiped at his eyes and looked up, startled to remember that there were other people in the carriage. When he opened the first book, a collection of poetry by Shakespeare, he had to squint in the low light filtering in from the windows and the jostling of the carriage. Mrs. Worthington tapped him lightly on the knee, like a bird lighting on a branch.

"Here, dear, try these," she said and handed him her

spectacles. Richard accepted them with a bow and when he placed the wire and glass on his nose the words came into focus.

"Thank you, my lady," he breathed, and she beamed back at him. He began with the first line and felt his hand clutch at his heart. Oh, for God's sake, books. He wanted to cry and curl up into the seat and put his head in Thomas's lap and read to him these sonnets. He looked over and Thomas was studying him. Particularly his glasses. Richard was, at first horrified, that he now knew his vision was not as strong as his body. But a small smile spread on Thomas's face before he covered it with his hand and turned, once more, to stare out the window. Richard wondered if Thomas knew how much this meant to him. He didn't want to feel any more affection for or confusion over the man, and yet, here he was, practically falling in love.

"Well? Do not keep them all to yourself. Read to us something!" Mrs. Worthington tapped Richard on the knee. He looked up from the book with a blush. The doctor was already fast asleep. Thomas did not budge from his study of the city as it turned into countryside.

"I do not wish to disturb anyone," Richard said quietly, glancing at the sleeping doctor.

"Nonsense! That stone of a man will not wake until the ferry. He does this on every journey, so as to not have to discuss politics with his mouth-forward wife. And I'm certain the future duke would be soothed. He looks far too sullen for a day this fine."

The voice of truth from the small and aged woman caused both Richard and Thomas to startle and stare at her. Richard looked at Thomas who scowled.

"I would not read, my lord, if it would disturb your peace."

"Do not concern yourself with my peace," he said. "The lady has made a request, and we must strive to be gentlemen at all costs."

"It will not interrupt your thoughts?"

"I shall weather it, for the lady's sake," Thomas grumbled and turned to look out the window, his head in his hand, closing his eyes as if in pain. Richard was going to put the book down at the cold reaction, but the lady struck his shin with her husband's cane.

"I prefer Shakespeare!"

"Ouch, ok!" Richard grumbled, set down the rest of the books, and pulled out the new but ancient small book. He opened on a random page and was one line in before he wished he'd picked a different poem.

14

SHAKESPEARE, SELF-DOUBT, AND RESOLUTION

Thomas wished they were alone. It was torture waiting for Richard to take the package. Then the slow unwrapping, then the deep-seated, gut-wrenching worry that what he found would not be to his liking. What if he studied books of science, diagrams of naturalists' papers, mathematical equations? He was a reeling idiot to have chosen poets and philosophy. He knew he had chosen poorly when Richard remained quiet as he sifted through them. But when he looked up at Thomas, tears in his eyes, the happiest, most emotional he'd ever seen the lion of a man, he wished they were alone and that he could pull Richard close, kiss away every tear and reassure him, that he understood the feelings in his heart.

Then, when Mrs. Worthington insisted that Richard read, and had given him her spectacles, Thomas nearly jumped out of the carriage. Richard without them was a dynamic beast of a man, a warrior on the field. In glasses he was studious, in a heart-pounding and sensual way. Thomas scooted away; he crossed his legs to hide his reaction. Even after the morning's passion letting, there seemed to be new reasons in every moment to find him even more attractive. Richard's voice, after squeaking when the woman struck him, was deep and even toned. Thomas closed his eyes and listened to a million different reasons in every intonation to fall deeper into peace. Richard's voice was quiet like a caress over the words, soft like a wind through the moor, deep like the rush of the sea. Thomas imagined laying beneath a tree, leafed out in spring green and renewed, his head in Richard's lap. Listening to the words …

> Let me not to the marriage of true minds
> Admit impediments. Love is not love
> Which alters when it alteration finds,
> Or bends with the remover to remove.
> O no! it is an ever-fixed mark
> That looks on tempests and is never shaken;
> It is the star to every wand'ring bark,
> Whose worth's unknown, although his height be
>   taken.
> Love's not Time's fool, though rosy lips and cheeks
> Within his bending sickle's compass come;
> Love alters not with his brief hours and weeks,
> But bears it out even to the edge of doom.
> If this be error and upon me proved,
> I never writ, nor no man ever loved.

Thomas couldn't stand the ache. Couldn't breathe, couldn't think straight. Love bears out even to the edge of doom. Were they not on the edge of doom? And wasn't Richard still there? A loyal and patient lion beside him. Richard closed the book. The lady had fallen asleep under the gracious and sweet spell of his voice. Thomas looked at Richard, who was caressing the binding of the book and shaking his head.

Thomas wanted to say something but no words would suffice. He wanted to kiss Richard. He wanted to trust in him, delight in his company, feel free to be themselves with one another. He wanted so many things that were not allowed. It burned like a fire in him and made him both frustrated and broken inside.

"Shall I continue, my lord?" Richard asked softly, still not looking at him. Thomas clenched his teeth.

"Do not torture me further," he whispered and turned away. Richard nodded, and slid to the other side of the carriage, as far away from him as possible.

Richard's heart was breaking and if he could jump out of the carriage he would. His only hope was that the portal by the inlet crossing would carry him far away from here. Oh, how Thomas's words cut him. That he'd hated him reading the poem. That it was torture to him! Had he thought he'd done it on purpose? He was torn between wanting to apologize and wanting to hate the hot and cold treatment that came from Thomas. This was the man who was supposed to love books, and poetry, and the arts. And yet he behaved as if it was an affront to his very soul to be in the presence of it. Perhaps he was resolved to denounce the truth in his own heart.

It wasn't the poem. Perhaps it wasn't the book at all, Richard thought with a tear rolling over his cheek as he feigned sleep against the far wall. It was him. He was an affront to the future duke. He'd gone too far that morning. He'd misread the signs, and in dreamy sensual sleep had acted out. He'd shamed himself. Richard hadn't felt ashamed of who he was since secondary school. He gently touched his cheek, the scar beneath. The reason for his magnificent beard. He was always hiding, in some ways, even in more modern times. He should have disappeared. He shouldn't be here. He let a small sob out before quieting his grief and staring at the passing countryside, waiting for the end of this terrible journey like the next breath underwater.

~

The journey was longer than it would have been without the heartache. Whatever would Thomas do? He'd committed to taking Richard back with him, sent word that he wished to honor the man's bravery. Now, just sitting with him in the carriage was torture. If they'd been alone would things have been different? He closed his eyes. He told himself that God held no space in his thoughts, that in his mind he was free. What would Thomas's life look like if he could have all he wanted?

He would want to not be constrained by the bounds of society. To not be expected to have a family to be fulfilled. He would be able to travel, to experience different countries and cultures. He would spend hours looking at art, painting the way his sister was allowed. He would read, constantly, beneath the shade of deep and woody trees, in the lap of a lover. A lover with a voice like dark silk, who knew the cadence of poetry could direct the palpitation of the heart, and guide it to be stronger and truer.

If he had such freedom, he would put his head in Richard's lap and listen, soft breezes beside them, the rustle of leaves above, the quiet of being in the presence of someone who calmed and cared for him, just as he was. He sighed, felt a sob tug in his chest. They would part ways with Doctor and Mrs. Worthington at the inlet. Both groups taking separate ferries.

He would be alone with Richard. For a very brief journey across the bay and another carriage ride until he was home again. How would he stay distant? It hurt so much to see the man's face fall after his beautiful reading. He had to cut him, did he not? So that there could be no confusion as to what their arrangement meant. But Thomas did not want the estranged distance between them. He wanted to be curled into his arms. A sob escaped his throat and roused him from the inner turmoil of his thoughts. The carriage was slowing as it approached the bay of the inlet.

Thomas looked out the window first, trying to avoid looking at Richard. The Doctor was rousing, his wife too. When he chanced a glance out the window on Richard's side of the carriage, he saw the man, quite relaxed and composed, carefully reading and turning the pages. So calm. Even as the storm was raging in Thomas's heart, just watching Richard read, made him feel calm.

Richard had dried his eyes and sobered his thoughts as they made their way across the countryside. He was not here to fall in love, or to engage in any affair. He was here to ensure that Thomas was kept alive, at least long enough to put in place the progressive and educational policies that would keep Great Britain from becoming an apocalyptic nightmare. He must take his heart out of the equation. Even when it was just healing from its sacrifice, even if the pile of books was the best medicine he could have received. Even if Thomas had chosen a book of romantic poetry and had put it on top of the pile.

Why was the man torturing him, if he hated him so? Richard chanced a look at him, eyes closed and arms crossed over his broad chest. His brow was furrowed, his mouth turned down. The beautiful bow of his lips, angry. Pouting nearly. He was guarded as if he could shut off the world and the carriage by closing his eyes and withdrawing. He watched the way Thomas's pulse jumped in the muscles of his thick neck. He was also angry, and in turmoil. Men of the era who did not have outlet to their emotions were bound to do stupid things.

Get into duels. Rage into battle. Throw themselves from the tops of cliffs. Anything but face the truth in their own hearts.

Richard could not allow it. But how could he keep the future duke safe from himself? From his inner conflict? From the feelings of shame that, quite possibly were the cause of his initial self-harm on the battlefield?

Be soft, Richard's mother's voice spoke in his head. *Be patient. Be kind. Not all of us know what our hearts want and not many of those who do, accept it. Be soft.* Richard sighed, relaxed his body closer to Thomas, picked up one of the books, donned Mrs. Worthington's glasses once more, and began to read William Wilberforce's philosophy on abolishment of slavery. Every small dip and jostle he allowed his body to move and be limber, until he was nearer to Thomas and relaxed in his state. He could protect the man without being his lover. He could keep Thomas safe from his own feelings by not shunning them nor encouraging them. But by being a safe harbor to the storm inside of his head and heart.

Doctor Worthington suddenly came to. "We're nearly there then? That was quicker than I thought!"

"It is because you fell asleep not two minutes from the livery!" Mrs. Worthington chided her husband and he smiled sweetly back at her. Richard watched them over the tops of the glasses with a smile. It was a beautiful thing, when love worked. He imagined it had more to do with friendship and the ability to be flexible, and the willingness to grow together. When the lady looked at him, he blushed, smiled and took off her glasses.

"My lady, I cannot thank you enough for the use of your spectacles."

"Oh, please do keep them!" She waved her hand at him, nearly annoyed. "I rarely read, I let Will read to me, as I'm not fond of the work involved, but I do love the story telling."

"You are still precocious," the doctor teased and nudged his wife's knee with his own. "I will read to you, for all our days, my love." He smiled and they exchanged a fond look. Both Richard and Thomas looked at them, then briefly to one another.

"How lucky in love you are," Richard said softly. "Thank you, my lady, I owe you a favor, to be sure."

"Keep this young philanderer out of trouble! He needs someone steady," she said and the carriage pulled to a stop. "I look forward to meeting you again at the wedding."

"The pleasure will be all mine," Richard responded. He leapt out of the carriage to give them both assistance down.

Thomas watched them walk down the cobbled streets to find a meal before their ferry departed. He looked down at Richard from the open carriage door.

"I do not need to be kept out of trouble," he grouched. Richard smiled up at him, at ease in his purpose. So at ease that he hadn't even thought to find the portal. He would see this adventure through, until he was certain Thomas would fulfill his promise to the future.

"Of course not, my lord. It is only my wish to keep you alive."

"Why do you have such care for my life?" Thomas said suddenly. Richard squared himself to Thomas and looked up into his piercing blue eyes.

"You may not understand now, but your brilliant mind is essential for the future."

"My brilliant mind? I'm a soldier, not a scholar. I do not converse with books," Thomas grouched again. Richard stepped into the carriage deftly and forced Thomas back into his seat. He looked up as Richard loomed over him.

"You do not know of your brilliance yet, because no one has ever seen it. If they have seen it, they have not appreciated it. But I do. You will do great things, Thomas Alexander. Great things that are not dependent upon who you marry or who you sire." Richard's eyes fell to Thomas's lips and Thomas leaned forward, into the gentle study. The world shrank and expanded.

"Now, shall we continue to the ferry?" Richard asked softly, and leaned near, his beard gently grazed Thomas's chin as he picked up the pile of books from the seat next to Thomas in his one hand.

Thomas stared at him and touched his chin. Richard understood that he was desperately trying to build up walls, and drive him away. *Be soft.* It would do no good to force the connection and risk alienating Thomas. Perhaps Thomas's cutting comments should have driven Richard away. Instead it only served to make him more calm, collected, and steady. The future duke needed a port in stormy seas and this was a time of great confusion for Thomas. Richard smiled and left the carriage. When he looked over his shoulder, Richard saw Thomas following him reluctantly and they gathered their possessions from the back of the carriage.

15

DOCTOR SHAW ALSO HATES BOATS

The ferry journey would take most of the rest of their day, and deposit them on the other side of the inlet in the dark hours of the morning. From there, it would take them another two days by carriage. Which meant that Richard had approximately two nights and three days alone with Thomas. He needed to make the most of them, and take advantage of the slight sense of freedom and to encourage Thomas to embrace the things he loved and stood for. The arts, a compassionate society, and focusing on the things that built up the working and poor class to create a better country on the whole. The ideas of art and philosophy that encouraged critical thinking were important foundations of an advanced society.

He also knew that he must shake away the feelings of lust that seemed to flood him anytime Thomas was near, and to think more of how he could influence the future duke to do what was best for the country. Perhaps in the way Doctor Blackwood would have. The brief thought hit Richard that perhaps Doctor Blackwood and Thomas had become lovers. Thomas and Matthew. The vision started to form, but he could not imagine the story far. Matthew had only one heart, and it was reserved for Lillian. Still if Matthew was as dreamy as she'd claimed, perhaps he'd still been able to influence Thomas to better patterns of change. He must have been a good man to deserve a woman crossing time to be with him.

Here in this place, Richard suddenly missed Lillian. In their kindred adventures and the faith it took to fling oneself into the unknown, she was the one link to both history and his present that he had. She too had found herself in the precarious position of being out of time, but knowing her actions were important. She too had felt lost. She too had probably desperately missed indoor plumbing and her Spotify playlist. Though beside Thomas, Richard still felt alone and only someone who had attempted this foolish course would understand. He wished he could see her once more. Maybe he could. If he got through this disastrous plan to save his country, he would find the time to seek her out. It would do his heart good to know she was well. Would she remember him? Richard felt homesick and lonely all at once.

"Are you ill?" Thomas asked from beside him as they watched the approaching ferry.

"I am fine."

"You look far away and lovelorn," Thomas said, quickly clenching his jaw to stay silent.

"I am missing home and dear friends," Richard confessed, not lying this time.

"A woman."

"No."

"Lover?"

"No, my lord. We have already discussed this. I do not ... have a lover," Richard paused. "My interests lie elsewhere," he said. Thomas seemed to stop all breathing from his words and held, statue still, at his side. "I have a dear cousin, Lillian, who I have not spoken to since she married and I am missing her. She always seemed to know what to do in strange and challenging situations."

Thomas nodded his head. "My sister, Natalie, is also this way. She has a strong head and heart. She has always brought me peace in troubling times," he whispered. Richard studied his face and the realization dawned that she must be his ally. Perhaps if he could get Thomas safely home, his sister could help to further persuade and support him. So that Richard could go home.

"God overdid creation with women. They are miraculous."

"Indeed," Thomas said stiffly.

"They deserve our respect and care. The mothers of our nation, the greatest minds we could hope for." Richard said, planting a small seed. "Men would not be born without them, nor taught compassion and resilience."

"All true," Thomas said, studying Richard with a scowl. "Which is all the more surprising that you have not found one to wed and sire lots of beautiful cubs with," he said suddenly. A tease. Richard smiled into it.

"No woman can have me," he whispered and stared pointedly into Thomas's eyes. "It does not mean that I do not respect their fierceness and intelligence." The call to board the ferry interrupted them and Thomas paused to nod to the strange and leading thought as they climbed on board to be taken across the inlet.

For a moment, Richard had forgotten he was not at all comfortable on boats. He quickly remembered when his feet touched the worn wood and felt his weight shift to and fro even with his legs firmly planted. He held out his arms for balance. Thomas looked over at him with a brow arched in study. He shook his head.

"Do you not do well on boats either? How is it you have travelled anywhere at all?"

The truth was Richard *hadn't* travelled much at all, by car or plane or boat, definitely not by horse. He'd been in the same region for much of his life. He didn't do well on most locomotion, save a train. And trains wouldn't be commonplace for another fifty years.

"I prefer to walk," Richard grouched back, trying not to drop his books as he ambled past the other passengers towards the middle of the boat. His mother had always said the center was a better place to be. Thomas followed, hands behind his back and balanced.

"Well, as I don't believe you are the son of God, walking over the inlet might prove to be quite difficult." He smiled into Richard's scowl.

"How long will it last?" Richard asked, even as he took a few breaths in. Even docked, the rocking of the boat turned his guts.

"The journey is not long."

Richard groaned and looked over the side, wondering how many times he could vomit and not pass out. "Please distract me. What are we to expect when this hellish journey across the inlet is over?" Richard grunted, trying to find a hold on the balusters and railings. His shoulder hurt from trying to grasp something solid.

Thomas smiled at him and leaned against the railing without qualm. "We should arrive in the dark and early tomorrow."

"Lodgings?"

"There is at Mortimer Crossing. We can and should rest there. From there it's another two-day carriage ride to my family's lands and my father's manor."

"In Marlborough," Richard sighed and nodded, trying to focus on the maps in his head rather than the way the boat dipped and swayed as they waited for all the passengers before departing. Thomas gave their fee to the captain and Richard looked at him as the man took the money and went to the next passenger. "My lord. You are too kind, to pay my way for all of this journey. And the books," he paused. Looking into Thomas's eyes made the queasy feeling subside. He felt more grounded. Thomas looked at his lips and Richard nearly lost his reasons to be aloof. God, he wished he could kiss the man before he left this time. Just once.

"You saved my life," Thomas said simply.

"A life you were trying to leave behind. If anything, you should be punishing me for causing you to live." Richard said, not sad but direct. Thomas moved closer to lean beside him. Their hips touched and Richard felt warmth spread in his loins.

"You tell me I have things to live for," Thomas said. He unfolded his arms and put his hand on the railing behind them, his thumb delicately touching Richard's flank. Whether subconscious or out of a need to connect, Richard wasn't sure. After his cold demeanor in the carriage, he never expected Thomas to be affectionate again. The man was conflicted. It was a constant ebb and flow of attraction between them, and he was hard-pressed to find a balance. Richard leaned, ever so slightly closer.

"That you do. You have an ability with your station and your power, along with your mind and fortitude, to do great things. I want to see you do them all," Richard said softly.

"Is that so?" Thomas asked, one brow arched in his direction.

"I'm rent with anticipation, my lord," Richard said, his eyes dropping to Thomas's lips.

"As am I," Thomas whispered and gently dipped his head, a hairbreadth closer, before the clanging bell startled them both and the ferry took off. The journey was rough for the first hour, getting out of the bay and into the smoother waters between the two ports. When things had evened out, they sat. Richard was lost once more in his books, but this time, without being bidden to and without permission, he began to read the philosophy book, pausing on the particularly important points that he thought might needle into Thomas's brain.

He made a point to read aloud the passages on the nobility of helping one's fellow man, the purpose of compassion, the overreaching balm of being a blessing to other human beings.

Thomas kicked his feet up on a bench, folded his jacket beneath his head, in a not very respectful way of the time, and lay his head down, next to Richard's lap. Richard tried to focus on the words and not on the way Thomas's curls touched his thigh.

"Shall I stop?" he whispered down to Thomas who shook his head.

"Never. Keep going. You are the teacher, I shall be your student," he smiled and closed his eyes again. Richard's hand fell from the book's cover for a moment and touched the soft curls at Thomas's forehead before drawing away to continue again. When the porter came by with simple provisions, Thomas sat up. They both stood, stretched and looked out into the blue gray waters. Fog was covering the distant horizon and Richard wondered how cold and wet the journey would be.

England seemed to see much more rain than Wales. He was ill-prepared for this trip. There wasn't much in his bag. He took off the glasses and tried to gently clean them with the tail of his shirt. Thomas purchased bread, cheese, onions and fruit, pickled garnishes and a small crock of mustard. With two tankards of ale they sat, the ploughman's lunch between them on the bench, as the wind teased at their hair.

"This is actually quite delightful," Richard said, nodding to the distant horizon.

"You are not going to be sick?" Thomas teased.

"Not until I have something in my stomach, probably." Richard smiled back and popped a radish into his mouth. When Thomas watched him eat, it made Richard feel self-conscious. He probably should not overdo it. But Thomas kept pushing more food at him.

"Well, fill it up. You've been without sustenance for too long in the last few days and you need to rebuild your strength."

"I'll rebuild my girth if I'm not cautious."

"I like your girth," Thomas said, darkly. "You—" he paused blushed looked away to the distant shore. "You are a stunning man. Strong. You must keep your strength up," Thomas fumbled.

Richard sat up, the words from a man he so admired, the truth in his tone, the way his eyes fell to Richard's chest and the heat that rose in his body.

"You are as well, my lord. So—"

"Beautiful?" One of those damn perfect eyebrows arched. Richard looked away and took a drink of ale. "I've never been called that before, by woman or man."

"I was practically unconscious from blood loss," Richard countered.

"They could have been your dying words," Thomas teased.

"I would not have changed them," he said. Richard wasn't sure if Thomas knew how far under his skin the future duke's teasing reached. A man that could keep up with him, undid his brooding, and made light of things that felt far too heavy for Richard to carry, was dangerous. There was no multitasking with Thomas. When he set his conversation and attentions on Richard, it was if the rest of the world ceased to exist. All the more reason to save his life and get back to his own world. Richard sighed and looked out on the water, thinking of home.

What would he do in a library after all of these adventures? He didn't even know if he'd make it back to his world. He could be lost to time. He could die of some common virus. He could drown this very night. He just had to do the best he could in this moment. That meant attending to Thomas.

"Tell me, what battle comes when we enter the gates of your home? Tell me about your parents and your brothers."

"Only if you tell me about your father." Richard's head turned quickly and his gaze was angry. "Did you think I'd forgotten?"

"No, I do not suppose you would have. You are far too clever at times."

"Why so surprised, what with my beautiful and brilliant mind?" Thomas teased him further. Richard's cheeks burned and he moved to stand but Thomas's strong hand was on his thigh and stilled him. "Find ease, Richard. I am merely delighted by the way you speak so freely, even if it is from blood loss. You are safe with me."

Was he? Richard felt the constant push and pull of all the things he wanted and all the things that his body tried to reach for to the detriment of the future.

He wanted the future duke to trust him enough to listen to his counsel and so he must give something of his own vulnerability to ease the exchange. An olive branch, a white flag. A bridge over the gap of their mutual uncertainty. His purpose was to not love the man but to love his country. Yet his heart was falling inexplicably into love just the same. He couldn't seem to separate the importance of Thomas's place in history and the way he felt. All at once on fire and at ease in the man's presence. If anyone would be a safe place, he supposed it was Thomas. A man he could very well disappear from, in only a few days' time. When that happened, Thomas would never see Richard again. Whatever secrets he divulged would die with Thomas in some distant years, before he would even be born. Richard took a deep breath and decided it was a greater gamble to not share.

"My father was a strong man. Physical. He was—an iron worker."

"Thus your build." Thomas said, over the edge of his ale. Richard nodded, hoping that the physicality he'd inherited from his father was not matched with the blindly led violence. Though if his deftness with a club and ability to strike were any indications, perhaps he had gotten some of the worst parts of his father.

"He was good at pounding metal into shape. He was equally as talented at pounding his son into shape," Richard said, but avoided looking into Thomas's eyes. He looked towards the back of the boat, now far away from where they'd set off. The last portal that he'd seen on the map. He squinted into the memory, across the water and into the falling light of the day. There was no going back now.

"What shape did he try to make of you?" Thomas asked.

"A man. A hardened man, like him. One that would not get so lost in books and art, and stories. One who appreciated and used his physical strength. To dominate."

"And here you are, physical, hardened and still liking books." Thomas said, but his tone was softer. "Did he hurt you?"

"Often," Richard said into his chest, sniffed back the tears and shook his head. "When I was old enough, I left my family and attended university. I decided that I would not use my fists to build the world, I would use my mind."

"You seem to do alright with your fists as well," Thomas said.

"Yes, well. Only in the direst of circumstances."

"Defending what you love?" Thomas's voice was low, his finger gently traced the outside of Richard's thigh before settling on his own cup of ale. Richard's eyes bored into his. Awfully assuming, the young lad was, to think this was love already.

"Love, my lord?"

"I speak of your country, of course."

"Of course."

"What happened to your father? Your brothers? Your mum?"

"Tell me about *your* father."

"Not much to tell, he's cold and calculating and plays his role to The Crown well. I do not hear from him often, but for the occasional letter berating me for still being in the service, when there are more noble pursuits to attend to. I know that his health is failing and as such he is anxious for me to come home and take my place. I know he will be just as horrible when we arrive as when I left, perhaps more so with the event of my sister's wedding. All of his children, save me, will be wed and it is a stain on his reputation. He always has an opinion of what I should be doing with my life."

"Is he not proud of you for your other attributes? Being in

service to The Crown? Of the battles you've won, the way you fought the French on their own land and here, when they dared invade? Does the work you've done to save the country not mean anything to him?"

"You seem to have perhaps too profound a knowledge of my history," Thomas said. Richard swallowed. Oh, the things he wished he had knowledge of.

"Your reputation precedes you, Thomas," he responded. Thomas sat back, stared into the horizon, and took a deep breath, much as Richard had to do.

"He would be happier if I would assume my responsibilities at home. I must always be in preparation to take over the title, especially with my father's increasingly poor health, even though my middle brother is much better suited for the disastrously boring duties of nobility. My father is angry that I have failed at no less than three proposals in the last five years."

"Seems like a decent record," Richard chuckled. "What happened to make them fail?"

"What happened to your father? Is he still with your mother?"

"My mother had enough of his flagrant abuse, and kicked him out of the house." The truth, innocuous enough in his own time was a shock to Thomas who sat back mouth open.

"How is such a thing possible?"

"She is a strong woman, who refused to be cowed anymore. The night after he—" Richard stopped and shook his head "after he'd gotten too rough, she drew a hard line and enforced it with one of his hunting rifles. He left at gunpoint."

Thomas's eyebrows rose in surprise. "But how did she survive, in such a time with children on her own?"

Richard looked at Thomas and thought of the social systems and programs that had kept them all fed and in school. Supported through the event, so that they did not have to stay with an abusive father to survive. Social systems that began with a young duke centuries before.

"We had help," he whispered. "From neighbors and our town."

"A community," Thomas said softly, lost in thought for a moment and Richard did not intrude. These were the seeds in need of planting. Thomas looked back at Richard. "Did he not also beat your brothers?"

"Not like he pummeled me." Richard wanted to throw up suddenly and he held on to the railing.

"But why?" Thomas's soft voice begged. Why indeed? Richard leveled his eyes on Thomas, wished he could tell him through the pain of the experience, the scars, the way he'd nearly died at the hands of his father, at the tender age of sixteen. For loving boys instead of girls.

"I displeased him. In all my pursuits. Not just about books." Richard said and looked down at Thomas's hands. He kept his from reaching out, in need to make the man understand. But it was Thomas who reached out and tilted Richard's chin up, his strong fingers on the soft brown beard, to meet his eyes.

"You will tell me his name and I will see to it that he never breathes free air again, if he breathes at all."

Richard's breath caught and he stared down at Thomas's lips. "What happened to your betrotheds?"

"I didn't think it was fair to tie them into a marriage where I could not love them. They were decent, likeable, intelligent women. Beautiful, I suppose too. But they, each one of them, deserved a man who truly loved them. One of them showed her real character by making sure I understood it was my money and title she as marrying, not me. Which made the decision even easier to make. The third, found her true love in my brother, and I couldn't be happier to call her my sister-in-law. We are amiable."

Richard smiled at this, the tension between them moments before had dissipated. "And now you are expected to go back and marry. In earnest this time?"

"Supposedly. My father does not have any other children to

marry off. He cannot die in good conscience while I remain free and full of sin."

"Are you now? Full of sin?" Richard chuckled and it grew into a huge and ripe laugh that shook through the other passengers and caused Thomas to laugh.

"To the brim, my friend. Nothing but sin and shame."

"How I prefer my friends," Richard remarked and they continued to eat. After a moment of silence, Richard continued. "I am sorry. Sorry that you feel you have to marry. Perhaps if you can find a friend in a woman, it would not be so terrible."

Thomas shook his head. "I've no qualms with women. But," he sighed, set his shoulders and looked at Richard, "I cannot fathom belonging to a woman." They stared at each other.

"To whom do you belong?" Richard asked.

"To myself, to my country. To the men who have saved my life."

Richard groaned and tried to turn away but the future duke took him by the shoulder. And shook him. "Come! Let's find a bunk and get some rest. The night will continue with or without us."

"Below deck?" Richard's stomach asked.

16

A ROCKY NIGHT AND NIGHTMARES

Thomas took Richard by the hand until he rose and gathered their things. Thomas led him down the narrow stairs at the front of the boat. There, in the darkness, families were stacked in bunks haphazardly. Thomas handed a portion of his pouch to the sailor below and the man nodded and led them to a more private bunk towards the back of the ship.

"It's no tent on the ground, but it will have to do. Beggars such as ourselves cannot be ones to choose," Thomas said and motioned for Richard to lay down.

"My lord, you should take the bunk." Richard refused to move.

"And I shall, once you are settled." It was a small bunk by any standards but larger than some of the ones the families shared. And it had a curtain.

Thomas held his breath. It was bold, but it was necessary that Richard slept, rested, stayed healthy on the journey. And he knew the giant would not take a bed if he was not also sleeping. He watched Richard's tired eyes sink. The mattress was soft, there were clean linens, and practically anything was better than trying to stay awake when you were being rocked by the waves.

"My lord—"

"It's an order."

"I beg your pardon?" Richard scowled back at him. "I am no soldier. You do not order me."

"You want me to live. You insist that I do?"

"Yes, of course."

"Then stop being a child and get in the bed."

"But this morning—"

"I'm not concerned with this morning. I slept better than I had in a long while last night. We're both weary and if I do not sleep with my trusted advisor beside me, guarding me from the obvious legions of ruffians upon this ferry, then I might just perish." Thomas smiled.

Richard groaned and buried his head in his hand impatiently. When it looked like he would not budge, Thomas's eyes narrowed on him.

"Or I might just step off the side of the boat, and sink all the way down with the heavy stone of my heart leading me to my death."

Richard looked up at him, anger in his eyes. "Saints, you are far too accustomed to getting your own way. Get in the damn bed!"

"You first!"

Voices hushed around them. If someone did recognize Thomas and his position, though he'd removed his coat and tucked it inside out under his arm, there was a risk that if they made a scene, there would be talk. Talk led to scandal, and scandal would surely make its way back to Thomas's father.

Richard breathed out through his nose and ducked into the bunk, its one window to the outside showing the moon rising off the water behind Richard's silhouette. Thomas knew it was not the soft comfort of last night's bed, but it at least it was not the back of a horse, so Richard had little to complain of. As soon as he got settled, favoring his shoulder Thomas noted, he groaned.

He must be in dreadful pain. Where Thomas was used to a more nomadic lifestyle, the doctor of books probably missed a bed.

Thomas came in shortly after, tucking his coat and boots at the foot of the bed with Richard's. He was excited to lay down and when he'd collapsed into the pillow next to Richard, he barely raised his head.

"Pure torture, is it not? To lay down after a day of travel?"

"Present company may make it torturous indeed," Richard grumbled, not opening his eyes.

"Ah, you do not like me. You think I'm beautiful and the future savior of the country, but you simply cannot stand to be given orders by me."

"You are lovelier when you are silent." Richard's eyes opened and he turned his head to stare at Thomas who arched his eyebrow and smiled.

"Pity there is nothing to put in my mouth to keep it busy." He said matter-of-factly and then turned away from Richard with a chuckle.

"Bollocks," Richard groaned and threw his arm over his face.

"Those too," Thomas whispered.

"Saints, you are intolerable," Richard said but the laugh was too much to keep in and it rumbled through the bed.

"Goodnight, Richard. I look forward to the measure of your surliness tomorrow morning."

"You do not have a big enough instrument to measure how surly I will be."

"I think I might," Thomas yawned.

Richard nearly cried. What the holy fuck was this man trying to do to him? He turned as far away as he could, with his injured shoulder and tried to let sleep carry him away from the tension and want he had. He must not, under any circumstances, give Thomas something for his mouth to do.

Despite his propensity for seasickness, Richard fell asleep to the calming sounds of Thomas's breaths and the warmth of his body next to his. He was too weary to think of much else and was in pain. It seemed when his body stilled, his muscles and nerves like to remind him that he had, in fact, been stabbed, by an old, rusty and probably germ-infested blade. The stitches were starting to pucker and they itched but he hugged himself to keep his hands from scratching at them.

Sometime, hours before dawn, Thomas thrashed next to him, sat up, and punched the air with a cry. Richard sat up to find him shirtless, heaving in great breathy sobs, slicked with sweat, fevered with the memory of some battle that had stirred horror in the cells of his brain, whipping them into a storm, even on the docile sea.

Richard was not a therapist. He did not know how to deal with post-traumatic stress disorders, or the effects of war on a man's mind. But he knew about nightmares and surviving pain that should have never been yours to carry. Damning the consequences, he reached out a strong hand and gently ran it over Thomas's bare ribs. Richard was present and awake enough to detect the slightest signal from Thomas if he did not wish to be touched.

"Thomas," he whispered softly. "Come back. Come back to me now," he crooned and Thomas's breath caught and sputtered.

When his hand grazed the warm and sweaty skin of his back, Thomas shivered, sobbed and leaned down, curling into Richard's arms and nestled his head into the crook of his good shoulder. His strong hands clung to Richard's shirt and he pressed his body safe against the length of Richard's. He continued to quietly sob into his chest.

"So many, so many. The blood ... hearts stopped, never to love again—" words inconsolable and only comprehensible in the context of war and bloody loss, shook quietly through their private space.

"My darling, I know, I know," Richard whispered. "You are here now, you are here with me," he stroked Thomas's trembling arm and held him close. He sighed out a breath and gently kissed Thomas's forehead. Thomas slung his thick leg over Richard's hips and held him tighter. "I'm so sorry. I wish I could take it from you. I am here." Richard said and kissed his temple.

Thomas felt his heart slow, and the night reappeared before him. The quiet and dark cabin, the steady heartbeat of the lion beneath him, so much comfort and warmth, holding him safe from a thousand different horrors that he could keep at bay in the daytime, but that found him when the night descended. The battlefields he wandered alone, brains, and hearts, and guts scattered, blood stinking up the air. The loss of a million thoughts and hopes, bleeding into the ground.

He never wanted to kill, he only wanted to escape his father. He only wanted to find peace in his own skin.

"My darling, I know. I know," Richard said into his hair. Kissed his forehead. Thomas leaned into the touch like a man dying of thirst. He wrapped his leg around Richard's hips. He was large enough, that he could stop Thomas from getting too close. He would surely stop him from this foolishness. But Richard didn't, he only held Thomas tighter, whispered apologies as if he felt his pain, as if he was sorry that he'd been through such a brutal scar.

Thomas nuzzled his nose under Richard's chin, traced the soft hair of his beard to his jaw line. Dried his tears on Richard's cheeks. He would stop him. He would push him away. Richard wouldn't allow this. He was a man.

17

THE RELIEF OF WANDERING HANDS

Thomas slowly moved his way up, from Richard's chest where his shirt was damp from tears and sweat, to his neck. His nose gently teased the pulsing beat that started to climb. His mouth, nudging Richard's jawline, led the soft breath against his ear, his cheek. Thomas pressed his cheek to Richard's, their lips gently waiting. Surely Thomas would pull away, ashamed. Surely he would. Richard waited.

Thomas sighed, a broken breath from his sobbing and his mouth touched Richard's, soft at first, a move easily mistaken. But Richard did not mistake it. His hand reached up, onto Thomas's chin and held him to it. Richard's beard and mustache brushed against the sensitive skin of Thomas's lips and he pressed closer, opened his mouth. Thomas tasted his bottom lip and sighed in pleasure as Richard's hand tightened on his back.

Richard groaned softly, held Thomas's head as he gently explored the hard lines of his lips, taking the bottom one between his teeth to softly nibble as his hands caressed his trembling skin, from hip to shoulder. He wanted to eat him alive, he wanted to tighten his fingers and bring Richard closer, touch every trembling muscle.

Thomas's breath caught and pulled, and he moaned when Richard bit his lip. His cock grew hard and Richard shifted Thomas's body, closer, so it fit into the crease of his thigh and hipbone. Richard's hand caressed down to cup his backside and draw him up and down, against his thigh. They moved in time while their lips explored. Biting and kissing and exchanging breath and heat. Richard bit Thomas's jaw and worked his hungry mouth down his throat. Thomas's hand slid, strong and pressing, down from Richard's chest below his straining hips to feel what his eyes had only seen. When he touched the hard and pulsing muscle, Thomas gasped and Richard felt his cock release a small, excited spurt of liquid.

"Richard," Thomas groaned and buried his face in Richard's neck. Richard's hand stilled on his backside, he felt the heat swell and rise, and knew Thomas was close. Thomas slowed his hungry stroking of Richard's excited cock and he shivered. He moved to put space between their bodies.

"I am vexed," Thomas's voice shook, tears clinging to his long blond eyelashes. "I am sorry." He started to turn away and Richard held him, by his hip, keeping them facing each other and stopping him from running away.

"Look at me," he commanded. Thomas shook his head but Richard grabbed his chin and made him meet his eyes. "Look at me." When he'd met his eyes, Richard kissed him again, purposefully, with gentle and loving slowness. "You've nothing to be sorry for. You are passionate and beautiful. I am not here to make you feel anything but good. You'll find no expectations or judgments in my bed," he whispered softly. Thomas started to cry.

"Listen," Richard took Thomas's hand and placed it on his pounding heart. "Where we lay is our place alone. It does not belong to the outside world. You are safe. With me you are safe. There is no god, no church, no father. There is only us. And our two hearts. Our bodies only." Richard lifted Thomas's hand to kiss his fingers. Thomas nodded, sobbed and kissed him, firmly, taking Richard's head in his hand and tugging on his dark curls, desperately.

He grunted and sighed and Richard let him explore with his tongue and teeth, biting his jaw and neck, his collarbone, even as his hand slipped behind to cup his well-muscled ass. Thomas cried and his hips surged forward, Richard held his backside close and felt the tremor shock through Thomas's body, felt the warmth against his own stomach.

The darling man, Richard thought. He had never known a lover's touch. He was never allowed to be free, to feel.

"You have been without love for so long," he whispered and kissed Thomas sweetly.

"I—I apologize," Thomas gasped, eyes closed, still shuddering with the shock of climaxing.

"None is necessary," Richard said and kissed his forehead, stroked his free and soft curls. "None at all." Thomas kissed him.

"Can I not do something for you?" he whispered and his hands slipped down, undid the ties on Richard's breeches. When his strong and calloused hands circled him, Richard grunted. "I would return, in kind, your generosity."

"Saints," Richard grunted, the tightening of Thomas's fingers, the sliding over his swollen and hot length, gently pulling and caressing the tip, pushed Richard up and over the edge. He cried out and Thomas swallowed his loud response in his own mouth, even as Richard bucked and strained into his hands. When he broke the kiss, Richard shivered and shook, finding it hard to catch his breath.

"The world may not exist outside this bed, but they can still hear a lion through a curtain," Thomas whispered and kissed Richard's sweaty brow. Richard's resolve was broken, burned and left behind. He had no control. Quickly he rolled Thomas over, crushing him into the mattress and kissing him harshly. Thomas groaned, surprised before taking Richard's hot and demanding mouth just as eagerly.

Richard wanted to cry and shake his fists at the gods to lead him to such a man, such a love. His tears mixed with Thomas's and he collapsed into the bed, gathering him close, holding him possessively. He had always planned to die for the duke. Now he wanted to live for him. Their bodies calmed, quieted, rested and fell into deep and dreamless sleep.

18

THE MORNING AFTER

The time was too short from when they fell asleep, a tangle of limbs and soft breathing, to when the ferry came near to the shore. Richard roused first and watched, for a moment, Thomas's composed and calm features. Was there ever such a beautiful man? He had always thought so, even in pictures that did not capture the light of his eyes or the glow of his skin. The stubble now coming in on his chin, boyish mischief and god-like physique. Thomas's chest was exposed but already Richard had begun to take count of all of his battle wounds. Thomas roused, moaned, rolled over. Richard was not accustomed to being the first one awake, but then again, Thomas had been through a great ordeal last night. Between the nightmares and the subsequent stretch of trust and care. He wondered how he would react when he woke. Richard prayed it would not be with guilt or remorse.

Richard quietly snuck from the bed, righted his clothing and put on his boots. He went up top, feeling a strange wobbly sensation in his legs and guts as if anything slightly suspended could not account for the rolling waves that grew deeper the closer they got to the shore. He found breakfast; a couple of rolls and fruit and a pot of tea with two plain cups. He paid with money from Thomas's pouch. Such was the life when you had a sugar daddy, Richard chuckled at the thought. He brought the simple breakfast into the curtained bed. Thomas was sitting up, looking out the window, hands clasped around his knees, staring at everything and nothing. Richard cleared his throat.

When Thomas had awoken, to an empty bed, his first thought was that Richard had been overcome with guilt and had jumped overboard. Taken his own life for the sin that Thomas had saddled him with. He meant to follow. He had put Richard's pillow to his nose and inhaled. At least he'd known passion perhaps even love, before his demise. He'd best act quickly, if he were to have enough sea to drown in. They'd be docking soon enough. If, however, Richard had simply risen to relieve himself, what could he possibly say to the man to ease the tremendous events of last night?

Thomas had no words, no reassurances. He only had doubt. Doubting Thomas. He hugged his knees to his chest and stared out the small galley window. The curtain opened. Richard was there, tea and food in his arms. A guarded but curious look on his face.

"My lord."

"Richard," he said. He looked away, reached for his shirt and covered himself. He could not meet Richard's eyes. He felt shame creep up into his cheeks and warm his chest with a tightness that threatened to stop his heart.

"The rules of the morning, stand the same as they did in the night, Thomas." Richard said softly. He climbed into the bunk, barely able to sit without hitting his head, and closed the curtain. Thomas swallowed, he felt hunger in his stomach, in his body. Hunger for more of whatever Richard had to give.

"Come, you must eat something." He poured the tea and put the biscuits and fruit between them, in his shirt he carried a small jar of jam. Thomas cocked his head. "I might have stolen this." Richard shrugged. "No one was using it."

"You are a criminal."

"Am I?" Richard's question was marked by a raised eyebrow. "When no one with stones and a judgmental heart sees what they perceive as a crime, is it a crime?"

"God sees."

"God does not create that which is not meant to be, otherwise he would not truly be a god." Richard countered. Thomas stared at him, deep line between his brows, in thought.

"God sent you to me."

"I suppose—"

"He sent a criminal."

"What? To reform?" Richard shuffled in the bed uncomfortably.

"No. He sent you to me, to steal jam for my biscuits." Thomas smiled. "To steal away my sadness," he added softly. "And my time spent in self-loathing, and my worry. To steal thoughts of leaving this world when there is still beauty to be found here." Richard reached out and touched Thomas's roughened cheek, but Thomas pulled away quickly. "It's awful. I have not shaved."

"I like it." Richard breathed and cupped his cheek. He let the sharp prickle of Thomas's hair gently scratch his fingertips.

Thomas leaned into the touch, and realized that although he had fought in countless battles, had been trained in several forms of combat and war, slept on cold dirt patches and hard wooden beds, rode for miles, marched for leagues, his body abused and struck in a million different ways, he had not been touched. Not nearly enough. He wanted to absorb all of it. He wanted to take everything and anything that Richard wanted to give. It was precarious.

"Please eat, my lord. You'll need your strength."

Thomas said nothing but smiled at Richard and for once, did as he was told.

. . .

They did not speak much more. The hustle and bustle of the other people rousing in the sleeping quarters kept them busy and in the company of others. Thomas remained stoic as did Richard, barely looking at one another. When they parked on the dock, both allowed the women, and families to go first. Thomas put on his regiment jacket again and tied back his hair. They would find a place to freshen up before the carriage ride.

The morning was cool and soft, a thick layer of fog clung to the low valleys beyond the green fields and Richard took in a deep inhale. All his life, his lungs had never breathed air so clean. All his life, he'd never felt more alive, in all of its give and take. The pain, the aches, the being present in a world that was quiet of engines and noise, devoid of distraction and demands from interconnectedness. He only knew four people here. Andrew and Thomas. Doctor and Mrs. Worthington. His world had shrunk down, and yet as he gazed over the fields and open spaces, it had also grown larger.

"Are you now afraid to walk on solid ground?" Thomas teased. He was already standing on the dock. Richard shook himself out of the philosophical stupor and walked down the gangplank, sure it would buckle over with his weight.

"I've never been here before," he said. "It's beautiful country."

"But you come from Oxford." Thomas said. Richard's heart started to beat harder in his chest. He went through his geography, internally until he realized the grave mistake he'd made.

"I do," he said, stepping down onto the dock and immediately wobbling to the side with the after effects of the boat.

"So, how is it you did not come this way towards Wales?"

Richard had to think quickly and make the simplest explanation possible. "I have not. I was traveling south from Gloucester when I stumbled upon the battle."

"What's in Gloucester?"

"Family," Richard lied and began to weave his way down the empty dock towards town. "I was visiting family. One of my brothers."

"And you just happened to go nearly all the way to the coast to 'stumble upon the battle'?" Thomas was following him now, not hurrying but marching in determined steps just behind Richard.

"I love the sea, I thought it might be my only occasion to travel that far. I'd heard from people along the way there had been a battle at sea, and on my way back home, when I heard the commotion I ascertained it had moved on land." Richard tried desperately not to lie. His brother did live in Gloucester, it was not a complete falsehood, he did know where the battle was fought. They were all just small mis-truths separated by a couple of hundred years.

"And were you hoping to watch the blood and gore?" Richard stopped and turned. Thomas was following him, brow drawn down, and his smile gone.

"No," his breath caught in his throat. "I was on my way home, traveling by foot, I saw the battle, tried to go around the outskirts of it, but then I came upon you and the general. I recognized your emblem. I knew of you. I did not want you to die."

"Knew of me?"

"From Oxford" Richard stammered.

"No one in Oxford knows me," Thomas narrowed his eyes, touched his belt. Richard felt his neck erupt in sweat. He glared back at him.

"They know of you. Of your family.. Your picture hangs in the walls of Belamor Hall, with your family. I knew of you."

Thomas stopped, he swallowed, looked down at his feet.

"Misjudge and distrust me, will you now?" Richard said, swallowing the hurt in his throat as he adjusted his pack, touched his stitches self-consciously and continued on towards the livery. Thomas's thick footsteps followed him but he did not say a word.

When they reached the livery, the horses were just being fed and watered, getting ready for a full day with the ferry's arrival.

Richard leaned against the fence beside the building, his head hanging. He still had to accompany him. He still had to make sure that history turned out right. But the look of distrust and the idea that Thomas would think he'd have anything other than his best interests at heart, hurt him terribly. Maybe he could just jump into the 1400's and die of the plague or better yet 2050 when the world would already be burnt, or frozen, and annihilated from greed. What was the point?

Thomas paced in front of him. "I'm sorry," he said, after a few tense moments. "I am confused and concerned."

"Over what matter?" Richard asked. Thomas looked to and fro, the livery men were busy readying carriages and the people in the town were troubled over their morning routines and the latest gossip in town. They paid the two men no mind.

"Over the matter of last night," Thomas blurted out suddenly. He started pacing again.

Richard sighed. He knew that his own guilt had run deep, especially while he'd kept the secret on his own. It was only by coming out to trusted people, having a loving mom who supported him, and who had gotten him away from his abusive father, did he start to come around to accepting himself as the beautiful human he was. Richard did not have years to get Thomas through this. He did not have therapy or a supportive family. He only had himself.

He pulled himself from the wall and marched across the street.

"Where are you going?" Thomas grumbled behind him.

19

NOTHING LIKE A GOOD SHAVE TO SET A DUKE RIGHT AGAIN

Richard entered the barber shop, nodded to the man and took a chair. The man put a cloak over Richard's dirty clothes, and proceeded to wash his face and trim his beard. Thomas watched with his bag in his hands, shifting his weight uncomfortably in the doorway.

"Man needs a shave, mate," Richard said gruffly and to the barber, and nodded for Thomas to take the chair beside him. The barber's assistant came, sat Thomas at the chair next to Richard and with hot towels he washed and dotted Thomas's face with cream. Thomas instantly relaxed as the warm towel was pressed into his face. When the barber took a comb through his curls, dusting them with a nice smelling powder and setting them back in a pony tail Richard could tell he was starting to feel better. The razor probably took away the itch of his stubble. After the hot towel was taken from Richard's face, the barber combed through his shorter hair, dusted it and eyed his beard. But when he turned to grab the cup of suds Richard leaned back and put his hand out.

"The beard stays," he said gruffly.

"You should consider a shave," the barber needled.

"No," Richard said simply and stood, removing the cloak.

"Why not?" Thomas asked.

"I will not deny who I am." Richard responded, and waited until Thomas was done. He came out of the chair, his shoulders more relaxed and his brow eased. Thomas paid and they went back to the livery where their carriage awaited them. They stepped inside. Thomas sat opposite of Richard and folded his hands between his knees. Richard took his books from the satchel, donned his glasses and began to read.

"Are we not going to discuss the matter?"

"Are you going to *discuss*, or are you going to yell at me?" Richard said, over the top of his spectacles. The carriage started to amble through town, the hoofbeats and city noise keeping their conversation private. The blinds were open and Thomas looked out at the cobbled streets and bright doorways as they passed.

"Last night was—"

"Beautiful." Richard said.

"A sin."

"Thomas, I cannot do this," Richard huffed, took off his glasses, tapped them on his knee and sat forward. "I cannot undo the years of abuse and hurt you have suffered. Not in a day of riding boats or carriages, and certainly not when we arrive at the source of it. I can only assure you that you are not alone. You are not the first man to fall for one of their own. It is not something that we chose. Any more than our hair color or our height."

"But the word of God—"

"Has been interpreted and reinterpreted by hundreds of men in power who sought to repopulate the earth with the poor and pious, as to remain in power."

Thomas was silent. "Richard—"

"They do this with fear. Not for the love of a god, but the fear of his retribution. And it keeps us all subjugated. Do you honestly believe a God would make you, perfect as you are, and mistakenly lead you to sin? That love, in all its fantastical and natural forms could be wrong?"

"I do not know."

"You are a learned man. Think on it." Richard said, put his glasses back on and began to read. The carriage jostled and swayed as they left the smoother cobble stone streets of Bristol and tracked onto a dirt road. Richard tried to focus on his book. It was poetry, a love sonnet to be exact, that could have been meant for man or woman, or anything in between. He'd said the word *love* to Thomas. And he had not said anything in return.

It was silly to be in love after a week. But Richard had known Thomas for so much longer. Hadn't he wished he could meet a man like that in his own time? When there wasn't a chasm of hurt to travel across to reach him.

> Love is not love when it alteration finds, or bends
> with the remover to remove.

"It is an ever-fixed mark," Richard whispered and stared out the window. Thomas sat, arms still crossed over his chest, eyes on the road that stretched out behind them, the rolling green fields. The silence and the gentle sway of the journey taking him deeper into his own thoughts, where Richard could not follow.

Thomas let the rhythm of the carriage settle his mind. Richard could not change the years of abuse. But he could offer him a safe place. Thomas had been a great many things in his life. Rich, strong, kept and shaped. But never safe. He looked up, Richard was still staring out of the window, biting his bottom lip and thinking over whatever verse he'd just read. A warrior body, a scholar mind. Damn, if he did not love the man. He wanted to know more. He wanted to spend years learning what made Richard Shaw such an enigmatic mystery.

He would not get to know him in silence. Or from so far away.

"Make space," Thomas grumbled and came over to Richard's side of the carriage.

"My lord?" Richard began but Thomas gently nudged him to the side and sat down, swinging his legs up on the seat and laying his head in Richard's lap. Richard lifted his arms in surprise and looked down at the scowl on Thomas's face.

"Well?" Thomas asked.

"What is it you expect of me?" Richard asked, his throat bobbing with a hard swallow.

"Read to me, Doctor of Books," Thomas whispered, folded his hands across his stomach and closed his eyes. Richard smiled, the weight and warmth of Thomas's head on his thigh bringing such a beautiful sense of ease. He began soft, even, and intoning the rich grace of a man who knew the power of words. His hand fell to where Thomas's were folded and he caressed his fingers. Soon, Richard's hand was heavy on Thomas's and his eyelids were closing. He took off his glasses and set them carefully on the bench. Thomas curled into his warmth and felt Richard gently caress his forehead, brushing away his hair and his worry.

The carriage rocked them to sleep. The nightmares did not come to Thomas, just the gentlest sense of peace. They were here, they were safe.

20

MOMENTS OF RESPITE

Both Richard and Thomas sat up quickly, wrapped in each other's arms. They parted as the carriage stopped. It was midday and they found themselves at a pub. Richard groaned and got out of the cramped space quickly. When he and Thomas had stretched, with nary a word exchanged between them, they walked into the pub and stood at the bar. Thomas fidgeted with his uniform. He should have had an occasion to launder it before they reached home. He looked over at Richard's clothing, which simply would not do to meet his family. He must have been scowling because Richard scowled back.

"Are you cross with me?"

"Just your clothing." Thomas said, and nodded to the barman for two pints and a plate of food for them both.

"What's wrong with—" Richard looked down, he'd been riding and sleeping in it for days, there were stains and stiff corners, some from blood, some from his own excitement. He was a mess. But frankly, in a world with barely any running water he'd been trying to lower his expectations. "It's dreadful. I'm dreadful."

"You are traveling. And neither one of us is presentable,"

Thomas smiled and they both stood at the bar, to get the blood back into their legs while they ate and drank. The meal was meager and Richard would have killed for some fresh vegetables. He stopped, bite midway to his mouth. He would kill. He had killed. The sudden flash of visions filled his head and he closed his eyes. The iron smell of blood, teeth flying through the air, the smell of gunpowder and bodies opened to the world. He closed his eyes tighter.

Richard thought of his mother. The woman who had prohibited violence in her home. Who had protected her sons from it. What would his mother say of him now? What would his father? Would he be proud? Was Richard any better than the brute of the man? He put the fork down and sighed.

"Is it not to your liking?"

"It's fine, I'm just not hungry."

"You? Aren't lions always hungry?" Thomas said, closer, quieter, confidential. Richard smiled from one corner of his mouth.

"I am—road weary."

Thomas studied him. "It is understandable. You have been through much in the last week. And I have been remiss in checking your shoulder. Does it vex you?"

"No, my lord," Richard whispered, even though it twinged and ached, it was nothing compared to the torment currently residing in his head.

"You can call me Thomas, you know." Thomas paused and leaned in, "Though," he conspired while the bartender stepped to the back room, "I would be lying if I said I didn't like to hear 'my lord' on your lips." His fingers grazed Richard's hip bone before he reached for his ale. Thomas's change in demeanor helped to lift Richard out of the bog of regret. He took a sip of the ale.

"The next leg is a mere thirty miles. We'll rest tonight in richer accommodations and then you will allow me to have you fitted for a suit."

"Excuse me?" Richard said and scowled.

"You will not be meeting my parents looking like some roadside ruffian."

Meeting his parents. Richard huffed. He'd only met one set of parents in his dating life and it had been rather a disaster. They'd loved him, but their son turned out to be a bonafide asshole.

"But am I not a roadside ruffian?"

Thomas sat back with a hand to his chest in shock. It might have been the gayest thing Richard had ever seen him do.

"You are a scholar! A doctor! A learned man in the employ of Oxford."

"Who bashes men's heads in with a club," Richard said softly. The memory of it came back to him quickly and he put his hand to his mouth, shook his head and his eyes filled with tears. He'd been ignoring it. He'd been hiding and burying inside of himself and the complexities of his feelings for the future duke. He had not been facing what he'd done.

But if Thomas was any model of the men of the era, he knew he could not express the regret so openly in the broad light of day. Thomas had cried to him, that night in the safety of their bed. He had found solace. But that was in private. In secret. He was looking at Richard now. Eyes narrowed and his cheeks growing warm with color. Richard needed to rein in his emotions before he embarrassed them both.

Thomas's voice was low when he spoke. "It is never easy to live with the aftermath of such a necessity. But that is what it was, necessity. I know your soul, Richard Shaw. You would not take a life if it did not threaten yours first," he paused, looked down at where his hand had taken Richard's, "or mine."

Richard nodded. He knew the logic was sound. But in the quiet, unrested and tired moments, his irrational brain was winning.

"Tonight, we shall rest and change your bandages. You will be much improved by morning." He said and pushed the food closer. "Please do eat something."

How it came to be that Thomas was now taking care of him, seemed an odd twist of reality. But because Richard could not bear to see the concerned and worried lines across Thomas's brow, he did as he was asked. After their short lunch, a trip to the loo, and a quick washing of hands and faces, they got back into the carriage and ambled down the road. Richard did not know what to say to Thomas. But the food and washing, and probably the ale, helped to calm him. He was drifting in and out of sleep, when he noticed Thomas lean against the window, opposite him and seem to be caught in hard study of the land outside.

"What is on your mind, my lord?"

"Nothing to concern yourself with."

"I am quite recovered, from this afternoon, if you are worried that I cannot carry more."

Thomas said nothing. They swayed with the movement of the carriage for a few quiet moments.

"What is kept inside, like infectious rot, will fester." Richard said, flipping pages in his philosophical study.

"It is my father. And my younger brothers."

"They are unkind?"

"They are expectant. They have always questioned my loyalty to the family name."

"Because of your lack of bride?"

"In part. But I truly have no desire to be a lord over land or inherit the title. I feel as though those in power use their title to hide behind it, instead of using it for good. They like the prestige, but never suffer the mantle of responsibility. Truth be told, my sister would make a much better leader than any of us," Thomas smiled.

Richard smiled too. "Of that I have no doubt. What is she like, your sister?"

"Gregarious, and unrefined."

"My favorite," Richard said, a spark of joy in his eyes.

"She must have found a decent man who would encourage it. I cannot see her marrying otherwise."

"I hope that is the case." Richard thought of Lillian's story. Of how marriages tended to work, especially for women in this era. He hoped, beyond hope, that Thomas's sister was marrying into a loving and respectful situation. "Her name is Natalie?"

"Yes, Natalie." Thomas looked far away. "I was the oldest brother but I always found more comfort in her company than in James's or Michael's. My brothers were rough and tumble and often cruel. But she was quick, and smart, and strong. So kind. So willing to stand up for what was right even though she was always the smallest in the room."

"I see that in you, my lord." Richard said softly. "It will be good for your heart to see her."

"Indeed."

"And for her to see you. I'm sure she has been missing you and in worry for your safety."

Thomas nodded, and Richard could tell that he did not take in to consideration how his death wish would affect the one person he cared most about in the world.

"She will most definitely be intrigued to meet you." Thomas smiled.

"I worry I will disappoint."

Thomas shook his head with a narrowed glance. "Come here," he grumbled, nearly a command and less a request.

"What?"

"Come here. Now." The strong command of his voice sent a shiver up Richard's spine. He didn't like taking orders, but my god when that tone hit his body, it seemed to melt him. What he wouldn't do for his duke. Richard came over to his side of the carriage. "Lie down."

Richard did, placing his head on Thomas's strong thighs, and looking up into his eyes. His breath quickened, if he turned, if he nuzzled into the warm juncture of his thighs, could Thomas be persuaded? But Thomas did not give him the opportunity or even suggest it. He merely placed one hand on Richard's head and began to lovingly run his fingers through his thick dark hair. He stared meditatively out the window and Richard watched him.

Was he being petted? Maybe. Did he care? No. His eyes fell and he allowed himself to feel every caress, every gentle tug of Thomas's fingers. The way his hand would fall to his beard and he gently explore the length of it. Richard had always kept it neatly trimmed and though the barber had helped, it was in need of more care since his week of living in relative squalor. But Thomas's fingers explored and caressed without hesitation. Richard moaned with the delicious feelings of being at once turned on and relaxed. He felt his groin pull. He did not feel it right to ask or push. What had happened on the boat was intense enough. This was daylight, with a carriage driver mere feet away, and windows open to the world, even if all they saw were cows, and pastures, stone fences and the occasional farm house.

Sometimes it was best to just enjoy what you had in the moment. And in this moment, Richard felt like he had the world.

After a short rest, more reading and a rousing conversation of why Richard should try to at least shave his beard once, the carriage came to a halt in front of their accommodations. Richard expected a similar and simple inn and was not prepared to step out of the hated carriage to the sight of a large, manor-like building, in the heart of the city.

"This is no inn."

"I promised you something comfortable. This is our last night as free men," Thomas said, and Richard wondered if he meant it as more than just two soldiers away from their families. "It is a summer manor of one of my dear friends and they are currently not occupying it. I was told I could come and stay whenever I had the need."

Richard looked up at the building, between other similar stone dwellings filling up the entirety of the block. It was indeed grand by his limited experience, and large bouquets of flowers lined either side of the stairs up. They were still looking fresh, even with the heat of the day that was now waning in favor of an evening rain. Richard asked what the name of the town was and Thomas looked at him as though he'd taken a blow to his head rather than his heart.

"It's Westbury, of course," he said "home of some of the finest lands in the county. I sent word ahead to ready our rooms at our last stop."

"This is Westbury?" Richard whispered and looked around quickly as if Lillian might pop around the corner at any moment. "How far is Westbury Manor?"

"Oh so you do know of the town?" Thomas teased. "Westbury Manor is to the south."

"And who is in residence at the Manor?"

"I am uncertain. I have been away for a great, long time. It used to be a Colonel Mayfield I believe, then his nephew, Fitzwilliam Byrne has probably inherited it."

"Do you know of Miss Lillian Byrne?" Richard said in a hushed tone. Thomas scowled.

"I do not. What is so importantly special about this Miss Byrne? How do you know of the lady?"

Richard could not contain his smile he shook his head, over the moon that Lillian was alive and in the same time as him. Richard suddenly felt less alone. "She is one of my dearest friends."

"And yet you are uncertain of where she lives?"

"When last I heard she was to be wed to a Doctor Matthew Blackwell."

A strange look came over Thomas's face, as if he were experiencing déjà vu.

"The name is familiar," he postulated and rubbed the stubble on his chin. Richard looked at him and wondered how much energy and information passed between timelines and dimensions. Could it be that Thomas and Matthew were two people meant to be together? Richard did not want to believe that. He shook his head.

"Well, I know we are on a schedule, but perhaps I will go for a visit sometime, after the wedding." Richard smiled, almost giddy and clapped Thomas on the shoulder. "My dearest Lillian."

"Perhaps I can invite her to my sister's wedding," Thomas said with no small amount of jealousy and hurt in his voice as he came closer to Richard. "Are you sure you are not in love with the woman?" His face turned discerningly as if to study Richard's happiness.

"Are you in love with your sister?"

"I love her as deeply as a brother would, and no more."

"Then this too is the affection I have for Lillian. I once helped her find and be reunited with her Matthew. Oh, she was miserable without his love. It was my favorite love story. So far at least," Richard said, he looked at Thomas who looked away quickly and nodded to the footman to take their bags, ragged and small as they were, to their rooms. When Thomas did not respond, but followed the man up the stairs to the large and ornate foyer, Richard continued on.

"It would be lovely to see her."

"Well, finally something I can give you to look forward to."

Richard stopped as they approached the stairs. The footman kept going. Thomas kept going, until he realized that Richard was not following. Apparently he had not heard the anger in his own tone, until the same anger came out of Richard.

"For the entirety of the trip, you have told me how unpleasant your family was but you still insisted I accompany you. Now, when I find joy and solace in seeing an old friend, maybe my only friend in this god forsaken time, you seek to tarnish my joy with your jealousy?" Richard said. The footman halted his progress and turned to look down at them. A maid came out of the servant's door below them to watch.

"Let us discuss this in private." Thomas commanded through his clenched teeth.

"Fine," Richard said, even angrier that he would call him out in public but would not argue his case. They both huffed, unspeaking and in a determined march behind the man and into a grand master suite. Surely Richard would be getting his own room, but Thomas quickly dismissed the footman. Richard didn't speak a word except to thank the footman before he left. Thomas slammed the door.

2 1

A FIGHT, A CONFESSION, A LESSON

"You dare to call me jealous in front of—"

"You dare to think I would love a woman after the night we shared? After I have been most forthcoming with you? And what have you ever been with me? Dancing around the truth of your family. Avoiding telling me anything too close to what you want or what you hope for? About how you really feel for me?"

"Feel for you?"

"Perhaps I'm just an object of your confusion. A lucky player at the right place and the right time for you."

"That's not all you are to me—"

"That my saving your life meant nothing, that I love and believe in you so fully that I could not live in a world where you ceased to exist? That all of the miserable hours we've spent have been for noth—"

Richard did not finish. Thomas rushed him and took his face in his hands. He kissed him, hotly, his teeth biting to silence the words. His breath came in gasps as he tore into Richard's mouth begging to taste the anger of him. The truth.

Richard was knocked back three steps and in such shock that his first reaction was to push him away, but as Thomas's hot and wet mouth silenced his words, so too did it silence his thoughts. He groaned and made a halfhearted effort to push Thomas away by his hips but the man pressed into him, pushing him across the room and up against the wall of the suite. He bit at his bottom lip, licked and teased and tasted Richard as though he was dying of hunger. Desperate gasps, a need uncontained, came from his mouth. He moaned when he felt both of their bodies respond. Richard wanted to yell at his own animalistic reaction. He was trying to make a point!

But Thomas was burning, and hard, and pressing against every inch of him. The smell of his heated skin, the strong and roving hands that sought out the shape of Richard's body, were an unrestrained force. His chest was firm and muscled and seemed to crush against Richard's ribs. Richard brought his hands up, to push him away and Thomas grabbed his hands, slamming them into the wall beside his head.

Richard yelled angrily and Thomas bit his neck.

"You dare to tell me you love me?" Thomas gasped and thrust his hips harshly into Richard's. Richard groaned and fought weakly against him.

"Why does it anger you so?" Richard wanted to cry. He wanted to run away. He wanted to drop to his knees and show Thomas how much he loved him. The rough foreplay was not something he was accustomed to. Weren't men of this era supposed to be gentle? Thomas continued to lick and bite his way across Richard's chin, he paused, breathing heavily and pressing his forehead to Richard's.

"Because you do not. You cannot love me. You do not know what rages inside of me. If you knew the thoughts in my mind, the things I wish to do to you, you would rightly label me a monster and have me stoned to death. I wish you would. It would put me out of my misery."

Thomas drew away suddenly, stormed into the separate bathing chamber and slammed the door. Richard was breathless. His lips hurt and were swollen. He was sure he'd have bite marks on his neck. He did not like the control Thomas had over him, or how they'd left one another incapable of doing anything but obsessing. He took three deep and measured breaths.

The only way to show Thomas that he was not alone, in his so-called perversions, was to instruct him. Richard did not knock; he did not use the door handle. He simply ran at the wooden door and shouldered it open. It banged against the wall and Thomas came up from his seat on the bath, red faced, crying and still suffering a painful erection.

"What in the hell are you doing?"

"Sit," Richard seethed, brown eyes blazing with fire as he came closer to the future duke, took him by his shirt front, and pushed him back down on the edge of the large marble steps of the built-in bath.

"What do you think you're doing?"

Richard held his shirt. The stiff knot of his fist in Thomas's chest kept him still. He used the hand of his wounded shoulder, which should not have taken a door at that speed. Even now he could feel he'd pulled out stitches and blood began to seep through his shirt. He ignored it all, and stared only into Thomas's hurt and angry face. Thomas did not fight him, not even when Richard knelt down, unfastened the draw ties of his breeches and pulled them down past his muscled and tight ass. The thick and sinewy length of his legs. The proud and thick member that pulsed in time to the beat of Thomas's racing heart stood expectantly.

Richard breathed heavy, shook his head with how disastrously horny he was and hoped he had the control to not completely ruin the man. He bit and licked his way up the sensitive and quivering flesh of Thomas's inner thigh. His mouth watered, god, he wanted to taste, to feel Thomas in his mouth. With the other hand he held one of Thomas's shaking thighs down as he looked up into his uncertain blue eyes, and took his girth into his hot and wet mouth hungrily.

"Gods," Thomas breathed suddenly, crying and grunting, hips fighting to rise from the marble seat. Richard held him down, fingernails into flesh while he took him into his mouth in deep, savoring strokes. Richard pulsed his tongue along the underside of his cock. "Richard please," Thomas ached and arched and his eyes fell closed at the divine and hot heaven that was his lover's mouth. Richard stroked him, licked him, toyed with the tip with tongue and teeth, one hand coming up to pull and stroke his engorged balls, circle the base of him and squeezing. Thomas's moans became gasps. His body contracted, Richard felt the wave building fast and terrible in the trembling flesh of his thighs.

"Yes, cum—" he gasped, before taking his cock once more into his mouth and sucking hard and fast, the length of it hitting the back of his throat and sliding over and over against the cradle of his tongue. The hot fluid released with Thomas's strangled cry, every muscle shuddering. Richard licked and sucked and swallowed it as if it were a gift from a god, his god. He continued until the yelling cries of Thomas's release became whimpers and soft sobs.

"Fuck," Thomas groaned. Richard kissed his thighs, he pulled on the tight and sensitive skin of Thomas's sack until he seethed and pushed his hands away. "Fuck you," he gasped, his head fallen back on the edge of the tub.

"That will come later. This was only your first lesson." Richard said, his eyebrow raised at the future duke. He would not let him become a martyr to his own desire, and he certainly would not put up with his pouting.

"Lesson?" Thomas said between gasps.

"I'm going to teach you, everything you should have learned about being pleased." With that he rose to his feet, his own cock still swollen and hurting, and he rang the bell for the bath to be filled. "Take off your clothes."

"You're to give me orders now?" Thomas said, too relaxed to be angry, too pleased to argue. "You take off yours."

"Fine." Richard said. "When your bath is ready."

He stepped away, handed Thomas a towel and went to answer the door for the porters, now carrying buckets up in a line. When the tub was filled and the servants gone, Thomas cleared his throat.

"Well? Your clothes."

"Yes, my lord," Richard said and undressed. His chest was still heaving and Thomas's eyes were drawn to the stitches that had broken and the blood that was running down.

"Richard," he breathed, concerned.

"We'll worry about it later. Blood washes off," he said and took down his pants to kick them into the pile of dirty clothes. All of their clothes heaped together. Completely bare before each other. Thomas's eyes fell to Richard's cock, engorged and standing erect. Thomas swallowed. His eyes were wide.

Richard sensed his hesitation. "You aren't going to do that to me," he looked serious.

"Do you not like it?"

"I do, but I—am a lot to take in and you are not ready."

"I do not like being told what I cannot do." Thomas said. Richard knew he was never one to back down from a challenge. Thomas fell to his knees in front of Richard, but Richard stepped away and covered himself with his hands.

"No."

"But you are surely in pain."

"I am."

"Then don't be stubborn! Just let me."

"Pleasure doesn't always have to be repaid. And I enjoyed every fucking second of what I did to you. I can't wait to do it again. But it was intense for both your body and heart and you need to settle."

Thomas moaned and came closer to him. A future duke on his knees.

"Please at least let me taste you." His whisper was a groan, an ache. A shiver rocked through Richard's body. Fuck he wanted him to. He closed his eyes, took a deep breath and loosened his hands. Thomas pulled them away. He studied it, curious and Richard watched his fascination, as he took it in his hands and traced his long and hard tongue up the underside, delicately teasing the seam. As if he'd never gotten to explore and was flush with curiosity. He would either be Thomas's ruin or his salvation.

"Saints," Richard moved to pull away but Thomas dug his hands into the flesh of his ass and took him nearly all into his hot mouth. Richard groaned in shock and Thomas withdrew to cough. "You see?" Richard moved to step away but Thomas stopped him. With a deft move, no doubt learned in the fields of battle and the training yards, he grabbed Richard by the foot, knocked him to the ground and pinned him down, his body opposite facing. "What the hell are you doing?" Richard groaned

"You will hold still and let me taste you," Thomas said roughly and this time, took only the tip of Richard's member into his mouth, pressing it between his tongue and the roof of his mouth, gasping and licking it until Richard let out a great moan. He was voracious and eager, but it was driving him mad. He wanted it deeper. He needed more and Thomas was not ready.

Richard grabbed both sides of his tight ass in his hands and lifted him away as if he were lifting a bar at the gym. The tight release of Thomas's mouth caused Richard to groan and Thomas fought the sudden separation by wrestling him, naked on the cold marble tiles of the floor.

"I was not done!"

"There is such a thing as consent!" Richard bellowed and pinned him down. Breathless he glowered into Thomas's angry face.

"Did you not like it?"

Richard kissed him, the salty sweet taste of one another mixing. His kiss was soft but pressing, not the angry kisses of Thomas before, but one of a calming, nestling, comforting.

"I wish to bathe," Richard said quietly, gently laying a large blanket of patience over Thomas's confused and writhing body. He continued to kiss him softly.

"Richard," Thomas breathed, perplexed by the composed sweetness. As though they were lovers not animals. Caring for one another, not just in the midst of beastly delights. "Do you not want the same pleasure?"

"I want this," Richard whispered, kissed him for another few minutes and then slowly drew away when he felt Thomas's tension give way to ease. When he rose, his body was calm again. The warmth of their bodies entwined was comforting. And even when skin connected and heartbeats found each other there was something deeper than the heat and want between them. "Come to the bath."

Provided along the edge of the bath were salts, and soaps, oils and potions and Richard scratched his head at them. Thomas concocted a tea of sorts and when it broke the steaming surface of the water the scents of herbs and lavender, sea salt and olive oil, moisturizing, ache relieving and something to bathe away the stink of several days travel. Thomas held out his hand to help Richard up the steps and into the warm pool. Richard hesitated.

"Do you wish to bathe alone?" Thomas asked.

"No, unless you do. Then I will do as you ask."

"Oh, for *this* you will do what I ask?" Thomas quirked a smile, not quite joking. Richard puzzled over the man, but in the calmness, he realized what it was. The future duke, Thomas Alexander the Third, fifth in line for the throne of England, with all of his grand ideas of social justice, was still a bit of a spoiled brat. He was pouting for not getting what he wanted. Richard clucked his chin, noting the stubble that had again appeared.

"In time."

"We have so little," Thomas swallowed and his eyes started to glisten. He watched Richard climb into the bath and settle with a sigh and a groan. He touched the crusted blood on the stitches that had come undone. The area was bruised and turning green in its healing process. Thomas stepped in after him, the steam and warmth a sure sign that heaven existed and that they were privy to it. They sat, facing one another, legs crossed.

Thomas stared at the wound that would have killed him, painted forever above the heart of a man who loved him.

This strong and virile man that existed around such a horrible wound, a gentle giant who had the capacity for such beautiful brutality. He'd knocked down a damn door to get to him. To pull him from his shame and make of it a gift of pleasure. His whole body began to relax, his eyes went far away.

"What is on your mind? I'm sure it must be something. You seem to have thoughts holding your tongue." Richard said and leaned his head back to rest. Thomas felt his legs run the length of his own as he sunk deeper into the water. What was on his mind? The world and nothing at all.

"So much. I—I am unmoored, I think."

"What do you mean?" Richard opened one eye and looked at him. His hands fell below the line of the water to gently caress the rough and worn soles of Thomas's feet. "My god, what I'd give for a pumice stone," Richard whispered, his eyes heavy as he continued to gently massage the tired and tense flesh. Thomas lived on his feet, always prepared to battle. He'd never had them caressed. Thomas groaned in pleasure.

"It's just that, in all of my years of searching, fighting, aching. Trying to be what everyone has asked, it is only now that I finally feel at home in my own skin."

Richard smiled and opened his eyes.. "And? This is not a good thing?" Richard led. Thomas sighed, his hands took Richard's feet. But he was quickly distracted from the topic.

"My god, but your feet are so soft!" he said and sat up, pulling one out of the water and nearly dunking Richard in. He looked at Richard's foot in the fading light and ran his fingers over the smooth heels. "It is like a babe's!"

"I take care of my feet!" Richard laughed in response.

"I'd put those in my mouth they're so pretty," Thomas chuckled. Richard flexed his toes and Thomas felt his body shiver.

"So I am pretty now? Fuck, but you are trouble." Richard said and rolled his eyes back to closed. "Tell me what else? What is the dilemma with feeling at home in your own skin?" Thomas put his foot back in the water and sat up. He covered his face with his hands.

"Just as I feel like I'm getting my feet under me, we are destined to head back into the fray. And I am remorsefully sorry."

"What on earth for?"

"For dragging you along into this ill-fated plan."

"Meeting your family, being there for your sister's most joyous day doesn't have to be anything more than what it is."

"There will be expectations!"

"Oh, most assuredly." Richard nodded, not worried, eyes still closed.

"They will want me to make a decision about my place in the family."

"And so you shall." Richard said. Thomas sent a great handful of water into his face and roused him. "What the devil was that for?" he coughed and sputtered.

"If I chose to marry, to take my place as duke, where will that leave you?" The silence after the last words echoed and rang throughout the room. Richard, water dripping from his beard, stared at him.

∾

Thomas's question hung in the air without answer. Where indeed would it leave him? He thought about the journey he'd taken to be here, the unexpected twist that landed him in the bath with the most amazing, strong, beautiful man in history. Who sought his counsel. Who was, like so many men Richard knew and loved, lost and in need of steady ground. He reached beneath the water, grabbed Thomas's legs and pulled him into his lap, face to face.

"I will not leave you until you tell me to. Married or no. I am your confidant, I am your protector. Titles and marriages are contracts to be met but—" Richard circled the firm flesh of Thomas's ass, and drew him close. Thomas wrapped his legs around Richard's waist and tugged at his hair, meeting his eyes. "Love knows no such boundaries."

It was wrong of him, he supposed, to be so open in heart. But he needed Thomas to not only trust in him and his advice, but to learn to trust and value himself. To know that he was loved, and capable. So that he could make the decisions that would build a better world in the future. His eyes fell to Thomas's lips. It was no lie. Love. He reached a wet hand up to touch Thomas's stubbled chin, thumb grazing over his bottom lip. Thomas's eyes went soft.

"Oh, and my wife would be content to share a bed with us both?"

Richard smiled and shook his head. "Brat," he said softly and kissed him. "You have no wife yet. That is a worry for another time."

"But I am to sire children with her," Thomas said between kisses, and Richard felt him shudder. He pulled away.

"It is not my wish that you should ever lay with anyone else." His eyes narrowed. "I would have you to myself for a lifetime of lessons, if fate were in my hands. But you are worrying about a future not yet made. And you may not know, but as a doctor of history—"

"I thought you were a doctor of books—"

"I can tell you with much assurance that some of the greatest leaders of the past did not prefer a woman in their beds." Thomas pulled back, scowled. Richard pulled him back in and bit his lip, kissed his chin.

"Surely you jest."

"Surely I do not. The great explorers Lewis and Clark, probably? Sir William Drummond Stewart. Shakespeare himself some would say … Walt Whitman, Oscar Wilde to be sure."

"Who is Oscar—"

"Oh—he's not born yet, but you'll love that cad," Richard said with a chuckle but then stopped suddenly mid kiss. He'd gotten too comfortable.

"I don't understand what you're saying."

"I'm saying that there will be a way, Thomas. Do not worry. Not here, in my arms, not so long as we are near each other." His voice was soft, he put his forehead on Thomas's "I will keep both your body and heart safe."

Gooseflesh rose on Thomas's arms and back. His breath quickened. He kissed Richard. "I fear I do not know how to love," he whispered into Richard's lips. "My heart is at constant war with itself."

"You needn't love me," Richard shook his head even as his heart felt like breaking into a million little pieces. "But I beg of you, trust me."

"I do," whispered Thomas. "I do." Richard kissed him. Thomas threw his arms around his broad back and leaned his head on Richard's shoulder. He flinched and Thomas drew away. "You must let me see to those."

He took the soap, and gently washed away the blood, the pus, the oozing anger that was working its way out of Richard's body. It looked less red than it had, and Richard hadn't suffered a fever in the last day. He hoped it meant that some of his twenty-first century vaccines had come into play. Thank God for his tetanus booster last year after that knitting needle debacle. He shouldn't have left his project bag on his chair.

Richard watched the concentration on Thomas's face as he attended to his wound. The stitching was becoming dry and brittle. He put some of the oil on his fingers and rubbed it into the line of them. Richard watched, his heart beat ticking up. Thomas looked at him.

"What is it?"

Richard looked at the bottle, his brain conjuring up the possibilities, wanting but not trusting his desire just yet, to keep Thomas safe. "Nothing. I'm hungry. We should get dressed for dinner."

Thomas's stomach growled in approval and they washed more thoroughly. When Thomas's hand dipped below the water to take Richard's shaft in its soapy grasp, he found him still half hard. "I wish you'd let me just fix this."

"It is not broken," Richard gasped, even as Thomas's soapy fingers continued to stroke him. "You are incorrigible," he laughed and took his hands away.

"What exactly are you trying to prove, being so stoic?" Thomas laughed and rinsed his hair.

"That I have control."

"I want you to lose control with me," Thomas said. "Do you think me not strong enough?"

"You are strong, but you should not have to be strong, or withstand something from your lover. You should accept and welcome it." Richard washed and rinsed his hair with the water that was now quite dirty. It was still better than the state of his skin before he'd gotten in.

"I want to accept it. Willingly."

Richard looked at the oil on the bath edge and back into

Thomas's eyes. "Someday you shall. But not this night, because I'm hungry and tired, and I'm bound to be a right lion."

"A lion in need of new clothes. I will send ahead for the tailor to meet us in the morning."

Richard groaned as he got out of the now cold water and took a clean towel. Thomas was already drying off and stood, naked and unafraid before him, rubbing at his wet and curly locks with fervor. Richard did the same, not abashed in front of Thomas, which was shocking for a man who was constantly comparing himself to other men and coming up short in his own eyes. There was comfort in their temporary circumstances.

"But what will the lion eat tonight?"

"Ale to be sure, and something warm. Haggis? Pie? It all sounds delicious. I'm starving."

Thomas bounded out of the broken doorway and into the sleeping quarters to hunt in his small bag for something clean. He came up with two shirts but only one pair of clean breeches. "Guess you'll go without pants. Pity," Thomas shrugged and threw him a clean shirt. Richard scowled. Thomas's eyes fell to Richard's groin. "Maybe I'll just have a large and lovely banger."

"You are absolutely unbelievable. It is as though you have been living on the battlefield with nothing but men. You must remember your manners before we arrive." Richard laughed and jumped into his less dirty pants as quickly as he could. Shirtless, he tied them tightly and made sure he was tucked away. The bulge still showed. Thomas smiled, a naughty man, unleashed.

"Perhaps it will make my father choose my brother. A wiser decision, if he knows what a derelict I am."

Richard shook his head. "I will protect you, my lord, even from yourself."

22

A GENTLE NIGHT INTERRUPTED BY THE TAILOR

Richard fell asleep nearly as soon as his head hit the pillow. They'd had dinner, a drink and quiet conversation. Thomas had given him a short rundown of who would be there upon their arrival. Most of the older staff he'd known as a boy had passed away or moved on. But his father's right-hand man, head of the household staff, Barnaby seemed to never age, and through letters with his sister he had learned, was still in excellent health.

Richard's eyes were heavy. Thomas quieted his conversation and nodded for the house's small staff to clear away the plates. When he'd taken Richard upstairs, the head of staff had asked if Thomas prefer they put Richard in a separate room. Thomas's skin felt hot as he stared at the man, knowing he must proceed with caution.

"No. I'm under orders from his doctor to keep a close watch on his wound. He is not yet healed enough and could face complications if not attended to."

The butler had nodded, unfazed, and helped Thomas with the door to their sleeping quarters. Thomas helped Richard get settled on the bed before he checked his stitches and, finding them in good condition, he loosened his coat and had every intention of pleasuring Richard to release. He wanted to. He ached for it. He wanted Richard to trust him as much as he trusted Richard. But despite his wants, he could see that the man was tired.

The journey with his injury had been much more difficult than he had shown. He was pale and seemed to be fading before his eyes. So Thomas helped him into bed, took off his boots, loosened his clothing and covered him with the blankets.

"You're coming to bed aren't you?" Richard said softly, his hand reaching out to hold his.

"I'll be along presently," he whispered and kissed Richard's forehead which seemed a bit hot. He stepped outside, made arrangements with the staff for the morning appointments and the meal plan, and came back. He bolted the door, drew all of the curtains. He disrobed completely, relishing the cool and sensitive way his naked body felt as he slipped between the sheets. He rolled over to watch the even breathing of Richard and how his face fell into relaxation. His brows were thick but well taken care of, a long bridge of a nose, his beard that had grown scraggly in the past weeks. Thomas wondered what he would look like without it. How much age was under it. Was he young-faced and that's why he insisted it stay in place? So that people would take him more seriously? Thomas smiled. His gaze moved down from the thick dark lashes and soft brown beard to Richard's lips. Thomas shivered and gently traced the pink fullness of the bottom lip. God, he loved kissing him. The pressure of it, the taste, the way his mouth was at once so warm and so profoundly sensitive.

He loved all the things that mouth was capable of. Thomas closed his eyes. They both needed rest, and he needed to regulate his thoughts. He needed to show self-control like Richard had. For the sake of his health. The next few days they would be parted, in separate quarters. They would be bombarded with people and family … and prospective wives.

Thomas traced Richard's jaw with his finger and his brow fell. This was all the time they were guaranteed. And he wasn't going to waste it. Quietly and with stealth, he slid close to Richard, beneath his good arm, and laid his head on the steady rise and fall of his chest. He slung his leg over Richard's warm hips, and kissed his chin before settling down.

"My love," Richard said softly growling and squeezing Thomas close enough to kiss his forehead. "Where have you been my whole life?"

Thomas felt the tears come but did not try to stop them. He sniffed and kissed Richard's chest.

"I have always been here. Right here. Waiting for you," he whispered back. They fell asleep like this, warm and safe, away from a world that would soon seek to separate them.

The morning rose slower than normal. Richard felt like the universe was conspiring to keep them in bed longer. And he had no mind to argue. The room was dark and quiet, even with the stirrings of the town starting to filter in from outside. Richard kept his eyes closed, willing the dream to continue. Thomas was holding him, from behind, the heavy weight of his arm across his shoulder. He'd slept on his wounded side and it ached. Pain was the strictest reminder that he must move sometime soon. He groaned into the pillow. Thomas's hand tightened and then released.

"Oh god, I've turned you over. How is your shoulder?" he breathed, sleepy and eyes half closed. He pulled Richard over to lay on his back once more and inspected the wound. Richard watched him push his curled and unruly hair away from his eyes and squint into the dimness.

"How does it feel?"

"Fine," Richard breathed. Everything was fine. If the world ended tomorrow, he had the memory of the future Duke of Marlborough, leaning over him in sexy sleepiness, concerned for him. His naked skin was warm next to Richard's. His body woke to the hundreds of ways he wanted to make this morning last.

"Only fine?" Thomas scowled.

"I am not concerned for my shoulder."

"And therein lies the problem. You did not tell me it was causing you to suffer for the entirety of the journey."

"You already had enough on your mind. I am fine, Thomas."

Thomas scowled at him once more and leaned down to kiss the tender and puckered skin along the stitches. All thoughts of his world outside this bed were lost. These were the last of their beautiful moments. Everything outside of this bed, this room, this moment, was a world that would not accept the love they kept. Thomas kissed him and fought tears that threatened. Richard's muscles tensed and flinched. Thomas gently bit his chest, his breathing coming quicker with every hot kiss.

"You are all I want on my mind, presently." Thomas whispered, continuing to kiss across his chest, until he reached his taut nipple. He wondered, grazing it with his thumb, why God would give nipples to men. Were they not for feeding babies? And yet, when Richard's hips rose from the bed when he took the bud between his teeth and gently bit, maybe God gave them for everyone to enjoy. Maybe God gave them each other … to enjoy. Richard took him in his arms and rolled him over with a guttural growl.

"What are you doing, my lord, besides torturing me?"

"I'm in need of another lesson," Thomas said. "I'm afraid I won't learn all I need to know without your help." He smiled up at Richard still sleepy and disheveled. "Take for example, the odd and curious notion that these would be so sensitive," he caressed both of Richard's nipples at once, pinching, kissing, teasing.

Richard bucked into his open hips. Rubbing his straining body against Thomas's.

Richard's eyes opened and he stared down at Thomas.

"Where are your clothes?"

"I have burned them."

"In truth?"

"No, they're in a pile at the base of the bed, where I left them when I crawled in next to you last night."

"I'm sorry I fell asleep," Richard said softly. One hand came up to trace the strong jaw of Thomas.

"Your rest was more important."

"More important than lessons?"

"More important than anything. Your rest is your health and I want you living for a great long while."

"Is that so?" Richard breathed softly and leaned down to kiss the crook of Thomas's neck and shoulder. Thomas's hands caressed down his back and cupped his backside.

"If I had my way," Thomas gasped, "You would live longer than me, so I'd never have to know a day without you."

Richard pulled back, his eyes filled with tears. "My lord," his heartbeat rose. Was this what it felt like? When someone reached into your soul, took one look at all of the broken and wonderful parts and said they wanted it in total. That they couldn't bear the idea of life without you? Why you'd travel through time and risk your own life, just to be in their orbit.

Thomas reached up and kissed him gently. "What's my lesson?" He whispered into his lips.

"How open of mind do you feel?" Richard said softly, nuzzling his chin, kissing and biting his neck again, the clean and fresh smell of him driving Richard mad. His words of love and thoughts of forever, causing his whole body to sing with the need.

"Whatever the master asks, the student will give," Thomas said softly.

Richard groaned and his member strained against his breeches as he moved against the length of Thomas's strong thigh. Thomas's nails dug into the flesh of his ass and pulled and pushed him against his body, his breath coming in heavy gasps. Richard slowed his pace, shook his head, caught his breath, kissed Thomas.

"Slow down, love," he whispered and bit Thomas's ear lobe. Thomas gasped and arched up beneath him. "I want to find all of those delicious spots that make your body sing for me," he whispered and gently nipped at the sensitive skin of his throat.

"My body is on fire with song. I am in agony, my lion." Thomas nearly sobbed, teeth clenched. Their breathing was loud and gasping in the room where the sun was now peeking through window dressings and the stirring of the town sounded below them.

Richard took his mouth in a kiss, hot and demanding. There was no other time than this, he would be gentle and slow and controlled, he promised himself over and over again, even with every kiss that became more biting and desperate.

A loud knock on the outside door rang through their intimate moment, shattering the world into a cold harshness. Richard jumped. Thomas held on tighter. They stilled, held breaths, listened. It came again, more insistent.

"My lord, it is Mr. Marcus Bennett, the tailor?" came the pinched voice from behind the door. "You asked that I come early?"

"Bollocks," Thomas groaned into Richard's shaking shoulder. Richard muffled a cry into his neck.

"We will have to continue this at another time," Richard said, taking deep breaths and trying to contain his desire in a practiced measure of control.

"I don't know how you calm yourself so quickly," Thomas grouched as they both rose and put on clothes. It was a pity; Thomas's body in the morning light, strong and scarred, was something Richard desperately wanted to study. He wanted to know all of his scars. He wanted to show Thomas his. Even the most painful ones. They dressed quickly. Richard began tearing bedding from the large bed.

"What are you doing?" Thomas hissed, about to open the door. Richard fashioned a quick, makeshift sleeping place on the ground next to the bed. Thomas stared it, sad and angry, and then nodded in understanding. He opened the door.

"My good man, you are of your word. It is I who had misjudged the hour." He said, charming and with a dashing smile that revealed a dimple that Richard wasn't sure he'd ever seen before. God, to make him smile that way. To see that dimple every day, to know he was the cause of Thomas's happiness.

"I am sorry if I woke your lordship." The tailor, a slight man with impeccable style strode in. His suit was a deep navy blue and just ahead of the times, his shirt, crisp and white, his hair trimmed and clean. Shaven. Richard eyed him. The tailor eyed him back. The man swallowed harshly.

"Is this what I have to work with?" He circled Richard more than once, discerning and disappointed.

"I apologize, good sir," Richard said lowly. "I normally do not dress as thus. It has been a long and strange journey."

"My friend is a professor at Oxford and saved my life in a most fortuitous act of bravery. In the fray he lost most of his belongings. His clothing was bloodied in battle and he was forced, by my own selfish will, to cross the country in nought but rags. I am a poor friend."

"My lord," Richard said softly but Thomas held out his palm to stop his protest.

"We are to attend my sister's wedding next week and I promised him we would insure he had something to wear."

"At least until my journey home." Richard said. Thomas looked at him and his brow fell.

"For at least a few weeks. What can you do?"

The tailor nodded, taken with the challenge and renewed with a sense of vigor. "You have come to the right man, my lord. He is a large, brute of a man—"

"*His* name is Doctor Shaw, and *he* does speak English. You can directly address me," Richard said, scowling now. A visible shudder ran through the tailor's body and his eyes grew wide.

"Of course, my good sir. I meant no disrespect. It's just that you—"

"Are large."

"And—"

"My clothes are dreadful. Please, know that it displeases me greatly. I am putting the fate of my reputation in your hands," Richard said and leveled his eyes on the tailor. He wasn't sure, but he swore he saw a blush erupt on his high cheeks.

"You can put your utter faith in me, Doctor Shaw." The tailor said and nodded. Taking in a deep breath he turned to his case which held the cloth samples, some suits merely needing tailoring, and those he'd prepared after receiving measurements the night before. He spread out his options and inspiration across the room, and the process began.

While Thomas tried on the clothing the tailor had pre-fitted, and they'd made adjustments, Richard explored the various cloths, colors and materials. Mr. Bennett must have a fine shop indeed. Even Richard hadn't expected the level of craftsmanship and quality of fiber. Then again, this was an era when a suit had to last you for more than a season and they were mostly all hand-made by people whose life's work it was to clothe the body.

Richard enjoyed watching the tailor work, deft and long fingers with pins and needles and an eye for measuring that seemed to even be more accurate than tape. He'd fashioned Thomas a new, bright red, and brilliant white officer's coat that made the one he'd met him in look like rags. Richard still liked the old coat. It had a story and a history, and the miles of blood and dirt that Thomas had endured to be the man he was. But he still looked very dashing in the well fitted coat and breeches. He also had a full blue suit fitted for him, that made his eyes a deeper hue. A sea of brilliant blue below his soft brown curls.

Thomas stood in front of Richard, arms outstretched and asked, "Well then, what do you think?"

Richard could scarcely speak. How could he tell him it made his eyes look like sapphires and anyone who looked upon him in it would instantaneously fall in love. How could he say, *you shall wear that for me, and me alone*? How could he say, it made him want to take him to bed and never let him leave? He shook his head, Mr. Bennett looked at him, worried.

"It is…" Brilliant? Perfect? Spectacular. "It is a fine suit, my lord." Richard choked and looked away. Thomas quirked his head and nodded, confused but not dissuaded. Any fool could see that it was a suit meant for him.

"Good, now, let's get to work on this great mountain of a man," Thomas teased, began to take the suit off and faced away as if Richard had not seen him naked. Richard went to the windows to look out on the town. When Thomas had dressed in his older clothes, he excused himself. "I'm going to go see about breakfast. You work your magic, Mr. Bennett, I'm putting my faith in you that every woman at my sister's wedding will be clamoring for his hand." He smiled, with the damn dimple flashing before he headed out the door. Richard scowled after him and wanted to give him choice words.

"Most assuredly, they will," Mr. Bennett agreed with a nod and began his work. He had Richard stand on a small box to measure the length of the breeches but found he could not reach his shoulders from that height and needed him to step down again to measure out the extra material to cover his broad chest. The tailor's eyes fell to the stain of blood on his shirt.

"Are you quite well?"

"I am healing," Richard said, looking down at it to. "You are a tailor. Could you look at it? Are these stitches sound?" Richard pulled his shirt aside to expose the wound. He looking up to see Mr. Bennett turn white and swoon to nearly fainting. "I'm sorry!" he caught the man and helped him to a seat at the bench.

"I sew cloth, Doctor Shaw, not skin!" He laughed and dabbed at the sweat on his brow with a kerchief from his coat.

"My sincerest apologies, my good sir. I meant no disrespect." Richard knelt at his side, some of the stitches in his suit coat popping.

"No apology necessary. When the future duke said that you'd saved his life, I thought he meant figuratively."

"No, I stepped in the path of a blade meant for him." Richard hung his head. Mr. Bennett looked at him with kind eyes.

"You are a true and noble friend."

Richard shook his head. At times he felt so very selfish. He knew, that in some small part, he was taking advantage of Thomas's gratitude. And though he espoused that it was for the good of the future, the truth was, he was not angry that Thomas was taking care of him, and willing in his arms. He hoped it was not just because of some debt he felt he was owed.

"I was merely in the right place in the wrong, er, right time." Richard coughed. Mr. Bennett put his hand on Richard's shoulder, he made him meet his eyes.

"He is quite fond of you."

"He is too kind to me." Richard's eyes fell and he shook his head. Richard helped the tailor to stand.

"You have no idea the weight of a man's soul or what it means to the future, to save even one life." Mr. Bennett said and looked at Richard pointedly. For a moment, Richard thought of the Timekeepers and sweat broke out on his neck. He looked across the room, to his satchel where the map was. He hadn't checked on it in days. He hadn't even thought about it since the carriage. His heart started to hammer in his chest. Did Mr. Bennett somehow know who he was? When he was from? Their silent study was broken by Thomas entering with a plate of fruit and pastries, and a woman behind him with a tray of tea.

"Gentlemen, let us break this tedious chore," he said smiling, and set the table in the parlor room with breakfast.

23
PHILOSOPHICAL DEBATES AND
FAVORS RETURNED

After the light meal, a rousing conversation of the new political landscape forming after the defeat of the French and the proposals for new social programs that were being whispered about in the parliament was started. Mr. Bennett resumed his work with Richard, who stood perfectly still while the tailor moved around him with sharp pins and sharper eyes.

"What are your thoughts on the new state of the country?" Richard said, turning his head slightly to where Thomas was perusing one of his books. The one of love poetry. Richard smiled. He needed to make sure Thomas was not so lost to his own heart and loins that he forgot about his duty.

"I do not know."

"What do you mean you do not know? Have you not an opinion?" Richard asked. Mr. Bennett's eyebrow rose, as he adjusted the cuffs of Richard's sleeve on what was to be his third suit. This one was a deep forest green. Thomas looked up and studied the suit, his eyes rising to lock into Richard's, mesmerized. He shook his head and returned his attentions back to the page.

"I feel like too strong an opinion may incite a riot. Or alienate others from the upper class where I reside."

"No opinion at all allows men of lesser moral character make decisions for the country."

"Moral character?" Thomas said, glowering. Richard paused and cocked his head disapprovingly at the future duke.

"I mean that if compassionate and level-headed men do not speak up in the face of injustice, then the unjust will continue in worsening ways towards nefarious ends."

"What are *your* opinions then?" Thomas asked sarcastically, putting the book down. Richard watched him rise, cross his arms over his just shirt clad chest and stare at him curiously.

"I am merely a lowly scholar. My opinions will never sway the course of history." Mr. Bennett cleared his throat and poked Richard in the side with a pin. "Ouch!"

"Sorry!" he bowed his head.

"But *you* are to be a duke, a man of standing. Your voice carries weight in this world and in this country, so your voice can change the course of things for the good."

"The good of what exactly?" Thomas said, honestly intrigued.

"What do you think is right?" Richard returned. "I want to know what *you* think."

"Mr. Bennett," Thomas said. The tailor rose, nodded, and left the room. Such matters were delicate and Richard had forgotten that some subjects were not broached in the company of 'service' people. He hung his head and folded his hands in front of his waist.

"What does it matter?" Thomas asked. "What I think? What I do? I am but a mere soldier. A black sheep. The family's cast off."

"The eldest son of a noble family. A man of war, strategy, who has seen horrors, and does not wish for his country to continue along the path of suffering, poverty, illiteracy—"

"You know this?"

"I hope this," Richard said quietly, his eyes feeling moist as he stared down at Thomas from his box. "I have been without power most of my life. But I have always been grateful to the people, men and women, who came before me. To make sure that school was important, reading mattered, food for the poor, health for the entire country, decent pay and decent treatment, no matter where or how we were born. This has been a saving grace in my life. To have systems in place to take care of those who needed the help. That we lift each other up, that we elevate the lowest so that we may all rise together ... I don't know why you're looking at me like that, I know it's stupid and not in line with the monarchy and the colonial ideals of—"

Thomas pulled him down by his pinned shirt front for a kiss. "Keep talking," He whispered after taking both of their breaths away.

"My lord?"

"You never fail to amaze me." Thomas gasped for breath. "When you first stepped in front of the blade, your body shoving me—me! Of all the men on the field! —away, I was stunned. Watching you fell those men—"

Richard hung his head and looked as though he might cry.

"I thought I'd never seen a warrior in equivalent to you. I'd never seen a soldier as brave or strong, or determined. I fell instantly," Thomas stopped, his head fell and his hand was still tight on Richard's shirt. "When you read poetry, when you spoke so softly and eloquently to Mrs. Worthington. When you put on those damn glasses!" Thomas had to stop again shake his head. "I need to know more. Of what is in your beautiful brain."

"My lord, I ache to tell you all of it, but I do not wish to overwhelm you." Richard said clamoring closer for a kiss. Thomas obliged. A soft and slow kiss.

"Overwhelm me," he gasped against Richard's lips. "Sweep me up in every beautiful thought you have. In every moral dilemma, in every social construct, in every wanton desire. Overwhelm me," Thomas begged, and pulled him close, kissing him again until the pins pushed into Richard's skin and he gasped and pulled away to inspect them. Thomas grinned, a boy in love. "I'm sorry," he whispered and pecked his chin lovingly.

Thomas stepped away and called out for Mr. Bennett to again join them and finish his measurements. The rest of the appointment went slower than Thomas had wished. He wanted Richard alone. He wanted to know more about his thoughts on the state of the country. It intrigued him to see a path forward. One that would mean greater equality for the masses. One that would mean a better future for all going forward. He would listen to any theory or idea from Richard. He would listen for hours. Days. A lifetime.

When the tailor gathered his fabric and material, his own mind distracted with the artwork he would be busy with, Thomas stopped him.

"When can these be ready, Mr. Bennett?"

"Tomorrow before the noon hour, to be sure, if it a rush, my lord."

"Tomorrow?" Richard asked, putting on his dreadful shirt. Mr. Bennett watched him as if it hurt to see a body covered in rags after the finery.

"My good sir, please take one of the models," he dug in his bag and withdrew a clean, though not fitted, shirt for him to wear. "It is disgraceful that such a brilliant mind and faithful man be dressed in those rags." The tailor shook his head as if he was doing the whole of humanity a great service.

"But doesn't your family expect us tonight?" Richard asked Thomas over Mr. Bennett's head, even as he disrobed to put on the far nicer shirt. Thomas watched his chest flex and he took in a deep breath.

"It takes the time it takes. I will not have us coming into Marlborough estates looking like a couple of ruffian vagabonds.

Please do not rush if it means more worry to you, Mr. Bennett, my friend. We are quite content here, and it would do Doctor Shaw a great favor to rest his wound one more day before setting off into the battle of my family." Thomas teased, even though some seriousness settled beneath his words.

"As you wish, my lord. I will get them to you in good quality and in good time." He smiled at both men and gave Richard an odd wink before he left. Richard watched him quizzically and then looked back to Thomas, who had picked up his old shirt. He was tracing the outline of the blood that had been shed in him tearing down the door to get to Thomas in his needful state.

"My lord, we shall be late to your homecoming," Richard said with some regret and stress filling the spaces of his voice.

"I am grateful for the excuse."

"I know you do not wish to go back to the pressures of your life, but I think it's important for the worry of your mother and sister—"

"I am grateful for one more night with you." Thomas interrupted. "A whole day, and a whole night," he said and looked up into Richard's face. Richard sighed. Perhaps it was not such a tragedy. "Whatever will we do with such a gift?"

Richard looked down at him. A gift indeed. Thomas's generosity with the clothing, his willingness to listen and learn and be open to the expansive ideas beyond his own time, set Richard's heart and groin on fire. He wanted to soak up every minute of the unexpected hours they had been given.

"What is there to do in Westbury?" Richard asked.

"Besides stay in one's bedchambers?" Thomas replied, annoyed. Richard smiled and gently pinched his chin, the dimples of his face hidden in his scowl.

"I will make it worth the wait, my lord. The next lesson," he paused to take in a breath. "Will leave you absolutely spent, I fear." Richard shook his head and Thomas's knees buckled. What more could they do to each other? What other sweet pleasures did Richard know of? What could he teach him? How many more ways were there to bring each other to release? He desperately wanted to give Richard at least a dozen.

"I will take you out, on one condition," Thomas said, lifting his chin in a fit of royal stubbornness.

"I will hear your terms," Richard acquiesced.

"I want to play with you."

"Play, my lord?"

"Explore. I want to touch you, without rush and without interruption."

"My lord, we have an entire day to spend."

"I am only asking for a few moments. I have been hungry all morning." He said, a pout returning to his mouth. Richard saw in it a doorway to gaining trust and the unquestioning loyalty. Plus, he was not an idiot, he wanted the same thing. Desperately.

"How would you have me, my lord?" Richard whispered and gently caressed Thomas's strong jaw line.

"You have been standing all morning," Thomas said and nodded his head to the bed. "Take leisure." Richard looked at the bed and groaned. How much torture could he endure. The inexperience of the future duke had more chance of enraging him with desire than in quenching it. He'd not been with a virgin since he'd been one himself. He knew that Thomas's intentions were good and he tried to focus on how he'd felt, in his first moments free to explore.

Richard stopped his thoughts. This was a lesson too. He had but to ask for what he wanted, needed, and desired. Richard could lead him. Thomas was an apt pupil.

"Was I unclear in my request?" Thomas said sternly.

"No, my lord," Richard said.

"Then?" Thomas said and nodded toward the bed again. "Off you go, and undo your breeches."

"My lord," Richard gasped, trying to not anticipate what he had in mind. Thomas locked the doors, drew the blinds and waited until Richard lay, supine in bed, the ties of his pants undone his shirt rising and falling with his heavy breaths.

"Take off your shirt."

"Sir," Richard said, pulled it up over his head, and watched Thomas's pleased expression at being obeyed. "And?"

"Lay still."

"That I cannot guarantee." Richard groaned as Thomas stalked nearer.

"You will not remove me. Or stop me, or try to hinder my exploration in anyway."

"With all due respect, my lord, I have needs," Richard stuttered as Thomas came nearer, placed his hand on one of Richard's thighs and another deftly against his throat.

"I am aware. I intend to fulfill them."

"It can be delayed until tonight," Richard started but stopped to groan when Thomas's strong hand slid up his thigh to cup his engorged balls over his breeches.

"You are a virile man. It can be both." Thomas said. His commanding tone made Richard breathless with the idea that he should be the slave of the man. He never wanted something so much. Thomas's hand slid down to his bare chest, caressed the hair, nails grazing to the ties of his pants and loosening them more. He tugged at the fabric until Richard's groin and ass were exposed but the pants still kept his legs bound.

"My lord, I can disrobe."

"I want you less mobile," Thomas whispered, eyebrow raised.

"Thomas, what do you—"

Thomas placed a strong hand down over the straining muscles of Richard's stomach and licked his other palm slowly, with a tongue wet and warm. "Oh god," Richard gasped, threw his head back and moaned even before Thomas touched him.

"Would you like this?" Thomas asked, eyebrow raised.

"Yes, yes my lord," before he could breathe out the consent of it, Thomas's hand encircled the base of his tight and hard cock, and his mouth took the rest. Slowly, with warm and wet suction, enjoying the hard tip sliding eagerly deeper into his mouth and throat, Thomas kept the pressure, a tight ring of palm and fingers against the base of Richard's length. Careful to control the depth and intensity. To savor every thrust, to keep the pressure and intensity and make his mouth an instrument of praise. Richard had greatly underestimated Thomas. His hips left the bed with the pleasure that seared up his thighs and spine.

So long pent up, so long wanting, Richard felt as though he was at a distinct disadvantage to show control. God, the heat and the wet, the pressure of his mouth and tongue, the slight grazing of his teeth over the throbbing head of him. He felt the first spurt of excitement and Thomas licked it up with a satisfied grunt.

"There's … more," Richard tried to say but Thomas was on him again, hungry and suckling, and pulling him deeper inside with every delicious thrust.

"Thomas, Thomas," Richard burned and sighed as his hips came off of the bed and he arched. The ache became a surge, that then became a wave that pulsed and demanded. He lifted off the bed, the tightening of his whole body in clenched fists and toes as he yelled a guttural cry and came, hard and deep into Thomas's throat.

The warm rush of it, the sounds that Richard made, releasing his desire and passion. The way his hands threaded into Thomas's hair and held him there to take the rush of his climax, made Thomas writhe and swallow and beg for more with tongue and teeth until Richard was shaking and imploring him to let go.

"Stop, Stop!" he cried and tugged at Thomas's curls, the sensitivity so great. But Thomas wanted more, he licked and bit until every last drop had been spent. He took one of Richard's balls in his mouth and gently tugged at it. He bit at the inner thigh. He smiled into the shaking muscles of the man beneath him, and the way he sighed, and groaned, and sobbed with the after effects. He chanced a look up to where Richard was tugging at his hair and covering his tear-filled eyes.

"Was it not satisfactory?"

"Fuck you," Richard breathed and pulled him up and into his arms. "Where on earth did you learn to use your mouth like that?"

"I have a most excellent teacher," Thomas gasped, and kissed the hollow of Richard's throat. He still breathed heavily, like he might not come down, and reached for Thomas's swollen pouch. Thomas stopped his hands.

"Turnabout is fair play."

"Absolutely not," Richard growled and tore at the bindings of Thomas's breeches, teeth bared and looking into Thomas's eyes.

"Consent matters." Thomas retorted.

Richard turned and pinned him to the bed, in anger. "Are you honestly going to tell me that I'm not allowed?"

"Did you not do the same thing to me yesterday?" Thomas raised a brow, seemingly in control despite his hard cock pulsing into Richard's hand.

"Perhaps I was wrong then," Richard said, aching to please his lover.

"What? The great Doctor Shaw, wrong? Inconceivable." Thomas said and drew away, rolling out from underneath Richard with a smile and quirk of his perfect eyebrow.

Richard collapsed on the bed and sobbed into the pillow. He put his fist into the mattress, and Thomas watched the strong muscles of his back flex.

"Are you having an episode? Are you a toddler?" Thomas teased, putting on his clothing, his worn and old coat. "Come, get dressed we have things to do. Sights to see."

Richard leaned up on one elbow and looked at him through a scowl. "Tonight," he growled and Thomas stopped all movement.

"Tonight?"

"Tonight, you will consent," he said.

"To what?"

"What's good for you," Richard threatened, rose from the bed, and still half undressed, came to Thomas, to take his mouth forcefully. Tasting his own desire, the salt and sweat. He drank of Thomas's mouth, fervently until the future duke was weak in his knees and had to push him away.

"We shall see what's good for me," he said, a slight fear and excitement in his eyes. Richard dressed, ate the leftover fruit, and shared the last pastry with Thomas on their way out the door into the now past noon, sunlight.

24

RING SHOPPING AND VOWS
OF LOVE

Westbury was a thriving hamlet and one that Richard only remembered from his brief visit with Lillian, and the one stop he made at an out-of-the-way museum. Where he'd stolen a map. A map that had landed him in this mess. A map that would surely get him killed by the Timekeepers if they should discover what he'd done. The map was tucked safely into his coat. Close to his heart. When he glanced across the street and his eyes caught the residence that in his time had become the museum where he'd "acquired" it, he shuddered and pulled Thomas to the other side of the street.

In fact, he became increasingly nervous. Lillian had said her father claimed there was an office of Timekeepers in Westbury. If there were Timekeepers here, he wanted nothing to do with them. They would tell him he had no right. They would make him leave and he still had a few precious days to set his world right again. Thomas glanced at him curiously as they walked side by side. Richard didn't want to think about the moment he would have to leave. His heart tugged against his mind. His stitches hurt. His whole body hurt when he thought of leaving Thomas. He leaned softly against his shoulder before backing away.

What he wouldn't give to hold his hand in this moment, as they walked along the busy street, its crowds and vendors unaware of the rush of love and worry that lay between the two stoic men.

"Have you considered a gift for your sister?" Richard asked, as they passed by a jeweler. Both stopped to look into the window display. Fine silver candlesticks and hairbrushes. Jewel-encrusted hair combs, and ruby and diamond necklaces. Plain silver rings, engagement settings twinkled up from displays. Someday, Thomas would have to pick one out for a bride. Thomas's eyes fell on them and he grimaced. Richard knew their minds were on the same fate.

"Come, let's go in and see." Richard said, resigned to the fact that he could not stop the world from marching on, and he could not save Thomas from this one particular fate. But he wouldn't ruin what little time they had together by worrying over a future he could not be a part of.

Richard walked along the displays and Thomas searched through the various hair combs, ivory brushes, and cameo necklaces. His sister must not have been a jewel person. Richard stopped before a display of men's rings. They were all carved and molded in patterns of the times. But one.

He leaned in to stare closer, retrieving his glasses from his pocket and looking at the ornately carved pewter ring, a lion with emerald eyes. Next to it, a sparkling blue sapphire set in the center of a Tudor style rose. If ever there were two rings that resonated, he thought with trepidation at how perfect they were, these were them.

"May I help you, sir?" The attendant said, with a frown towards Richard's clothing.

"No, I'm merely here in support of my friend," Richard leaned back. The attendant looked to Thomas and his jowly face brightened with recognition.

"Certainly, sir, forgive me. I did not see the duke's son."

Richard's mouth turned down in a frown. Prestige had some perks.

"What do you think of this one, my lord?" Richard asked, and pointed to the sapphire rose. Thomas came over to look as well. His eyes landed lightly but he exhaled quickly.

"My, but that is beautiful," he said, blue eyes stuck on the fine craftmanship. Richard watched his profile, the strong jaw, the soft lips, the concentration between his beautiful brows. How would he ever live in a world again, without Thomas? He felt tears come to his eyes and he sniffed them back.

"It is indeed," he said softly. He didn't know how, but he would find a way to leave Thomas with something to remember him by.

"What have you decided for your sister?" Richard said, clearing his throat and his mind of the disastrous sorrow of his impending loss. It took a moment for Thomas's eyes to pull away from the ring.

"I think that fine silver set there," he nodded to the brush, comb, mirror and powder box in the window.

"A fine choice, sir." The attendant nodded and went about wrapping it carefully in fine paper and ribbon. As Thomas perused, Richard leaned in towards the attendant.

"How much does the rose ring cost?" His voice so low and deep that the attendant became an instant coconspirator.

"It is no matter."

"I know that I look quite disheveled, but it is only because the battle and journey were long and we are awaiting new clothes from the tailor. I assure you that I can pay you—" Richard said, not really knowing how he would actually accomplish that.

"It is no matter, because I will give the ring to the future duke as a gift for patronizing the store and because you seem to know his heart. It would be an honor to have him wear it from our shop." The attendant whispered back.

"Sir, your generosity is greatly appreciated," Richard nearly cried. The attendant deftly boxed the ring up, and slipped it to Richard. Richard, in response, took out his metal wrist watch from the satchel and handed it to the man. "For your kindness."

The attendant looked at it curiously. "I've never seen anything of its measure," he breathed. Richard wondered what wrench he'd just thrown into the art and science of timekeeping by handing it over. Lord, did he just create a ripple? The attendant fumbled quickly into the case and took out the lion ring, he boxed it and handed it over just before Thomas strode up. "It is only fair, and I think it suits you," he nodded.

Richard bowed deeply. "Thank you, good sir."

"Are we ready?" Thomas said, morosely. Richard nodded and so did the attendant, trying not to seem conspicuous. Thomas glared at them. "What mischief are you up to?" he asked Richard on their way out.

"Nothing but the best kind, my lord." He smiled and they walked the town, visiting the markets and the shopkeepers. It was, in short, the loveliest afternoon Richard had had in a long while. They stopped to inspect the food vendors and the scribe's shop, the bookseller nearly took two hours and Thomas had to pull Richard out of the door. Still, he purchased him an additional six books.

"You needn't do that," Richard had protested.

"I must keep my lion in a library," Thomas teased and they strode down the streets until the lamplighters came out. "It is nearly time, is it not?" he said softly, his shoulder bumping Richard's.

"Where did that day go?" he sighed in response.

"To the best of company," Thomas said. "I truly cannot remember a better day," he stopped and touched Richard's hand, head bowed, the streets cleared of most pedestrians.

"Nor I," Richard said. "Thank you," he whispered, and wished desperately to kiss Thomas, soft and slow, savoring every second they had before they were to return home.

"Luckily it is not quite over yet. I believe you have promises to keep." Thomas said and looked up, his eyes falling to Richard's lips.

"Do I?"

"Lessons. On what is good for me." Thomas's blue eyes darkened and Richard's breath caught and pulled. Thoughts of holding his body, of gripping the taut muscles of his hips shuddered through him and Richard's mouth watered. He did not wish to wait another second.

"Only if you consent, my lord," Richard said softly and leaned closer.

"I shall strive to be your most faithful student," Thomas said and smiled from one corner of his mouth. "What is on your mind?" Both of their breaths quickened.

"Simply that we cannot return soon enough to our sanctuary."

"Agreed," Thomas said, nodding but not able to look away from Richard's mouth. They walked quickly back to the stone building of their quarters. Its warm lamps beckoned in the growing dark.

"Are you hungry?" Thomas asked over his shoulder. Richard walked close behind him.

"Only for you," he growled lowly into his ear. Thomas's teeth clenched. "Food can wait. Unless you are in need."

"I have only one need," Thomas said quietly back as they ascended the stairs.

"I ache to satiate it," Richard said, his fingers brushing Thomas's as they approached their chambers. Tumbling inside, and locking the door, their packages were dropped to the side and Richard pushed the coat off of Thomas's shoulders, even as he took his mouth in a hungry kiss, biting into his lips as if he'd been thinking of nothing else all day. Once his hands were freed, Thomas began to strip Richard's jacket, untied his shirt front, untucked it and ran his hot and calloused hands up his torso.

Grunting into the kisses, unable to get enough of the hot and tender attention.

"Thomas," Richard breathed. "What I have in mind is intense," he gasped and whispered and held his face away, to meet his eyes.

"I am willing," Thomas gasped.

"The moment you are not, or do not feel comfortable, you must say so. You must tell me at once. Promise me," he whispered, brow furrowed.

"I do. I promise." Thomas nodded.

Richard pulled him to the bed. He kissed Thomas's cheek, and his chin, even as his hands went to work disrobing Thomas's body. Richard ran his hand up Thomas's naked thigh and gently caressed the velvety hardness of his shaft, until Thomas's hips rose from the bed and a sigh rose from his lips.

"Wait here," Richard whispered, He left only briefly and returned from the bathroom with the bottle of oil, and stood, watching Thomas, recumbent in bed, lightly touching himself, turning his head to catch Richard's loving gaze. Richard took off his remaining clothes and joined him in bed.

Without a word, he tenderly kissed up Thomas's long legs, the scars, the hard muscles, the story of a body abused by life. At the juncture of his thighs, he took Thomas in his watering mouth and teased him to the edge with deep and slow strokes.

"I know this lesson," Thomas gasped, hands threaded into Richard's thick hair.

"I want you to be just as excited as I am, my lord," Richard said softly.

"I am. God how I am, please, Richard—" Thomas writhed in the sheets. Richard slowly turned him over to his side, kissed his neck, his back, kneaded the tight muscles of his ass, with the oil in his palms. His hands slid over Thomas's thighs and upwards, then he oiled his own hard cock and returned one hand to Thomas's engorged member.

"Is this what the oil is for," Thomas gasped and smiled over his shoulder. Richard tenderly bit him, let his body find a rhythm into his hand, as his cock gently pressed between Thomas's firm backside.

"And this," Richard whispered softly as he gently slid inside of Thomas, slowly, achingly slow, with gritted teeth and listening as Thomas gasped and pressed back towards, not away from, the length and hardness.

"Richard," he gasped and threw his head back.

"Is this alright?" Richard groaned, not moving, but letting Thomas adjust. God. He was tight and Richard wanted to thrust, relentlessly into the heat of him. But he held back, and gently withdrew, only going slightly deeper the next time.

"Fuck, how does it feel so good?" Thomas groaned, and Richard's hand tightened on his cock, stroking deftly. "Richard," Thomas cried and moved his hips back, taking Richard deeper inside of him. "Don't stop. Please—more. Give me more of you." Richard moved out, slid in again, deeper with each slow and delicious stroke, matching time and pace with Thomas's body sliding between the tight grip of his fingers.

Thomas was only slightly in shock, when he felt the warm and hard pressure enter him. But Richard was gentle and sweet, pressing kisses to his neck and back, and caressing his excited cock in even strokes. He wanted more, he wanted deeper. To be filled, to be taken. He pressed back into Richard's hips felt the delicious sting and pleasure as he drew out of him. Only to delve deeper each stroke. Fuck ... it was so good. Thomas's mouth watered and he groaned and seethed and bucked into Richard's hand. Every thick stroke inside of him built up the need more intensely, cresting in his loins like a tidal wave.

"It's coming, I'm—" Thomas's guttural cry drove Richard deeper. He thrust deep inside of him, grabbed his hair with one hand, bit his neck and stroked and pulled at his thick cock until their mutual and undeniable climax rocked through them both, exploding the world in a fury of heat and noise. Both of them came in tearful gasps and grunting release. Richard removed his hand to hold Thomas's body close to him, kissed him over and over and over again, sobbing into his shoulder blades.

"I love—" Richard cried. "I love you, Thomas." He held him tighter, and his arms shook around Thomas. He felt tears against his shoulder blade where Richard's head rested. Warmth rushed over Thomas, and he shivered and shuddered when Richard gently slid out of him, to an ensuing groan of pleasure.

"God, Richard," Thomas gasped, trying to catch his breath even as his body shuddered through with a shock of pleasure. When he felt Richard pull out, his whole body missed the warmth and fullness and he turned quickly to the downcast face of his lover. His confidant, awaiting remorse or guilt. Perhaps even punishment for what had just transpired. Richard would find nothing of the sort from Thomas.

"Do not look away from me," he shook his head and tilted Richard's chin up to kiss him gently. He kissed his temple his chin, his lips, the tears that continued to form at the edge of his eyes. Thomas began to cry too and took Richard in his arms and held him, his forehead pressed to the beating of Richard's heart.

"Was it, alright? Are you hurt?" Richard whispered, kissing Thomas's temple, running his strong hands over the length of Thomas's arms and back. "Are you in need of anything?" Worry lifted his tone and he shifted, casting his gaze on Thomas where he stayed buried next to the beat of Richard's heart. "Thomas, please—say something. Anything."

Thomas shook his head, beside himself with the emotional well that rose in his chest. God, but he would never be able to wed another. Never lie with another. Never love another.

"Thomas," Richard choked and began to cry. "Please—"

"It was beautiful. Perfect. I am not hurt," he sobbed, and sniffed.

"Are you certain? You sound hurt." He pulled away to look into Thomas's teary eyes. The beautiful hazel of them deep and searching his own.

"I do not know what to say," Thomas whispered. "You have upended me, in all the best of ways."

"Thomas, I—"

"I love you, Richard. I wish for us never to part. I cannot bear the idea of a life without you, in my bed, in my body … and yet, it is a world closing in around me." He cried, and shook. Richard held him tight in his arms. Caressed his skin, made soft shushing noises into his temple and closed his eyes. Letting his own tears fall.

"The world is not allowed, not here, not with us. Not on this night." Richard whispered. "I will protect you, my rose." Richard covered them with the blankets and held Thomas close in his arms, gently gliding his hands over his tired and shaking body.

"My lion," Thomas whispered, and kissed Richard's chin before they fell off the edge of the world together.

25

ARRIVAL TO MARLBOROUGH

Richard was roused from sleep by the pounding at their bedchamber door. Untangling from the warm mass of limbs and love laced sheets, he tugged on his pants and hurried to quiet the noise so that Thomas might sleep. Pulling on his shirt, he answered to find Mr. Bennett, arms full of packages. He did not say much but pushed his way in. Richard checked to see that his fake bed was still on the floor.

"I took the liberty of bringing new boots as well. I know the cobbler and I simply could not have my works of art be brought down by the shoddy nature of the—" he paused, looked up at a sleepy and shirtless Thomas yawning as he stumbled into the conversation.

"Your grace," he bowed. "I am dreadfully sorry to have awoken you. I assumed at this hour you would be—"

"Normally yes," Richard interrupted. "We—celebrated the upcoming nuptials at the pub last night, a bit too late."

"Ah!" Mr. Bennett said but his eyes fell to a love bite on Thomas's neck. He craned his head to peer into the other rooms, looking for the woman who had left it. Richard cleared his throat and stepped in front of his curious gaze.

"You said something about boots?"

They tried on the garments, had last minute adjustments and Mr. Bennett left with a smile, wave, and much heavier pockets then when he arrived. Thomas had been quiet all morning. Sullen. When the door closed Richard turned to him.

"What is on your mind?" he said, keeping his voice soft. Thomas looked down at the packages, neatly ready for their journey. He shook his head.

"I do not know."

Richard nodded and sighed from his nose. "It is to be expected. Last night, I should have—"

"Done nothing differently," Thomas interrupted. "It was perfect. I wish we could have it again. I wish for more. More than I deserve. More than I have any right to. We must pack. The carriage will be here shortly and my mother is expecting us."

"Thomas," Richard said, took his hand and caressed his knuckles with the pad of his finger. "Have we not, at least time for a bath?"

The corner of Thomas's smile lifted. "Yes, my lion, we do and we should."

They took their time, bathing one another, leaving the soiled clothing of the battle and their short history together on the floor. They were tender in their caresses, and slow in their kisses. Richard gently washed Thomas who hissed when the soap and hot water reached his more tender areas. Richard sighed and kissed his shoulder. "It will not always be this way."

"Would that I had more time to get used to it," Thomas said.

"Would you," Richard blushed, held Thomas's neck and looked at him. "Would you ever like to do the same to me?" Thomas's eyes narrowed. Richard watched his cheeks light with pink.

"I would. But not on this morning. My mind is busy and worrisome. I fear I would be too rough." Richard lifted one brow and thought that it didn't sound all that bad to him. But Thomas was right. There was a time for angry and hot sex, and now wasn't it. He needed love. Support. Care. And that's what Richard had given him.

When they loaded the carriage with their new clothes, gifts, and bags they seated themselves with a young, newlywed couple on their way towards Marlborough. Richard had to sit next to Thomas but it pained him to not be allowed a reassuring touch of Thomas's shoulder or leg. It equally pained him to be able to read, words of love, but not out loud. Thomas sat still by his side, gazing sadly out the window while the young couple held hands and gazed at one another with the newfound passion and love that stirred jealousy in the other hearts in the carriage.

Richard watched them, cleared his throat and went back to his books. Someday that would be his rose. Only Thomas would not be giggling with a girl and sneaking chaste kisses to her cheek. He would be straining with the lie, and aching with the fire of truth stuck inside his heart. He would be acting for the rest of his life, to appease the outside world. He wondered what Thomas was thinking. He glanced over. Thomas was watching the couple too.

Arriving at the gates of Marlborough Manor in the near evening felt like time had zipped by and Richard found himself wanting to cry the nearer they came to the house. This was it. This was the place he would have to set aside his feelings for Thomas. He would at least stay for Natalie's wedding, and see to it that the seeds of his work had taken hold. His sole purpose had been to know that Thomas would go on through history making a better life for others. Once he was assured, he must return. Not just for the sake of a better future world. But because he now knew that he simply could not endure a lifetime of watching the man he loved live a lie. And it would not be fair to stay, putting Thomas in the position of constant heartbreak. It would be best for all if he just left.

With time, Thomas would forget him, perhaps take a different lover in the shadows of a preordained marriage. Thomas got out of the carriage first. The servants unloaded their belongings and more met them at the gates to take them. They greeted Thomas warmly, expressed their gladness that he was alive and looking very well. Richard stayed in the carriage, dried his eyes, and sniffed back the emotion. He would be strong for Thomas. He would not falter. He would be the stoic giant at his side, and nothing more.

In all of his pep talking he didn't realize how long he'd sat. Thomas popped his head into the carriage.

"Are you coming? Surely you are not so frightened as to sleep in the carriage instead of facing my family?" Thomas smiled. Richard could not bear to look at the beauty of it. He gathered his books, tucked his glasses next to the map and followed Thomas out.

26

A MEETING OF THE FAMILY, AND A NEW PLAYER ON THE FIELD

They had arrived prior to drinks in the parlor. They had not missed supper and Richard suspected that Thomas was distraught about this. Led into the opulent foyer, Richard studied every detail of the manor. From the grand stone steps to the well-lit and beautifully decorated entryway, to the women in fine silks and brocades that greeted him. Thomas's mother, with the same curly hair, the same dimpled smile, bowed with a perfect curtsey.

"My lady, it is an honor," Richard said softly and bowed. He made a point of not looking at Thomas who watched him intently. Richard was greeting Thomas's grandmother with reserved warmth and utmost respect, when a sudden eruption sounded from the stairs.

"Is this him?"

All eyes swung to the younger woman, beautiful in golden curls and bright blue eyes, dashing down the stairs in her yellow gown, holding it aloft to not impede her progress. Richard's eyes grew wide as she came at him with the full force of a quarterback and tackled him around the waist, knocking him back three paces.

"Saints," Richard breathed, with a chuckle.

"You beautiful man! You savior!" She laughed. The rest of the room drew back in horror.

"Natalie! Please. Some decorum." Her grandmother chastised. Thomas simply laughed and Richard did not know what would be the best course of action. He cleared his throat and then calmly and gently patted the young woman's back with his warm hands.

"You must be Thomas's sister, Natalie. I am very pleased to meet you." Richard smiled and did not let go until she did. She curtseyed sweetly, cheeks pink. Richard bowed.

"I owe you a great debt of gratitude, sir," Natalie said and turned to her brother to hug him in kind. "I'm so happy you are safe and back home."

"Forgive her, sir, she is far too affectionate," Thomas's mother said to Richard and sighed. Richard put his hands demurely behind his back and shook his head.

"I am charmed. To know Thomas is so well-loved is a blessing," he said and bowed to the matron.

"Thomas?" The grand matron rose a thin eye brow at him.

"Forgive me, I didn't not mean to seem—"

"The man saved my life. He can call me whatever he wishes." Thomas broke in, glaring at the older woman.

"In any case, I'm delighted to meet you all. Thank you for welcoming me into your home. I know that you must want to spend some time with Thomas. You have been long away from him and in a state of worry no doubt." Richard said, bowed to each lady in turn. "I might retire to my quarters to freshen up, if that would be permitted?" He addressed Lady Marlborough.

"Of course, good sir. We will be in the parlor if you would like to join us before dinner." Lady Marlborough curtseyed. The ladies bowed in turn. Richard bowed to Thomas whose eyes narrowed on him.

"Thank you," Richard said and took his own belongings up, where a servant waited to lead him to his room. He didn't look back. He was overwhelmed enough, and worried he'd say or do something wrong. He needed space. He did not see Thomas watch his every step away from him, with worry and sadness.

~

"He's a man the likes of which I have never met," his mother said, as soon as Richard was out of earshot.

"Mother, it's good to see you," Thomas smiled and tried not to think about the kind of man Richard was, and how she would never know even half of his greatness. He planted a kiss on her cheek. "Grandmother," he bowed to the pinched-faced matriarch. He turned to his sister with a wry smile and Natalie launched into his arms once more. Thomas laughed and spun her around. "You are a wildling! You must settle down before your impending nuptials!" he chastised sweetly.

"Never! The baron knows I am wild and loves me all the more for it."

"Natalie! Decorum." Grandmother shouted again. Thomas set her down and kissed her forehead with a laugh.

"Of this I am most happy to hear. You must tell me all about him and how he swept such an intelligent and free-spirited woman off her feet." Natalie went on to animatedly tell him every detail of their first meeting when she'd saved the young baron from being trampled alive by his own horse, which turned into a walk back to his stables, and dinner with his parents a few short weeks later. Thomas could tell by the excitement and blushing and the very unlike-Natalie way she wrung her hands as she recounted nearly every detail that she was deeply in love. It made his heart feel lighter to know she would be taken care of. An odd mixture of jealousy and love filled him.

"Oh Thomas, if you were to find a partner so loving and kind," Natalie's eyes swam. If only, Thomas thought and chanced a quick glance up the stairs.

"Something we intend to discuss, shortly." A tight voice came from down the hall. Thomas let go of his sister's hand and stood straighter as the ice blue eyes of his father pierced into his. Far from being elated that he was alive, Thomas felt that his father was sizing him up to pick apart any imperfections that the war had not solved.

"Father," Thomas bowed. He received no such politeness in return.

"I'm glad to see you are unharmed."

"Thank you," Thomas swallowed and wished his savior were here now. "I have Doctor Richard Shaw to thank for that."

"Yes, this man. I must admit, no one seems to have heard of him, but then again, I do not know all those who live at Oxford. I look forward to meeting this mysterious savior." Thomas's father, the Duke Alexander of Marlborough looked down his nose as if his son might have been better off if he'd died a glorious battlefield death, than living with the dishonor of having been saved. Thomas felt himself shrink, just as he had as a little boy.

"Well, I would not keep His Grace waiting." Richard's deep and powerful voice floated down the stairs. All faces turned. He'd changed into fresh clothing, washed his face, combed his hair, smelled clean and looked refined. His hazel eyes sparkled, as he descended the stairs in his new and fresh suit and boots. He stopped at the base of the stairs and Thomas's heart fell out of his chest. The pressure that had engulfed the room at the entrance of his father was released when Richard came to stand beside him.

"Your Grace, it is an honor to finally meet you." Richard said, effortless and emotionless. Thomas wished he could grab his hand, kiss it, and throw his arms around him. He hid his smile as best he could. The warmth of Richard's large body next to his made him feel ten times stronger, facing his father. "Forgive my lateness, I wanted to freshen up from the journey. I am indebted to you for the room and your hospitality." Richard said. So regal his countenance, so large his presence, put-together and at ease, he seemed nearly a different man. Natalie smiled up at him. The duke looked a mixture of surprise and disappointment, as though he had thought Richard would be less impressive.

"Isn't he wonderful, Papa?" Natalie smiled and came to stand on Richard's other side, putting her arm in the crook of his elbow.

"Indeed," The duke sighed. "I should be expressing my gratitude to you, sir." He extended his hand and Richard took it with a firm grip, and a bow. Richard's eyes never fell, and kept the man in his scrutinizing gaze. Thomas watched the challenge. The way he stood up to his father even in the undercurrent of his genteel behavior.

"Come now, let us visit and you can tell me all the gory details of battle!"

"Natalie! Decorum." Grandmother shook her head. Natalie led Richard into the parlor. He smiled at her gregariousness. Thomas smiled too. He had missed her bright and bubbly nature. It lightened his heart.

Richard could feel Thomas's eyes on him. When they entered the room, he felt Thomas gently touch the small of his back as he passed by him on the way to the decanter and brandy. A thank you, and the only touch he could offer in the present moment. Thomas's brothers, James and Michael, joined them with their wives and the room grew loud and rather hot. Richard bowed demurely and kept what he had to say brief and polite.

The ladies sat and the men stood as they conversed. After a few tense moments in the company of his brothers, Thomas came to sit beside his mother and she seemed to warm to it. Richard watched the strange and subtle language that played between all parties. Thomas's father was the most discerning and seemed to be judging not only Thomas but Richard as well. Even

Natalie. He would lean over to James with hushed comments and then look away.

Richard was pulled back to the circle of ladies by Natalie. He told of his timely arrival but nodded to Thomas before continuing the tale. "The rest maybe too much for polite company." A blush spread on his cheeks and he looked down.

"Nonsense, I heard you took a bayonet! Did it hurt? I heard that it broke off in your body. Who removed it? Did it bleed terribly? Can I see the stitches?"

"Natalie!" The duke approached during the story and chastised her. Richard smiled. Grandmother looked like she might faint. Thomas cleared his throat.

"I was in a man-to-man battle with the general of the French invasion. I knew that they would be merely the first in a long line of attackers if we did not decimate them on the shores, before they could reach the borders of the King's land. I was weary, having only returned from France a week before. I could feel my resistance fading," Thomas looked at Richard. His knowing eyes caught the truth in Richard's. They both knew how it was supposed to end.

Richard looked at Natalie, lowered his head, his gaze, and his voice. "The battlefield was a smoky hellscape. I had been skirting the edges trying to avoid the conflict and stay out of our brave army's way. I was unarmed, after all, and I feared I might be more of a confusion than a help. But I walked directly into these two men's conflict—"

"He lies," Thomas said, staring at Richard. "He did not walk. He ran! He saw that I had lost my weapon and the final blow was to be struck and he ran to push me out of the way." Thomas dropped his head, spoke softer. "He took the blade, not an inch from his heart, where it should have impaled mine."

The room fell quiet. All heads swung to Richard. His brow fell. Before he could speak, Thomas continued.

"The blade did indeed break off inside of him, but despite

that, he picked up a club from the ground and fought the encroaching infantrymen until I could rise to my feet. I've never seen such bravery and strength."

"My lord, you would have done the same for any one of your men." Richard tried to dissuade the attention.

"I intend to write a letter to the king, entreating you for an honorary rank." Thomas's mother said, with tears in her eyes.

"Your Grace, it is not necessary." Richard flushed and though he was honored, his mind went to the implications to history if such a thing should happen. He could not show up in history two hundred years before his birth.

Natalie interrupted. "Then what? How many did you kill?"

"Natalie!" This time Thomas stopped her. Richard's face went pale.

"I did not enjoy taking the lives of those men. But I could not leave your brother's side without offering him whatever aid I could." Richard said softly. He threaded his fingers together and squeezed his eyes shut to the memories he was only now starting to come to terms with. Thomas came to his side. He placed a warm hand on his shoulder.

"I would not be alive without you, to be certain."

"You are so very brave! Both of you, I do not know how I would ever even survive a scuffle on the street, let alone a battle."

"Oh, child!" Grandmother closed her eyes and sat back like she might pass away from embarrassment.

"Truth be told, I did not last long." Richard looked back to her and smiled. "Not five minutes after the French general fell, I fainted dead away, like a little flower," he chuckled. This lightened the mood and even Grandmother smiled at him.

"A heavy flower. It took four men to get him back to the medical tent." Thomas laughed, "And in the rough field surgery wherein I had to remove the blade myself, he came to and nearly struck me!"

"It hurt!" Richard laughed.

"All he said was 'ouch' then fell back to sleep."

"What a great bear of a man you are!"

"Natalie!" This time her mother, but with a softer reprimand.

"More akin to a lion," Thomas said and could not look away fast enough with his soft gaze. Natalie saw.

"It is a tale of bravery. You are lucky this man arrived. You have always been, by accounts, a lucky man." The duke spoke up, swirled his brandy and stared down at it. "A luck that will continue on this night, I should hope."

Thomas looked at him, softness gone. "Whatever do you mean?"

As if on cue the bells rang outside of the manor and soon after, the butler announced the arrival of Sir George and Lady Joanna Dougherty, and their daughter, a Miss Marianne Dougherty. The three arrived into the parlor, Sir Dougherty first, his wife, and then his daughter. Richard guessed she could not have been older than nineteen years of age. At least twelve years Thomas's junior. She was dark-haired and beautiful, with sharp eyes and a quirked smile as if she already had the world on a string.

Richard watched them, and rose when the ladies entered the room. He bowed as introductions were made and watched Thomas's face. Not even a day home, and they were already parading candidates about? Natalie rose from the couch, curtseyed and came to stand on Thomas's other side. Even surrounded by people who loved him, Richard could feel Thomas's tension. The parents of the room bowed and chatted like old friends. Thomas leaned over to Natalie.

"Seems father has been very busy while I was gone."

"Since learning of the battle, and your survival, he has put forth renewed effort." Natalie whispered back. "I do not understand why he is in such a rush to see you wed."

"I cannot take my place without a wife," Thomas said, and Richard wondered if it wasn't more. That maybe his father wanted him to fall into the lines of society to assuage any doubt of where Thomas's desires truly lay.

"Then why won't he allow you to find your own?"

"Because he knows I don't want to," Thomas said. Natalie looked up at him, smiled gracefully and gently touched his hand before chancing a glance at Richard, who was staring back at both of them.

"You *do* wish to find an amiable partnership, but only with a person deserving of your heart," she whispered. When it was Thomas's turn to be introduced, they both bowed and curtseyed demurely and Marianne's parents flitted off to take refreshment and converse with one another. Richard wondered if he should excuse himself. But Natalie took his arm in her hand and began to make conversation.

Miss Dougherty could not seem to take her eyes from Thomas, and Richard could not blame her. He was indeed handsome. But Thomas was cold to her. Indifferent, almost to the point of rudeness. This would not do. The ruse must be maintained and even Richard could see this was a pre-approved candidate for marriage. He asked leading questions. Found that the woman was well-read, strong-minded, and had a calling in helping the poor. Richard looked to Thomas between each revelation and found his face and tone nothing more than a mask. Thomas bowed, gently kissed her hand and excused himself. Richard and Natalie watched him go.

"You must forgive him, Miss Dougherty, the trip has been long and he is rather weary. It is nothing to do with the charm of your company. He has a great deal on his mind and shoulders," Richard reassured and excused himself from the room to find Thomas.

27

QUIET CONVERSATIONS AND DEALS MADE

The manor staff directed Richard outside to the gardens where they had seen the young master leave to take air. It was pleasantly quiet and the night was not yet cold. The fragrances of the budding flowers were soft and tentative. Richard found Thomas, standing beside a fountain, breathing heavily with his hands clasped around his middle.

"My lord—"

"Finished making friends with my future wife, have you?" he said coldly, not turning. Richard came up beside him.

"Thomas, please. Let us not be dramatic." He sighed and joined Thomas at staring into the gently pouring water feature. "I am only trying to help determine the character of the woman."

"What does it matter? I will not marry her."

"Thomas. Please consider—"

"My heart is taken!" Thomas yelled and his hands rose as if he wanted to throttle something. He paced madly around the fountain, gravel and rock shuffling beneath his feet. Richard wanted to cry both in joy and in pain. He caught Thomas by the shoulders, stopped his body, and met his eyes.

"As is mine. You are all that is in my heart. Your safety, your protection, and your future. But marriage does not have to be built on love or passion. It can be merely mutual respect."

"I cannot believe you are saying this to me," Thomas scowled.

"If it were allowed, our marriage would be all of those things," Richard said softly. Thomas's eyes filled with tears. "Love, passion, mutual respect, joy—" he stopped to choke back his own tears. "But we cannot have that luxury. Miss Marianne is a fine young lady, composed and smart."

"She is not you."

"I am neither composed nor smart?" Richard teased. Thomas huffed.

"You know what I mean."

"I do," he whispered. After a moment, Thomas's breath softened, Richard could see that he was thinking through the situation and understanding that a contract was not the same thing as a commitment of the heart. He sighed, cleared his throat and adjusted his cravat.

"I shall be pleasant and accommodating for this evening," he said with a nod. Richard nodded sadly, in pain for him. "Under one condition."

"My lord?"

"That you come to my bedchambers tonight."

"Thomas, you know how dangerous that could be."

"I need your advisement. In private." With the serious decree, Thomas left the garden and went back to the parlor. Richard had no choice but to agree. He followed him inside with a bubbling sense of excitement. Sneaking into his lover's bedroom should be frowned upon. But he found it strangely exciting. He could think of little else during the whole of dinner. Decorum insisted that he sit next to Thomas and that his future bridal prospect was placed across from them. She was fine enough. A lovely woman, a good match for any man who was heterosexual and breathing.

But not for his Thomas. No one would ever be fit for his rose, Richard thought, trying to not succumb to the anger even as he stared into his plate. He knew that it had to be done. Still, he did not have to like it. He worked especially hard to be cordial. To ask her appropriate but interesting questions. To remember which fork to use and to compliment Lady Marlborough on the fine dinner of venison and luscious gravy with roasted vegetables.

"And what of you, Doctor Shaw?" Marianne asked, barely touching her food, befitting of her slender figure. "Tell me about your family. Have you any sisters?"

"No, Miss Dougherty, only brothers. Three."

"What a wild household that must have been. Your poor mother! But your father must have been proud." Marianne said. Richard cleared his throat and tried to maintain his posture. Thomas's hand found his thigh beneath the table and caressed it softly.

I am here. You do not have to say a word of your father.

"Richard is quite the astounding scholar," Thomas redirected. "Why, even in his injured state, he was able to instruct me on some of the finer points of literary work."

Miss Dougherty nodded at Richard. "That is commendable. A learned man is a catch indeed! Have you a wife, Doctor Shaw?

"No, my lady. I do not."

"Why ever not? It is a pity. It seems you have the entire package of admirable traits," Marianne said.

"It's true, an entire package," Thomas agreed even as his hand trailed up to Richard's groin and Richard coughed before shifting away.

"I am," he paused to clear his throat. "I am merely waiting for the right woman." Richard lied. Thomas's eyebrows rose and he huffed a small laugh. After dinner they retired for games and drinks in the parlor. The parents made small talk and watched the new couple interact. Richard withdrew to converse with Natalie over the chess board to give Thomas time to find something redeeming about Marianne.

"What do you think of her?" Natalie said, moving the first pawn.

"She seems intelligent, well mannered, and is accommodating."

"Do you not find her attractive? She is beautiful too, is she not?"

Richard turned to chance a glance where she sat demurely on the settee next to Thomas. She was beautiful. If not slightly small featured. Delicate. A doll in pretty clothing. Perhaps even shrewd, Richard thought and tried not to let his feelings for Thomas skew his opinion. She certainly at least knew the advantage she was getting in this arrangement and she was working hard at seeing it through.

"She is to some, I'm sure."

"Not to you?" Natalie's eyes met Richard's.

"She is beautiful," he backpedaled. Natalie smiled.

"Not as beautiful as our Thomas though," she said and moved her rook into play. Richard countered and set up his next three moves in his head. He looked up at her.

"No. No one will ever be that beautiful," Richard admitted softly. It was an idiotic risk to take. He should not have said anything. But Natalie merely made a move with her bishop and gently touched his hand.

"My Thomas is special. He deserves a love just as special."

"Do you think she will provide it?" Richard asked, their hands still touching.

"I think she will provide him easement from our father's demands. A good standing in society, and children to the honor of our family."

"Of course," Richard nodded.

"But not love. I think for that, he has already found that gift elsewhere."

Richard met her eyes, the game stopped and they stared at each other. Richard wanted to cry. He did not wish to lie to

Natalie, but he could not risk hurting Thomas. If her faithfulness did not extend to the breaking of social propriety, his next words could be disastrous. Natalie leaned in.

"I have always known; from the time we were young," she whispered, eyes darting to where her father was in deep discussions with Marianne's father.

"Known, Miss Natalie?"

"Must I say it?" she sighed.

Richard bowed his head forward and closed his eyes. "My whole existence depends on Thomas's safety and wellbeing. Be it physically, emotionally, or within the boundaries of society."

Natalie smiled and narrowed her eyes. "You and I are of the same exact mind, Richard. And we both know, that despite his gentlemanly status and physical strength, that he is not interested in the fairer sex. And there should be no shame in it. It was simply how he was born."

Richard let out a long breath and Natalie took his hand in hers before continuing.

"My father suspects it but does not approve, of course. This marriage will secure Thomas's future and remove father's scrutiny from his life. It is, in many ways, tragic."

"But wholly necessary," Richard said delicately with a nod.

"Yes, I am sorry, my dearest Richard. I know that you love him. I saw it the moment you came down the stairs. And he is much in love with you."

Fear struck into Richard's heart. If Natalie could perceive their affection, hadn't everyone else as well? He'd been so careless. He shook his head. "My lady—"

"It is a secret I fear we will all take to our graves. And that is the real tragedy." Her eyes filled with tears and Richard offered her his handkerchief. The evening wound down and Thomas and Marianne took a short walk with Richard and Natalie behind them at good chaperone distance, followed by Thomas and Marianne's parents. Marianne's hand was tucked in Thomas's arm, her skirts swished against his legs. He looked down at her with a soft smile and his hand molded over hers in the crook of his arm, securing her to him for the group to see.

"I believe it is to be settled." Natalie whispered. Richard merely nodded. His only comfort in the gut-wrenching thoughts of Thomas moving on to marriage so quickly from his bed, was that he had been called to Thomas's chambers tonight.

It was late when he sat in front of his mirror, combing his beard and looking over the map. He had to give himself some direction. A happily ever after with Thomas would not be happening, and he was an idiot to suppose it ever would. Though the duke in his historical accounts never sired children, he was a proper man of society.

Had he even married? Richard tried to remember. When his life was saved by the good Doctor Blackwell in the previous timeline, Thomas had gone on to live a life of bettering other humans' lives. Becoming a champion for social justice and education. Had it just been the act of being saved that had given him purpose? What had gone wrong this time? Richard looked up into the mirror. He scowled ferociously at himself.

He had gone wrong.

He had saved the man, and fallen in love with him. He had distracted Thomas from the track he should have taken. He might have even just arranged him into marriage that would further depress and disempower the man. Richard looked away from the mirror to put his head in his hands.

Had he given Thomas an even greater excuse to die? By encouraging his natural but unacceptable tendencies? Matthew had probably merely pointed him in the direction of better work and, not having a love to expend his energies upon, Thomas had put himself into the fire of helping others.

But Richard had interrupted that cycle.

"Fuck," he breathed. He'd saved the future duke but he may have yet doomed the future of the country. Richard buried his head in his hands. The hour was late and his heart was heavy. He paced, trying to find another avenue to save his future. He withdrew the map and saw a shadow of a portal, not far from the manor. He wondered how close this one was to the portal that Lillian herself had jumped through. She'd ended up in a field. Some farmer's field, alone and far away from her love. She could have been, alone and hurting for the remainder of her life, if Richard hadn't helped her get back.

Which led to this chain of events themselves. In helping Lillian he had, in turn, doomed his own future, broken his own heart and Thomas's too. Richard wanted to die. How could he have fucked this up so royally? How could he have doomed them both to a life of—

A sturdy knock to his door roused him and his heart nearly fell out of his chest. Before he could call to the manservant that he required no further assistance for the evening, Thomas burst into the room, no coat, loosened shirt, and looking disheveled and angry.

"Did you not remember your promise to me?"

"Thomas I—" Richard paused and closed his eyes to shake his head. "Forgive me, I am troubled."

"As am I." Thomas said and slammed his door closed, hissing the lock into place.

"My lord—"

"You promised," was all he breathed before pulling Richard into his arms, desperate and hungry, alone and aching to feel the warmth of his kiss and the passion of his arms. Richard fell into him, despite the stern talking to he'd given himself earlier. He knew that he should not, and yet it had been a terrible day, away from the warmth of Thomas, the taste of his lips, the hungry and sweet noises he made as he kissed his way down Richard's neck, past the opening of his shirt.

"Thomas, we have much to discuss. Please," Richard begged, eyes closed in sighing from the warmth and the heat of Thomas's tongue along his collarbone. His body shivered from his bare feet up through his calves. Down from his shoulders, tickling his spine until the two ends met at the heat and pressure in his groin. Richard grunted and threaded his fingers into Thomas's hair pulling his lips closer, his body closer.

"This is the only way I wish to communicate," Thomas gasped, his roving hands finding every hard and straining muscle aching to be naked and next to his own.

"So much has transpired this evening, your parents, you father—" Richard's mind whirled when Thomas's hands took his hard shaft in a strong grip.

"I do not wish to hear words about my father," Thomas said, teeth against Richard's jaw.

"What of Mari—"

He did not finish as Thomas pushed him to the bed and tackled him into the soft cushions, pinning him down and tearing his breeches open.

"Thomas, please!" Richard tried to keep his voice low and his patience intact.

"Do you not want me?" Thomas cried, on the verge of tears. Richard put his shaking hands on his cheeks, forced him to meet his eyes. He helped to settle Thomas's breathing with his own. He tried to slow the world down.

"I want you more than I want air, or food, or any other life-sustaining gift. But I want you safe. I want you whole. I am worried that you are hurting."

"Of course I am hurting!" Thomas tore himself from the bed, pacing and pulling at his hair. "Do you think I want to marry her?"

"I know you do not." Richard said, coming up.

"And yet you insist that I do so!"

"I only insist that you do what is best for yourself."

"Then let me have you," Thomas said and came back and pinned him into the soft covers.

"I fear that is only what is best for me," Richard said and arched from the bed as Thomas held his hands to the blankets and kissed across his jaw and neck and chest.

"It is what's best for us both." Thomas whispered.

"I worry for you," Richard said. He stopped Thomas's attentions and rolled him over, to hold him down in his sheets. "What if I have done irreparable damage. I've seduced you, confused you, enjoyed every delicious inch of you. What if it is I who has damned your soul? Kept you from becoming the greatest man you can be?"

"Does that man need a wife? Truly?" Thomas said and looked up at Richard, he traced his beard with his thumb.

"Men can do great things married or not." Richard acquiesced. "But your father—"

"Pray, do not let my father into this bed with us," Thomas sighed and reached up to kiss Richard slowly, with sweetness.

"Then let us keep quiet counsel with one another," Richard said, watching the calm satisfaction of Thomas's features settle under the tender work of his hands. Saints, but he needed him, wanted him. It simply would not do to be put out of one another's orbits. Richard kissed his way down Thomas's firm stomach and untied his breeches.

"Not what I had in mind," Thomas sighed though his hips said otherwise, bucking up to meet the warm and wet pressure of Richard's mouth. He licked and suckled before coming up to meet his gaze.

"Oh? Did you want to discuss parliamentary procedure? The finer points of Queensbury Rules? Perhaps croquet—"

Thomas pushed his head back down with a chuckle. "I wish to have you take me, again," he whispered, even as Richard's mouth drew his throbbing head in. Richard teased, and gently ministered until Thomas was writhing with the need. He broke away, gently massaging his balls and teasing the gentle seam beneath his cock with his tongue.

"What of you taking me?" Richard asked softly. Thomas, eyes filled with desire and ache. He groaned.

"I do not have the necessary aids."

"I will find some," Richard nodded, "Until then, let us be mutual in our conversation." He disrobed and came to place himself facing opposite on the bed to Thomas. Thomas sighed in excitement and caressed Richard's strong buttocks and thighs as his mouth watered. As Thomas pulled Richard into his eager mouth, he felt Richard taking him in. It took all the control he had not to break away to gasp aloud.

The more excited he became, the harder and deeper he took Richard until he felt his body shudder, his flanks flex in Richard's hands and the warm jet of excitement spill from him, even as Richard pulled him in deep and his nails dug into Thomas's ass, pulling him in and out hotly until Thomas, too, gave a glorious groan and exploded. He muffled his cry into Richard's thigh and for a moment, they stayed still, gently licking and kissing and caressing one another. Richard drew away first, but only to come back to him, taking Thomas in his arms and pulling the blankets up over their now cooling skin.

"That was, indeed, a productive talk." Thomas sighed and nestled into Richard's chest. Richard laughed.

"You are quite the orator, my lord." He bit his lip and quirked his eyebrow up at Thomas. His laugh rumbled through his chest and they held on to one another in the dim light of Richard's dying lanterns. The hour was late indeed. No doubt there would be much to do tomorrow, more visits with family, and only a week to prepare for the wedding. There would be more courting of the affable Miss Dougherty. Richard sighed, kissed Thomas's forehead and gently stroked the length of his bare arm.

"Though this is the happiest I've been all evening, all day even, I should go back to my own chambers," Thomas said softly before nuzzling into Richard's chest and pressing the length of his warm body to his.

"I wish you did not have to."

"Would that not be the amazing life? Run around saving the world all day, laying in each other's arms at night?"

"The perfect love story, to be sure," Richard whispered and ran his hands through Thomas's messy curls.

"Nothing is perfect," he responded quietly. Richard felt the tears rising but did not wish to bring more sorrow. He sighed, watching Thomas's head rise and fall with his breath and the endless cycle Richard felt of disappointment and useless hope.

"No—indeed it is not. Were I a better man, I could do more for you."

"It is not a matter of you being better," Thomas sat up and looked down at him with a scowl. "It is a matter of the world not being kind enough."

It was too late, Thomas had seen the tears in his eyes, he brushed away the corners of Richard's lashes with the palm of his hand and shook his head.

"Good night, my lion. Sleep well." He placed a soft and warm kiss to his lips and Richard reached up for more. Selfish in his need to make the moment last longer. Thomas drew away, put on his shirt and crossed the room. He looked back over his shoulder, relaxed but not smiling.

"Good night, Thomas," Richard said softly and rolled over, his back to the sound of the closing door. The coldness with which Thomas withdrew was not the same as it had been from the shame he had shown before. It was … a resolution. That this was all their lives could be. And in this, Thomas was more practical than Richard.

If he was resolved, perhaps he was less in love. And less in love meant that Richard could leave. Without the fear of breaking Thomas's heart. Richard reached up to scratch at his stitches, felt the murmur of his heart and the way it seemed to ache more without Thomas nearby.

Perhaps the answer was in the wound he carried. A stitch at a time, he would pull himself away, until the wound would stay closed on its own. Until Thomas realized that he did not need Richard anymore. Until he knew that he could continue on with his life, perhaps taking lovers outside of his prearranged marital bed. Until Thomas realized that Richard was merely a stepping stone to the life he was supposed to lead.

Richard sobbed into his pillow and ached for the truth of it. There could be no other way. He cried himself to sleep, and had terrible dreams of being stabbed, over and over through the heart.

Thomas went back to his room, his body satiated but his heart an open wound. He wished he'd never come back. Better to have run away with Richard, they could have joined a sailing crew and headed off to some distant land, where the sun replaced the gray and attitudes towards love were open as the sky. Did such a place even exist? He washed, stripped down and pressed his shirt to his nose to fall asleep with Richard's smell. He knew he must marry. He knew it must happen within a month.

He also knew he'd rather die than be untrue to his heart.

28

THE REMOVAL OF STITCHES

The preparations and festivities for the wedding in the next four days kept them both so very busy that they barely had time to converse. Thomas's father had required and convened family meetings until late in the night. Thomas confessed that he was barely able to get any sleep for all of the battle planning that was taking place. Richard merely nodded, stepping away from him to help Natalie select the floral arrangements or to offer his advice on the wedding feast. After the last night they'd spent together, Richard knew that this had to be the plan all along.

To make sure that Thomas no longer needed him. One stitch at a time, pulling him out. In congruence, every time Richard turned around, it seemed Thomas's father was shoving Marianne into his son's arms or encouraging garden walks, or planning their meals with the entire Dougherty family. The budding couple began to sit next to one another. Richard was moved one seat farther down at nearly every meal. Until he was at the end of the table, closest to Thomas's brothers.

Michael and James weren't stunning conversationalists. James was such an avid hunter that the bloodlust in his eyes frightened

Richard. Still, he thought over his fifth glass of wine for that night, he could take the little man in a fair fight. Michael was quiet, reserved, and more discerning than he let on. Richard was well aware to watch his mouth around both of them, and be nothing but the reserved stoic he used to play behind the plexiglass of his safe librarian world.

Richard sat through this evening's dinner without talking or eating. The haze of the alcohol dimmed his pain, numbed his senses, until he was watching with a detached eye the way Miss Dougherty swooned and leaned into Thomas. Smiling and touching his hand lightly. The practiced way Thomas smiled down at her, as though adoring a future wife. Had he merely been entertaining his own experimentation with Richard? Perhaps with the 'right' woman, he would find his proclivities rested with both of the sexes. Perhaps Richard had become nothing more than a disgraced memory, an interloper. Unwanted. Certainly no longer needed.

These were not the thoughts of the rational man who had jumped through the portal intent on saving his country. These were the ridiculous notions of a jilted lover. He was being childish and his own thoughts embarrassed him. Richard finished his wine and rose quickly, knocking the table with his leg and woozily standing.

"Excuse me, my lords and ladies. I am ... quite unwell. I must retire." He knocked over the chair on his way out but did not stop to right it. Richard stumbled quickly through the hall and struggled up the stairs as the world swam around him.

"Doctor Shaw," the sharp voice commanded. Richard kept ascending. "Richard!" Richard did not turn, but he closed his eyes to the swimming of the ornate staircase, and briefly wondered if he should not let himself fall; hope for a broken neck and an end to this suffering.

"Are you well?" Thomas's voice was reserved, an actor in play. Richard did not need to turn to know that they were not alone.

He supposed it was Marianne, or perhaps dear Natalie, maybe even the duke, following his boorish exit from the dining hall. He did not want to see any of them. He could not hide his feelings now that the wine had stolen his mask. He could not look any of them in the eye and not allow them to see how in love with Thomas he was. He stayed still, facing the stairs.

"I am, fine, my lord. I am merely unwell and in need of respite," he whispered, steadying himself on the banister and continuing up the stairs in a slower and more refined manner. Thomas would dare not come after him in front of anyone else. And Richard was sure he did not wish to. When he arrived at his room, he closed the door and went to the mirror. He tore off his shirt and stared at the puckering red and purple scar, the threads growing into his skin.

How he wished the blade had made a quarter turn to the left. How he wished he would have just died. He scratched at the stitches. Maybe if he reopened it, he could finish the job himself. He took out a letter opener from the desk drawer. Not a soldier's tool but a diplomat's. Not nearly so sharp as he had hoped. Still, he thought stumbling back over to the mirror and donning the Mrs. Worthington's glasses, somewhat appropriate that he should die by such a silly instrument.

"Let us allow this heart to bleed out, shall we? At the very least, I will not have to sit through another horrid dinner." Only two days until the wedding and probably Thomas's proposal to Miss Dougherty. Two days. So at least two stitches.

But once Richard felt satisfaction in the sting of pain, two was just a good beginning. One by one, he pushed the tip of the blade beneath the stitches and twisted. Some of them popped open, some of them merely pulled, causing the blade to cut into the skin. None of it hurt as badly as watching Thomas draw away from him steadily for the whole week. Even though he'd promised to do the same.

"Keep going, you idiot. You have so many more memories to

pluck out," he grunted to the wild-eyed man in the mirror, now with blood trickling down his chest.

"Here's the one for the moment I first saw you." It was a hard stitch, it stuck, it pulled, the knife sliced alongside the puncture where the needle had tried to put him together.

"Here is our first kiss." That one popped loose and Richard cried. He poured himself another drink from the decanter beside his reading chair.

"Here's the first time you called me lion," to the stitch he said, and it stuck accordingly, "and the first time I had you in my hand."

Stitch after stitch.

"Your laugh," he cried. "Your smell. Your spoiled pout and demanding tone." Pluck, stick, sting, bleed.

"Your patience, your dimples, your h—heart." Richard yelled and slipped the tip of the knife deep into the middle of the wound, not steady of hand to stop it. The burn was nearly enough to shake him out of his daze, but so brilliantly beautiful he only wanted to plunge it in further. He grabbed the hilt with one hand and meant to hammer it in with the other.

"Stop!"

Richard whirled around, blood dripping down his chest, dotting his pants and staining the carpet below. He looked down, to where the knife was two inches in. Thomas rushed him, fear and anger in his eyes.

"What have you done?" he bellowed, enraged.

"I am trying to remove my heart, my lord." Richard said reassuringly, tears pressing out from the corners of his eyes. "I do not wish to live with you there ... inside of me. If I cannot have you, I do not want it, you see?" Richard's lips felt heavy, his tongue a weighted mess in his mouth. His arms felt weak.

"Help me tear it out, would you? You've already gotten such a brilliant start." Richard fell, the world, the drink, and the blood loss all doing their parts to render him unconscious. Thomas yelled his name and rushed to put his arms around him, catching him before he could impale himself on the floor.

"Doctor! I need a doctor!" Thomas cried, his voice booming through the hallways and out into the night.

29

THE ARRIVAL OF AN OLD FRIEND

The road was long and Lillian had not talked to Matthew nearly the whole way there. Each were stuck in their own thoughts about the severity of their actions. When Lillian had fallen back in time, and subsequently in love with Matthew, neither understood the ripple in time they would cause. Though they could never belong to another, their actions had ended up killing a future duke, before he could set Britain on the brighter course it needed. When the Timekeeper had appeared in their wedding chambers and explained that their love had a price, they both agreed to help set things right.

Under the guise of taking a wedding trip, they'd ridden off in a carriage, to an empty field twenty miles north of Westbury Manor. The Timekeeper met them there, gave them a map, and sent them three years in to the future. She did not give them many instructions. Just that Doctor Shaw had made a grievous mistake and was in danger of dying. If he died, the future was in danger of imploding, and that they needed to intervene. Matthew was nervous about the whole situation. Lillian less so, as she'd been through portals before. At least this time they had a

Timekeeper on their side, getting them to the right space and time.

The Timekeeper opened the portal, large enough that their whole carriage went through. It felt like an easier transition for Lillian. Perhaps the more one did it, the more one got used to it. Matthew had commented about the pressure and the horses were not at first pleased with the sensation. Lillian remarked that it was far better than falling down a set of stairs. Once on the road, they became quiet, wondering if this was the last time they'd have to set something right.

"I hope we'll be on time," Lillian said, her hands wringing nervously in her lap. Matthew reached his hand out to cover hers.

"We will do everything in our power to save your friend, my love. I promise. All will be made right again." Lillian looked to him with teary eyes. No matter the danger, no matter the time, she was just happy he was by her side. With that, and into the early evening, they continued on their way, set for another wedding, in Marlborough. Their cover story was weak at best, and neither was even sure how they'd get close to a family they had no connection to.

Just as they arrived at the front gates of the Marlborough estate, however, rather than having to muddle their way through some fabricated story, a cry arose from the bedrooms and halls above.

"A doctor! Someone, fetch me a doctor quickly!"

Matthew looked at Lillian, "Well, I guess the Timekeepers keep to their schedules with stunning punctuality, don't they?"

Not one to fear danger, Lillian barely waited for the horses to stop to exit the carriage. Matthew soon followed and greeted the gateman, saying they were passing by and heard the cries for help. The staff admitted them and Lillian wasted no time in hiking her skirts up and dashing up the stairs, leaving them to stare after her.

Matthew took his medical bag from the back of the carriage and nodded in apology to the dazed butler who barely had time to reprimand the young lady who'd rushed past him.

Called to the resounding cries, Lillian skidded into the room to find one man holding another, a knife protruding from his bare chest. Her first thought was of concern that the man was dangerous. But his eyes were filled with tears and he had no blood on his own palms as would be evident if he had done the stabbing. Matthew arrived behind her to the scene and they both approached the two men with haste but caution.

"Please! Doctor? Please help him!" the man gasped, laying the other down. Lillian noted how distraught he was. "I do not know how deep it is set or if by moving it we might kill him," he said and nodded to the knife. Matthew and Lillian came closer to assess the wound, and watch for the rise and fall of the bloodied man's chest. "My lady, surely you should not be here," the man said.

"She is the finest assistant any doctor could hope for and I need her at my side. No one else is of a calmer temperament," Matthew defended. Lillian felt a swell of pride that was quickly dashed when she looked closer at the man, unconscious on the floor.

"Holy shit," Lillian exclaimed before covering her mouth and dropping to her knees. "Richard? Oh no, oh no!" The breath and belief left her body. Her hands shook as she reached out to him. She touched his face lovingly. The handsome man watched her.

"Do you know this man?" he said, the fire of anxiety in his eyes.

"He is one of my dearest friends, sir. Who are you? What has happened?"

"I am Thomas Alexander and he did it to himself," Thomas said angrily. "I think he was drunk. Certainly not in his right mind. Please!"

Matthew took Thomas's place and Lillian sat on the other

side. Matthew studied the knife, not far in enough to be deadly but close to the heart. There was no way of knowing if it had pierced or nicked a life sustaining artery or vein. His brow fell. "The only sure way to know is to pull it out and gauge the bleeding."

Lillian nodded, tears in her eyes. "Someone fetch us clean cloths, boiling water, scissors, needles and thread, please." Thomas nodded and rose to find someone to help. A young woman swung into the door way.

"What has happened?"

"Please leave, Natalie!" Thomas bellowed. But she did not. She swept in and fell beside Lillian.

"Richard, my dearest," she said before Thomas pulled her back to her feet, and gave her a gentle shake to get her attention.

"Fetch the doctor clean cloths, boiling water, needle and thread. Now!" Natalie did not falter even at the harsh tone. She nodded and hurried to do her duty. Thomas dropped down next to Lillian.

"My lord, you should not be here," Matthew said.

"I will not leave his side," Thomas growled and took Richard's cold hand in his own. Lillian studied the plucked stitches, the small cuts that he'd given himself trying to remove them.

"What on earth was he doing?"

"Trying to take out his heart," Thomas's voice shook and he looked green. "Please, you must save him," he said to Matthew. The doctor looked closer at the wound, and nodded.

"I think the drink and the bleeding, along with whatever is affecting his mind has done the worst. It does not appear to be a deep wound." The bandages and sterile water with needle and thread arrived and they all braced. Matthew looked at Lillian, teary-eyed but resolute.

"I love you. Be strong," he whispered to her. She nodded, held the towels close to the knife and braced them against the wound as Matthew slowly removed the knife, angling it away from the heart. Richard moaned and shifted. Lillian applied pressure. The blood was a slow leak, not a bursting surge or pulsing explosion. They all held their breath as they watched the wound for a series of moments. Matthew let out his breath and nodded.

"Let us set him right." Together Lillian and Matthew worked to clean the wounds, take out the old stitches that were ready and trim the ones that were not. They applied salve and medicine to the small cuts and put in a few stitches to the new stab wound. Lillian, when the danger was passed, shook her head and glowered at Richard.

"What in the hell were you thinking, you stupid, brilliant man?" She smoothed her hand over his sweaty brow. Thomas kept his hand around Richard's for the entirety of the procedure, on his knees and holding in the ache to weep and howl.

"I am sorry I did not introduce myself properly," Lillian said softly and turned to him. From what the Timekeeper had told them, she had some idea of who this man was. She didn't know that her friend had apparently found someone so enamored with him. Thomas could barely tear his eyes away from Richard, his breathing shallow in worry. "I am Lillian Blackwell." She cleaned her hand on a cloth and offered it, not to kiss, but to shake. Thomas was hesitant to lose connection with Richard's hand. But he briefly shook it.

"I believe Richard has mentioned you. I do not know how or why you've come to his rescue at precisely the right time, nor do I care. I owe you a huge debt of gratitude," Thomas said lowly. Richard began to rouse. He sat up suddenly and they all had to back away. He looked first to the doctor with a confused scowl. Down to his chest where there were fresh bandages. Then to Lillian. His scowl lightened, his body wavered. He smiled.

"My dear, Lily with the sharp tongue. Whatever are you doing here?"

"Saving your life, you idiot," she whispered back. Richard

moved to reach out for a hug but found his shoulder on fire with pain.

"Lie back," Thomas barked, angry and shaking. Richard looked to him, his scowl returned.

"You should not be here."

"Where else on earth would I be?" Thomas retorted.

"With your soon-to-be wife," Richard growled. Thomas loosened his hold, rose to his feet, and even though his legs felt like jelly he stalked from the room. Lillian watched him go.

"Richard! That man saved you, and I daresay he's deeply concerned for your heart."

"That man destroyed my heart," he said angrily with his eyes fixed on the empty doorway. He started to cry. The servants and Natalie quietly left the room and Matthew and Lillian helped him into his bed.

"I don't know how you came to be here," he whispered and gently touched Lillian's cheek. "But yours is the only face that could bring me back from the verge of death."

Matthew cleared his throat. Lillian rolled her eyes at his peevish expression. She turned back to Richard.

"I have missed you terribly, and if it weren't for the Timekeepers helping us through the right portal, I would not have found my way in time." she said softly. Richard looked confused.

"The Timekeepers?"

"They came to us saying that you had gotten yourself in a bit of trouble. And here I thought Lillian owned the profession of troublemaking," Matthew said as he pulled his shirt sleeves back down to button them. "They opened a portal for us, and here we are." Richard studied Matthew, still processing all the information in the midst of his pain and sadness.

"Richard, this is my husband."

"Ah yes, the beautiful doctor, Matthew Blackwell. Of course." Richard breathed and groaned as he brought his good hand up to shake. "It is an honor to meet you. The only man who would deserve my fair Lillian." He smiled softly even as he felt his body giving way to the stress of the night.

"You should rest, sir," Matthew said.

"My heart," Richard said, eyes closed. "I wish you hadn't saved it." He cried softly until he lost consciousness. Matthew sat on the other side of the bed, took his pulse, and watched him breathe.

"Did he not want to save it because he loves you so?" Matthew asked her, a twitch in his jaw. Lillian sighed, shook her head and gently brushed Richard's hair from his forehead. She planted a kiss there.

"He doesn't love me in that way," she said. "He is from the future, my love. He helped me to find my way back to you. He's the librarian. The one who inherited Miriam's journal. I would have never found you if he hadn't kept it safe."

Matthew paused. His eyes grew wide. "This is the affable Doctor Shaw?" he sat closer. "How did he get here?"

"I imagine he stole a map. This was what the Timekeeper must have been trying to tell us."

"But why? I thought the common of us weren't supposed to meddle with time."

Lillian looked back at the door where Thomas had left. "He wouldn't have done so lightly. He was a staunch believer in historical record and the importance of not making waves in the timeline. He must have come back for a purpose."

They sat in silence for a moment before a small voice came from the shadows, followed by Natalie.

"I'm not sure what you mean by this strange conversation."

"My lady!" Matthew rose. She put a hand out and shook her blonde head.

"Richard saved my brother, on the field of battle. He said that he must live, that he must survive. That it was imperative for the future."

Lillian looked at her and then to Matthew. "Thomas must be very important to the timeline indeed."

"It is more than that," Natalie whispered. "I believe that his affections run so much deeper."

"His heart," Matthew said softly. Lillian looked at Natalie and back to the door where Thomas had stormed out.

"My guess is that he's very much in love with Thomas. My brother is expected to be betrothed soon, and I know it must be horrible for Richard." Natalie said wringing her hands.

"And is your brother much in love with the young lady?" Lillian asked.

"No—not at all." Natalie said. "But what choice does he have?"

They all stayed quiet and listened to Richard's breathing even out. He began to softly snore. Natalie leaned down, kissed his forehead and left. Lillian and Matthew stayed.

"It is not fair," Lillian said and caressed Richard's hand.

"There is nothing to be done," Matthew said.

"Nothing to be done?" Lillian returned angrily.

"Lillian," Matthew sighed, exasperated. "I'm not sure how things are in your time. But there is no leeway given for that kind of love." He rose, cleaned up the mess on the floor, gathered the tools and implements and placed them on the tray. She refused to look at him. He leaned down and kissed her crown. "I'm sorry, my love."

He took the tray of bloodied cloths and instruments up and looked back at her. "I will speak briefly to the family and see if they might have accommodations for us this evening." Lillian didn't look up. "He will be alright, Lily. When he wakes we shall make a plan to get us all back to where we belong."

Lillian didn't leave Richard's side. Her mind was a flurry. There must have been something she could do. She didn't want to live in a world where a man like Richard could not love.

213

30

PENANCE AND HEALING

Nothing could lift the guilty weight in Thomas's stomach. He thought he'd been doing what Richard had wanted. He thought that they could muddle through this awkward time and when the mess of the wedding was behind them, they would once again regain their rhythm. He had not been paying attention. He hadn't been paying enough attention. He'd only been appeasing his father and keeping the peace. Meanwhile, Richard had been waging war inside his own heart. Thomas remembered the unbidden reaction to finding Richard on the floor. The sobbing and wiping away the deluge of tears and blood on his cuff as he yelled for someone to help.

When the doctor, a blond and strapping man, ran in with the tall and graceful-necked woman, he thought two angels had arrived from the heavens to take his lion away. They got to work quickly and it took mere moments for Thomas to realize the serendipity, that this should be the woman, Lillian, that Richard had spoken so lovingly of. They worked efficiently; a team used to gore, and unfazed by the nature of the injury. Both of their hands steady, they had saved him and patched him up.

When Richard had so cuttingly told Thomas to leave, all the

words that followed came back to him. His hatred of his own heart. How Richard wished he'd never fallen in love with him, how he wished he could die rather than see him marry, Thomas thought to walk straight off of the balcony and to his death.

He nearly did.

Until a strong hand took his wrist and pulled him away from the wide and glassed doors. Thomas turned, angry and took back his hand. Matthew shied away.

"My lord, forgive me."

Thomas's face fell, his shoulders dropped. "I should be begging your forgiveness." Thomas said and looked down. "Thank you for saving him."

"My work is only as good as the next few hours and days. He needs care."

"I'm sure he will be fine in your and Mrs. Blackwell's capable hands."

"He needs care that I believe only you can provide."

"I do not understand what you mean," Thomas glowered, wondering what the doctor was insinuating.

"Sometimes in war, my lord, a captain's commands can bring the worst case back from the brink. Soldiers obey," Matthew said softly. He looked back at the doorway behind which Richard rested and Lillian sat in vigil. "I will need my wife back at some point this evening. Please take her place."

"I should not—"

"I will deal with your family," Matthew said and narrowed his eyes. Thomas studied his face. What was this man about? Stoic, beautiful, and an instant ally? How could it even be possible?

"As the doctor wishes," Thomas said. He went to his quarters, removed his bloodied clothes and changed. He washed his face, his hands, and tied back his hair. When he got to Richard's room, he knocked softly before opening the door. He did not know what he expected to see.

But he imagined what it would be like to walk in on Richard, kissing Lillian. Holding her hand, walking the room with her, or worse, naked in bed, enjoying his beautiful body. No wonder Richard had been driven to stab himself. Would Thomas be any different were their roles reversed? He came into the room. Lillian was resting her head on Richard's bed, beside their clasped hands. Her eyes were red and full of tears when she looked up to see him approach.

"Thomas," she sniffed.

"Dear Mrs. Blackwell. I do apologize for my behavior. I was—"

"Concerned, as was I. I am glad to see you have returned."

"The doctor insisted that he have his wife back for the evening." Thomas smiled.

"The doctor insisted, did he?" She rolled her eyes. "I can do as I please."

"Of that I am certain," Thomas smiled. He came closer. "But I would beg you to return to your husband. I can see how fond he is of you and know what it must feel like to be parted from the one you love. I would very much like to keep vigil with my friend."

"I would never part two people in love," she whispered softly with a smile and rose. "If he wakes and he is surly with you, you mustn't take him seriously." she said. "He is merely stung and trying to protect his pride."

"Such as a lion does," Thomas said softly.

"I do believe he loves you."

"Of that I am certain," Thomas's voice shook.

"Where does your heart lie, my lord?" Lillian whispered.

"I have never loved," Thomas said, dropping his voice and gaze to Richard's face. "Until Doctor Richard Shaw pushed me to the ground and saved my life. I have never known—" he gasped, "known such a loyal, passionate, beautiful man. I love him, greatly."

Lillian's tears sprung fresh and she shook her head. "I wish," she sniffed and cleared her throat. "I wish I could give you both more than a night. You deserve a lifetime."

Thomas nodded, sniffing back his own tears. "If the world were a fair place, my lady. Such would be the case."

"We must make it fair," she said and nodded to the bed. "At least for this night. I will lock the door," she kissed Richard's head and gently touched Thomas's hand before she left. "You must not —" she paused as she stopped at the door.

"Yes?" Thomas asked.

"Do not give up hope. There will be a way. We will find one. I will help. I rarely leave well enough alone."

Thomas smiled with a small laugh and she left, locking the door behind her. Thomas crawled into the bed, and cuddled his warm body next to Richard's. He stirred, grumbled, and turned his head.

"You're not supposed to be here," Richard whispered, pained.

"You're not to give me orders." Thomas growled. "There is no other place for me to be."

"Thomas, you idiot."

"Be silent and rest, you great beast," Thomas said and pulled him close, into his shaking arms. Richard sobbed softly until he fell back into sleep. Thomas held him the whole night, barely sleeping for the worry and the hurt in his heart.

31

WEDDING PLANS AND THE LION
HAS A GUARD

The house was quiet in the morning. Servants skittered about in their usual fashion, tending to the family and guests. But no one was allowed in Richard's room except the doctor and his wife. And Thomas of course. When the duke and duchess inquired about Richard's health, they were given perfunctory information, directly from Matthew. Richard's wound had become infected over the journey. The sacrifice he'd made to save their son had put him in grave danger. He must not be disturbed.

Thomas's father looked angrily on, whenever his son would help to carry trays and medical supplies up to the room where the interloper lay. The Duchess was much more worried for Richard's safety and offered to sit with him while he slept. Thomas felt renewed in his love of her, and in the simple act of her kindness.

Natalie snuck in whenever possible in the next day, even though Richard insisted that she go and spend time preparing for her wedding. She brought him samples of flowers, and materials, and asked his opinion.

"And what would man know of such things?" Richard asked,

caressing a particularly creamy swatch of satin that might have been made of angel's breath or butter, or a combination of the two in its softness. He had been instructed by the doctor to stand and walk the room intermittently to keep his lungs in good health. Thomas turned away from his pacing of the windows.

"You ought to have seen what this vagabond was wearing when I met him. As if he'd escaped the stage at the Globe Theater."

Richard scoffed and shoved Thomas playfully. "Was that what you noticed on my way to save your bloody life?"

"So much was on my mind upon seeing you," Thomas turned quiet and reverent. Natalie paused to watch them with the smile of a girl reading tales of bravery and romance.

"That surely, he was the bravest soul you had ever seen. And the most handsome, I dare say." Natalie winked. Thomas blushed and cleared his throat. Richard looked down. They hadn't touched since Thomas had cradled his body the night of the 'accident'. But Thomas had kept vigil on the settee beside his bed. He would not allow Richard to do anything that might tear a stitch. It was only patient cuddling, caressing, helping him dress and clean the wound. Thomas read poetry to him and insisted he eat. In essence the best time that Richard had ever spent. Richard looked back to Natalie who watched them curiously. He cleared his throat.

"Careful, or I shall steal you right away from the groom without remorse."

Natalie laughed at this and took her basket of wedding details from the room. "I shall have tea brought up. But not too soon," she winked and closed the door behind her. Silence descended between them. Richard, weak in his legs, returned to bed and sighed.

"My lord, we must discuss something."

"Is it about me pleasuring you into a right state of oblivion?"

Thomas said, with an arched brow. "Because you know the new regulations state that all stitches must be healed first." He was studying a flower arrangement, even while he calmly spoke of pleasuring his lover.

"But that shall take forever!" Richard whined, before he caught himself and cleared his throat. "I do not mean that. I mean, the future of your family. Of your marriage to Miss—"

"Please, do not. Do not speak her name."

"But she is to be your betrothed."

"She is nothing to me. She needn't be." Thomas threw a wilted lily into the dustbin with more force than necessary.

"We must think of—"

"You. I must only think of you. Don't you understand?"

"Thomas. Please. You know I care for you, but I will not let you face the wrath of your father—"

"So brave a man I once thought you were. Is my lion so cowardly? Did you not know that I am a hardened man of battle? That no sniveling man, hiding his weakness beneath brocade can sway me from the destiny I choose?"

Richard's heart leapt to his throat and he was speechless. "Thomas, please. I'm trying very hard to—"

"Leave me. I know. I'm not a fool, Doctor Shaw. You believe there is no hope and that we must part ways."

"It isn't that I want it this way."

"But the truth of the matter is that I will not survive without you."

"That is not true! You have so much to live for yet," Richard's voice rose. He tore the blankets from his legs and rose to angrily pace but his body refused. Thomas caught him as he nearly fell to his knees.

"Stop this useless struggling. I will not leave your side." Thomas looked to the pained expression on Richard's face and sighed. "But I will not hold you to any promises until you are at least strong enough to stand on your own," he whispered softly.

"You must return to sleeping in your own bed."

"No."

"Thomas, I am fine," Richard tried to sway him even as he needed help into his bed.

"I will not leave your side until I feel you can at least make it to your chamber pot on your own." He sat next to Richard, pushing his hair from his forehead. Richard leaned into the touch and his hand found Thomas's with warmth that felt like the only real thing in Richard's world. What would it really hurt?

"May I not at least have a kiss? Just one?"

"I cannot risk raising your heart rate, so the doctor says."

"The doctor is a prudish charlatan," Richard protested.

"I assure you, Richard Shaw, I have walked by the Doctor and Mrs. Blackwell's guest chambers, at all hours of the day. That man is in complete service of his wife, with much ... joyful abandon," Thomas said and blushed, he looked down at Richard's lips. Richard looked at his also. What in the bloody hell? Why did it matter how hard his heart broke? He knew he was living on borrowed time at best. He leaned in close, but did not touch his lips to Thomas's.

"If you insist on being of service to me, can't we not do so with joyful abandon as well?" he whispered, to the resounding and beautiful smile on Thomas's face.

"I must examine your stitches first." Thomas leaned down and pushed Richard's shirt away to kiss the tender and red skin. Richard inhaled sharply and held Thomas's head close. "They seem a bit raw."

"Would that I could show you raw," Richard growled, his hips rising from the bed. Thomas put a firm hand on him and pressed his rising need back down.

"Do you speak to all your lovers so tenderly?" Thomas smiled, wickedly up at him.

"I have none but you," Richard cried, no truer words ever spoken, from a place, so deep and long-held in his chest that he couldn't even remember a former lover in that moment. "I miss you," Richard whispered.

"And I you. So, rest today, and if you can make it to my chambers on your own, I will tend to you in every way you wish," he said and gently bit Richard's neck before the knock on the door, announcing tea, drove them both apart.

32

A CLOSE SHAVE, AND SCARS REVEALED

"Sit," Thomas commanded.

"My lord, it is not necessary," Richard said, trying to remain strong and stoic, even though he felt weak from his trek across the large manor to find his way into Thomas's quarters. He could not show weakness now. He shook his head. Thomas nodded back to a chair in his seating area.

"I gave you an order," Thomas's voice and eyes lowered and Richard felt heat coil in his belly. The intensity in Thomas's blue eyes was clear. Richard felt at once aching to comply and torn to resist. Richard did not try to fight the desire Thomas had sparked at the simple command. Despite the protest from his father, Thomas had not left Richard's side since the night of the incident. Until last night, when Richard commanded that he sleep in his own bed for more complete rest.

The rule stood with Thomas. He hadn't allowed them to pleasure each other until Richard was well enough to walk. It was only delicate kisses, holding, bathing, cuddling. Richard loved every moment but there were some things he really would like to do with Thomas. Miss Dougherty had been turned away when she had called. The tension between father and son had resumed.

"Do you disobey me?" Thomas shocked Richard back to the dawn-lit room.

"No, my lord." Richard breathed, and shut his eyes briefly. *I must remain in control*, he thought. But Thomas playing dominant and submissive was definitely not helping the glorious case of swollen balls he had currently.

"Well then?" Thomas nodded to the chair in the center of the room. The morning sunlight streamed brightly into the bedchambers and the household below them began to crank to life. It was the morning of Natalie's wedding. Probably a horrible time to take this chance. But Richard did not know how much time they had left.

"Yes, my lord." Richard said lowly and Thomas smiled to hear the compliance in his tone.

"That's a good soldier," he whispered and locked his chamber door. "I can't have my right hand man attend such an auspicious event with that monstrous beard."

"You know my rule about the beard. Besides, I thought you liked it."

"I do. But I want to see your face." Thomas paused and looked into Richard's ashen expression and walked slowly towards him. He picked up a cup and lather on his way to Richard. He held a sharp blade at its hilt. "What is it?"

"My lord, I—" Richard's palms erupted with sweat and his voice shook. He wanted to press on, but Thomas interjected.

"Surely you do not believe I truly find your beard monstrous. I was only speaking in jest. I actually am quite fond of it."

Richard looked into Thomas's smile; his perfect face lined just barely with age. And war. He did feel like a monster, compared to such a beautiful man.

"My lord, I am horrific. Beneath."

"Surely not," Thomas said, still with a smile. "Far from it. You are quite the handsome man. Inside and out." One step closer and Richard's heart ticked up in its beating. Still, he let Thomas approach with the cup, knowing this would end disastrously. As he got close enough, Thomas smiled down at him, a half-cocked smile. He thought he was handsome, inside and out. God, Richard rolled his eyes and closed them. Fire spread through his gut and down to his groin. Thomas lowered his brow.

"Come now, you aren't afraid of me surely? Are you?" His voice was low and sweet and Richard opened his eyes.

"I am only afraid of what you will find," Richard said as Thomas reached out to gently caress the soft hair of his beard. Richard caught his wrist in a strong hold. "My lord, I am— maimed. Scarred badly."

Thomas's eyes went soft, he looked across Richard's cheeks, freed his hand to turn his chin this way and that.

"Where? How? By what blade? Where do I find this man?" his gaze darkened.

"My lord, please, the beard helps to conceal it."

"Let me see," he said softly and peeled away his hand from Richard's grasp.

"Please, Thomas," Richard's broken voice was pained in the silence between them.

"My dear Richard, it is our scars that make of us men. Human and divine." Richard's eyes filled with tears. "They have forged you into the man you are, the warrior, who shows no fear in battle."

"I am no warrior," choked Richard.

"But you saved me, valiantly. More than once."

Richard looked up, Thomas was closer now, their knees touching. Thomas's hands reached up to gently caress the soft dark hair on his cheek. "I am only brave in the service of you." Richard whispered and closed his eyes.

He knew he should not re-engage. He knew he should keep their distance, but instead he pressed his heart and his cheek into Thomas's palm.

"Be brave with me here," Thomas whispered. "I wish to know

all of your secrets," his hand moved up to thread into Richard's hair and he nearly purred. Richard sighed and nodded.

"There now, my mighty lion. Let us free you from the heat of this scruff." Suddenly Thomas's hands were gone and Richard opened his eyes to watch as Thomas sharpened the blade and frothed the cream. He set a bowl of water, a towel and the razor beside Richard.

"Take off your shirt," Thomas breathed.

"My lord?"

"You don't want it getting thatched with hair," Thomas said. Richard hesitated. "That's another order. Do not make me add up the punishments." Thomas growled and watched while Richard sat forward. He knew if his shirt were removed Thomas would want to touch him and if he touched him, that would be the end of it. He'd been without his attention for too long and he would not deny either of them.

"Must I remove it by force?" Thomas asked with a smile. His voice and eyes lowered on Richard and his eyes fell to his lips. Richard's body was a traitor and he felt his groin fill with blood. His heart raced.

Yes, please remove it by force. Do everything to me, with your anger and pent-up need, he thought achingly. He was pained and hard.

"No, my lord." Richard whispered, not looking away from Thomas's heated gaze as he stood and removed the shirt. Thomas's eyes fell to his bulging groin with a desire that wouldn't be confused. Richard watched him bite his lip and stare hungrily at it. Richard felt his body break out in a cool sweat. They had seen each other naked before. He'd felt Thomas's teeth on his skin before. But there was something about being mere steps away from his family, in the broad light of morning ... naked and in hopeful anticipation that they might again touch one another.

"Sit," Thomas said again, husky. Richard stared at him

through a haze of uncertainty. When he saw the scar, how could he possibly still think him beautiful? Worse, it would be a sight for all of the revelers at the wedding to behold. Thomas's father, dear Natalie, Lillian and Matthew. All of the fine ladies and gentlemen would witness the cruelty of his father's mark.

"Do not falter on me now."

"I will be rendered horrific for the wedding."

"Do you doubt my skill with a blade?" Thomas teased and put his hand to the middle of Richard's chest, pushing him down in the seat. His hand trailed up Richard's neck, gently turning his chin to face the light coming in from the windows.

"What will they think of the scar? What will you?" Richard voiced his concerns.

"You are beloved. Scars and all." Thomas whispered and gently spread the foam over his beard. With patient and gentle strokes, he scraped closely down the side of Richard's face. Richard had always worn a beard, from the time he could grow one, so the skin felt strange and sensitive. The first side came off easily and Richard watched Thomas's face turn in concentration as he deftly took away the hair. He felt so exposed, cold, and unable to hide from the world. Moving from one jawline across his face, Thomas delicately took away the mustache and the hair from Richard's chin to move to the scarred side. Richard took in a deep breath and Thomas did too.

"There now, be brave," he whispered and began. He was extremely cautious and patient with his blade, rinsing it often and re-foaming Richard's cheek, careful to not nick the tender red line that spread nearly from below the corner of his eye down to the edge of his mouth. It was a horrid sight, Richard was sure. Thomas's eyes filled with tears as he exposed the red, raised line. Richard watched him.

"I told you. I warned you."

"I do not weep for the sight of it. I weep for the boy who took such pain. I weep in anger of not being able to offer retribution for the way he hurt you. What man did this?"

"My father," Richard said softly. Thomas's brow drew in and he gently traced the scar with the pad of his thumb. Cleaning up the remaining hair, he dabbed at Richard's exposed skin, and the strong jaw beneath, the boyish good looks below bright and intelligent eyes.

"My god, I cannot let you leave this room."

Richard's eyes fell and he scowled. "I told you. I am horrific—"

"If the world sees how stunning you are I will have to fight off men and women alike to keep you mine." Thomas finished, putting Richard's chin between his thumb and fingers to make him meet his eyes.

"Yours, my lord?"

"All. Mine." Thomas said, and took his mouth. What a strange feeling to kiss without the soft barrier of his beard. His skin was so sensitive and hot against Thomas's. It was like being kissed for the first time. Thomas's hard mouth explored and tasted his, gently biting at his lips, his exposed chin, settling in between his legs and wrapping his arms around Richard's bare shoulders.

Richard held on tightly to the bones of Thomas's hips, then curved his hands around his muscled ass and pulled him in closer with a grunt. Thomas's kisses trailed down his neck, biting at his collarbone and shoulders and Richard seethed.

"Thomas—it is morning—"

"It is my room, and I've bolted the door," Thomas grunted in response and drew away only to pull Richard by the hand towards the bed. "I made the mistake of trying to give you space, and look at the bloody mess you made. No more space. And now that your stitches have healed sufficiently, I will wait no longer. When we are alone, you will be within the heat of my body. No farther," he demanded and turned to face him as they reached the tossed bed and its tangled sheets.

"You have had a rough night," Richard said, looking past his shoulder.

"I tossed and turned, without you in my bed, really since the night I found you, bleeding and dying in your chambers."

"I was not—"

"Forced to touch myself, wishing it was you. But not wanting to hurt you further." Thomas growled. Richard felt a shiver run up through his body and he gasped. Thomas studied his newly exposed face. "Do not make me wonder, because I will consent without complaint if you still are not able. Please, tell me you are feeling well enough?"

"I'm here to serve, my lord." Richard whispered and pushed him back onto the bed, pulling Thomas's breeches down and licking his way up the tight and trembling muscles of his legs.

Before he could take him into his mouth, Thomas pushed him away and turned over, exposing his hard backside and Richard's mouth watered at the way his muscles trembled with anticipation.

"Thomas, I have no—"

"I do not care. I must have you," he nearly cried.

"I do care. I will not hurt you," Richard yelled back and slapped his beautiful ass. Thomas cried out and moved against his hand. Using the excessive watering of his mouth at the sight, Richard licked his palm and spread it around his throbbing cock.

"You will return the favor, my lord," Richard growled in Thomas's ear as he pulled his hair and his head back and bit into his shoulder. When he slid slowly inside of him, Thomas cried out with pleasure and bucked his hips back.

So long he'd been without love, so untouched and pent up with need that Richard was embarrassed at how quickly he came into the tight and fast strokes Thomas met him with. He yelled out and his hands shook as they bruised Thomas's flesh to hold him into the explosion. Thomas gasped, and shook, and moaned. Richard drew out, turned him over and began to lick and coat

Thomas's unspent and swollen cock until it was wet and throbbing. Richard watched it with rising desire as he took all fours and looked back at Thomas.

"I know not what to do," Thomas gasped, still shaking and reeling from Richard's fervent love making.

"I will guide you," Richard said thickly and reached back to help Thomas find his tight and eager opening.

When he pushed slowly inside, Richard could feel the shiver that ran through Thomas. So big, inside him, that Richard's hands dug into the sheets even as Thomas pulled him forcefully back, to plunge in deeper. Richard arched up and yelled. Pain and pleasure so close in the space that he didn't know if he wanted to cry for Thomas to stop or cry for more. Any gentlemanly sense of decorum he might have had, seemed to break inside of Thomas, he was a man possessed.

Richard was his, he could see the possessive look on Thomas's face when he looked back over his shoulder to where Thomas was staring down at his back. Thomas ran his hand up the straight line of Richard's spine and grunted before threading his hand into Richard's thick hair.

"Slow, slow down—" Thomas whispered, trying to control the pace, his hands pulling Richard closer and pressing back out, even as the rippling, driving heat searing up Richard's thighs and back.

"Deeper, Thomas—hard." Richard whispered, groaned and spread his legs.

"The way you speak to me," Thomas gasped, "makes me want to throw all sense of decency and—" he paused to grunt.

"Do not be decent. Take me—" Richard cried as he felt his own body respond and his cock start to throb again.

With a guttural groan Thomas pulled Richard to him, up to the hilt of his length, and drew out only to ride him with hip-bruising desperation until he felt his body shiver and shudder and his cock grow thick and large. He reached around to find

Richard hard again and stroked his cock as he exploded, coming deep inside of him. Richard shuddered in his hand, spurting into the sheets and Thomas's palm with a satisfied cry.

They fell into the bed, ruined and exhausted. Bare of lies and beards. No good for any other lover in the world, and only ever each other's.

3 3

THE WEDDING

They had to rouse, to clean up. To get dressed. It was a pity they could not stay in bed all day, making up for the time they'd lost. Richard stared into the mirror for a good long while, trying to recognize his own face. It had been so long since he'd seen that boy. The scar had faded with time, and with all of the healing he'd done both externally and internally. Thomas came up behind him, sighed, kissed the back of his neck and adjusted the shoulders on his forest green, velvet coat.

"You look fine. How will I ever keep you in only my bed?"

"Who else's bed do you think I would find?" Richard teased over his shoulder and turned around to help Thomas with his cravat and straighten his hair. "Are you alright? After this morning?" Richard nodded to the bed.

"No," Thomas said.

"No?" Richard's throat contracted in fear and he took Thomas's face in his hands, tearing up at the thought he might have gone too far, too fast. "Thomas, I'm—"

"I fear I shall never be able to bed another man. You have completely ruined me and I can't wait until we're together again tonight. And I am also distraught because although you look

232

divine in those clothes, I much prefer you naked," Thomas interrupted, his breath quickened and he reached to undo Richard's coat. Richard stopped him with a laugh.

"We have a wedding to attend, for which you are probably already late!"

Thomas growled and threw a small fit, tugging at the buttons and bindings that kept him from touching Richard the way he wished to.

"Let us not go."

"It is your sister's wedding!" Richard laughed, at his tantrum. "I would not, nor will I let you, dishonor sweet Natalie. Plus, there will be food and I am famished."

"Oh? Worked up an appetite, did you?"

"Didn't you?"

"I," Thomas stopped, closed his eyes, and Richard could tell he was remembering it all. "I did not know a body could feel so good. I thought I was going to die from the pleasure of it. You were so hot and tight—" Richard took his mouth in a fervent kiss. He broke away and stepped back.

"Do not talk to me in that manner or we will miss the wedding, and perhaps the entirety of their honeymoon." Richard laughed and patted his bottom. Thomas smiled.

"Would that I could take you away on a honeymoon."

Sadness descended between them, but was curtailed by the knocking outside.

"Are you quite ready, my lord? The procession is about to begin and your father says you are to attend the greeting line outside the church. We must make haste," the butler commanded.

"I am coming," he yelled back and gently kissed Richard. Thomas sighed, and pulled Richard into his arms to hold him for a moment.

"I will see you in the procession," Richard said, and quietly pulled away.

"It will be the highlight of the day," Thomas responded and

left the room. Richard waited and spent a few minutes calming himself down, he made the bed, checked his face again. Lillian would not recognize him. After the last few months, he barely recognized himself.

He wondered if he could ever go back to his old life. Ever go back and not be Thomas's. He did not wish for a life without Thomas, even for all the pain this one afforded him. On his way down to the stables, to share a carriage with Lillian and Matthew, he was stopped by Thomas's mother.

"Excuse me, sir, are you lost?"

Richard turned and smiled. "Pardon me, my lady, it is I, Richard. I shaved my beard at the request of the young duke and," he touched the fresh and tender skin. "It is quite different."

"Richard!" she gasped and turned his face this way and that. "So it is! Why you look so handsome! You may very well end up engaged before the night is over!" She laughed and escorted him to the front door where they found their separate carriages.

"What happened to your beard?" Lillian gasped, she too reached out and touched his face. Richard drew away.

"Is this how pregnant women feel? Everyone thinking they have a right to touch them suddenly?"

Lillian blushed. "I don't know."

"I would very much like you to know," Matthew said under his breath. Richard stared at them. There was a tension there. The topic was a heavy one indeed.

"Yes, I am aware. But we've only just gotten married and I told you, I'm not ready."

"I just want—" Matthew stopped and blushed. Lillian knotted her hands in her lap nervously. Richard cleared his throat.

"It is a big decision to be sure," he whispered. "When the time is right you shall both know."

"I suppose," Lillian sulked.

"And if you ever decide it is the right path, I will be the finest uncle ever." Richard chuckled and slapped both knees. "Until then it's the trying that's the fun part of the whole mess." He winked to Matthew who nodded with a small smile and softened in his tense posture. Lillian remained closed off from the subject even as the carriage went through the streets of the town towards the church. She shifted in her seat and looked at Richard.

"How long will you stay, Richard? How long can you stay? Is it safe for you here? And Thomas?" she asked. Richard was hit by the reality of it. It was one thing to daydream himself but to have someone who knew he did not belong in bring him back down to reality, was a dark cloud he'd been avoiding.

"As long as I can," he whispered and looked out the window where Thomas and his family were lined up outside of the church to greet their guests. "As long as he wants me. We will be careful, I promise."

"But Richard—" Lillian was stopped as the carriage pulled up and the footman opened the door.

"Do not take this moment from me, Lillian, I beg of you," Richard said. "I have so little happiness, I just want it for a little longer." He touched the scar self-consciously and she and Matthew watched him exit the carriage.

"What trouble will this bring about?" Matthew asked but Lillian could only shake her head.

"I fear the worst kind."

The ceremony was lovely. Quiet but for the laughing of the bride at various intervals. Thomas shook his head with a smile. Their father scowled and cleared his throat. Natalie had always been a joyful child and now her joy was manifest in the man she'd both fallen in love with and had chosen to spend her life with.

Richard sat next to Lillian and Matthew. He did not belong to a noble family and really not on either side of where the families sat, bride nor groom. Though he knew Thomas's mother was forever indebted, he had always known that Thomas's father regarded him with suspicion. Especially when he'd shown up at the wedding, clean shaven, and Thomas's smile had beamed brighter than any time before that day.

They'd been very careful, but the man was not an idiot. He did not rise to his station and maintain the dukedom by being a man who did not notice things. He looked back over his shoulder at Richard when he noticed that Thomas could not stop glancing his way. Richard quickly found the study of his fingernails most engaging. He wondered if Thomas would have to take over the manor upon his father's death or if he could travel to new places. In any case, they had time. Time before his father transferred the responsibility of land and title to Thomas. Time for them to travel. To get out of Marlborough. To maybe even try and find a portal.

So lost in his thoughts, Richard startled when the crowd burst into applause and broke out with oohs and aahs that accompanied the joyous announcement that Natalie and her groom were now wife and husband. He held back in exiting the church, not feeling close enough to follow the family out. He stayed close to Lillian and Matthew, and as he went through the receiving line, Natalie pulled him in for a hug.

"I quite miss your beard! It took me all ceremony to figure out who the man was beside the Blackwells. Handsome and mysterious!"

Richard blushed and kissed her hand. "You make a beautiful bride, my dear, and one who I know will do amazing things going forward. For the whole country itself." He warmly pressed her hand between his and then shook her groom's hand. "Take good care of her and always be acquiescing."

"I cannot be anything but. She is my sun and moon," the man said and looked down at her. Natalie, bucking the traditions of decorum, kissed him square on the mouth to the delight of the guests.

"At least wait until you are off the steps of the church!" her father reprimanded from the side. Thomas smiled from his other side.

"Of course, father. Because God would not approve of a married couple finding joy in each other."

"Do not speak with such disrespect! God does not find affection necessary!" His father retorted and Richard hurried past him with a bow. Thomas caught his hand before he could pass by him as well.

"Doctor Shaw. I thank you for being here." He said softly and bowed. Richard bowed back and realized that without his beard he could not hide the blush in his cheeks. He cleared his throat.

"The pleasure was all mine, my lord. It was a lovely ceremony."

"Someday soon you will see another," The duke said beneath an arched brow. "The young Miss Dougherty and my son, of course." Richard's smile faltered but he caught it and lifted it with a nod.

"Of course," he looked to Thomas who had blanched and looked like he might throw up. "That, too, will be a day worth rejoicing in." Richard bowed to them both, kissed Natalie's mother's hand and got out of the line as quickly as possible. He waited in the carriage for Lillian and Matthew to make their way through the line. He shook his leg nervously. What was he doing? The magic and chemicals of the morning spent with Thomas were wearing off. He was in grave danger, but what was worse, he was putting Thomas in danger too.

Depending on the offence, who was made aware, and the county of residence, it could mean anything from banishment to death, and certainly to social ruin, which was not much better than death in the time. For not just Thomas, but his family as well. Richard looked out the window where the crowd was getting in carriages to attend the reception at the manor. He watched the strange and beautiful dance of a society in the shackles of propriety. The carriage door opened and he startled. Thomas entered.

"I must commend you for not tearing my father's head off."

"You should accept the same commendation," Richard answered and quickly looked out of the window to see if anyone had seen Thomas get in.

"You are on edge," Thomas said and gauged the fact by touching his knee. Richard jumped with a slight whoop.

"I merely do not wish to have you slandered by my unacceptable affections."

"There is no one here," Thomas chuckled and ran his hands up Richard's inner thigh. The carriage door burst open and they both jumped apart. Thomas's eldest brother, Lillian and Matthew entered, squishing all in.

"Hello," Matthew said softly and stared at them both.

"Sir, Doctor, my lady," Richard said in turn bowing and looking out the window. Thomas's brother, James, sat next to him and forced them both to sit closer, thigh to thigh. Richard's body shook. They had almost been discovered. He bit his lip and stared out the window as the carriage carried them back to the manor. Once a place of respite, Richard now felt it was a den of snakes.

When he glanced over, he saw that James was keeping them both in his sight the entire way.

34

CONSEQUENCES OF LOVERS DISCOVERED

The reception was a delight. The flowers were fresh and spilling out over silver vases, the cake was nearly as tall as Richard from where it sat on the table in the center of the room. A portrait of the happy couple sat at the head of the ball room where a quartet played for the dancing crowd. People chatted and danced around each other. Lillian stayed close to Richard except upon the occasions when Matthew asked her to dance. Richard watched them with a soft smile. He never thought his friend Lillian could have such grace, but perhaps in the arms of love, one could learn to do most anything. Richard looked over his glass of lemonade, he'd given up on alcohol after the knife incident, and found Thomas conversing with his father. Miss Dougherty approached Thomas from the other side.

He would be asked to dance. He would have to oblige. And Richard would have to live with it. Now, more than ever, it was more important that they resume their distance. Especially in the company of others. James's eyes had been keen and he'd watched the acted indifference with suspicion. Thomas was not a fool. His position afforded him some protection. But Richard's did not. And the young duke had far too many important things to do after Richard left. He sighed, sipped his lemonade and made polite conversation.

"Richard, you simply must dance with me!" Natalie said, exuberantly coming to stand beside him.

"My dear, I regret to inform you that I am not at all skilled in the art."

"Surely you've seen *Pride and Prejudice* a few hundred times," Lillian whispered and smiled at him, coming off the dance floor herself, looking rosy cheeked. Richard blushed, surely, he had. He remembered parts.

"You cannot deny a bride on her wedding day!" Natalie smiled. Richard could not tell her no. She was Thomas's best supporter and the one who stood a chance at helping him survive and thrive once Richard was gone. He bowed and smiled at her.

"You must accommodate my clumsiness, my lady."

"We will keep you up on the steps," Lillian assured and took Matthew by the hand. The music was luckily a slower tempo and Richard caught on quick, laughing at his own mistakes and enjoying the spinning twirls. As was the custom, partners interchanged and he found himself face to face with Marianne. She smiled and bowed as did he.

"I have never properly thanked you for saving the dear future Duke of Marlborough." She said as they spun and turned back-to-back. "My future quite literally, depended on your bravery." Richard cleared his throat and nodded his head. He and Thomas were side by side now. Thomas met his eyes. Richard looked away quickly.

"It was my pleasure," he said, at a loss for words.

"A pleasure? To be stabbed?" Marianne laughed sharply.

"To come to the aid of such a great man," Richard corrected. Thomas bowed and blushed. "The world needs him, far more than it will ever need me."

"Surely you are right," Marianne said and narrowed her eyes at Richard. It cut and he gladly switched partners again, but not before catching Thomas's clenched jaw as he glared at Miss Dougherty. The dance ended and they all clapped politely.

Richard's guts turned, to leave him in the care of such a woman, may not have been the safest thing, but what choice did he have? He went to the table, feigned interest in the food. Thomas met him there.

"I apologize, Doctor Shaw, for Miss Dougherty's rudeness."

"You mustn't," Richard shook his head. "Her behavior is not yours to apologize for. You are not yet married." He smiled softly and stared into the flower arrangement, wishing a portal would swallow him up this very instant.

"Yet?"

"Thomas," Richard leaned in and shook his head. "We both know that she's the paramount hope of your parents."

"Yes, well, my parents are not the ones with the decision to marry her," Thomas said tightly and moved to accept a flute of champagne.

"I know she is not your ideal. But surely you can find some redeeming quality in her?" Richard said and made sure to put plenty of space between them.

"She is ambitious. But I'm not sure that's an attribute I look for in a partner."

They leaned back and watched the next round of dancing.

"What would you look for, my lord?" Richard asked, not taking his eyes away from Natalie and Lillian twirling around their partners, able to marry and devote themselves to one person, whom they loved. In sickness, in health, for richer and poorer.

"Loyalty. Strength of character, thick dark hair, and a rich reading voice." Thomas said softly. "A sense of humor and the nicest hind quarters I've ever seen." Thomas leaned closer and the air was warm suddenly. "Perfectly kissable lips, and the courage to put me in my place when I pout." He smiled and nudged Richard. "And you? Doctor Shaw? What do you look for in a partner? Your life mate?" Before Richard could answer, James, the duke, and Marianne's father came up to the refreshments table. Both men cleared their throats.

"Yes, Doctor Shaw, do tell us! It's always good to know what men look for in their women."

Their women, it irked Richard to hear the possessive words from the duke. "I hardly think my preferences should matter," Richard countered.

"Of course, how else will we find you a suitable bride to take back to Oxford!" Marianne's father slapped him on the back as though they were old friends. Richard scowled. He looked briefly at Thomas's father.

"Well, she must be well-read."

"Reading? Is that a quality that women even need?" James scoffed. Richard narrowed his eyes.

"I prefer my spouse to be educated so we can converse with ease, about any subject."

"It is not conversing you want to be doing with your wife, unless it is between the sheets," James said, looking back at Lillian on the dance floor with a lingering stare and licking the edge of his glass.

Ugh, men. Richard thought.

"We cannot be in bed all day," Richard said and stood taller. "They should be brave, compassionate. Giving, but strong-willed and able to withstand—"

"A man your size?" Thomas's father sneered at him.

"Hardships," Richard scowled at him at the crude remark. "And not become embittered and unkind because of them."

"You want a saint, not a woman!" James jeered.

"I want a partner I can talk to. Who I feel safe with and who feels safe in my arms. I want someone who tells me when I'm being an idiot and loves me when I have misgivings. I want someone who loves to be read to and who listens when I speak." Richard continued and the men seemed to shrink away. "Not just because I'm their husband but because they respect and love me, and they genuinely want to know what's on my mind. I would, of course, offer them nothing less in return."

"Good lord, no wonder you are still in want of a wife," James scoffed and downed his champagne. "You and my brother need to lower your standards or you shall be alone for the remainder of your lives. Wifeless, untitled, alone."

He sniffed and walked away.

"Being wifeless and untitled would not suit you, Thomas. Bear that in mind." Thomas's father shot a glance to Richard before leaving with Marianne's father. They watched the men go. When alone again, Thomas put his half-full flute down and sighed.

"I am no saint."

"You are everything." Richard whispered back, even as he stared at the ground. "Everything I could have ever wanted." He rushed from the table and out through the doors to the garden. He had to leave, he needed to get away from the heat and the people. The prying eyes and wandering glances that told him he was not safe and neither was Thomas. They would be found out. They would be killed. History would be changed for the absolute worst.

He would leave tonight. Thomas would be hurt but he would continue on. He would do what he had to and would persevere, bravely. Especially now he had his sister to love and guide him. Lillian and Matthew might even be of some service to his forward direction. He had to believe that it was at least better that Thomas had been truly loved at least once, than not at all. Richard wanted to believe that he was loved too. At least once.

The night was still and the revelers were staying close to the music and drink, enjoying the light-hearted occasion. Richard should have said goodbye to Lillian and Matthew. Surely, they were smart enough that they would put together what had happened. They would understand why he had to go.

He pulled out the map from his jacket pocket and took a look at it, under the light of the full moon. There, beneath the soft and blue glow, where shadows made funny shapes of every topiary and stone statue, he saw the twinkling. A portal. A doorway. The first he'd seen clearly since their arrival. It was just a couple of miles east of the manor. All he really had to do was start walking that way. The map must be telling him that it was time.

He hoped, that no matter where it dumped him, he would never again have to look upon Thomas Alexander and know he would always love him, but would never be able to be with him. Richard sniffed. He had to believe that he'd done enough. To stay any longer, to risk them being found out, to risk Thomas's reputation and good name? He could not.

He wanted to get a few things from his room before he left. He wanted to leave Thomas a letter and the ring ... Explaining and assuring him that he would have all he deserved in life and that Richard would always love him, no matter what time or space he ended up in.

He started back up towards the house, through the gardens and high walled shrubbery. He felt disoriented and full of grief, but still resolute that this was the only way. The revelers from the wedding were making joyous noise and Richard tried to be content in the idea that he'd been part of something. Something rather magical. He'd saved a man. Loved someone more than his own heart. Possibly saved the country. He'd never be able to tell the tale. But as long as he knew, and Lillian too, there would be a slight peace in his heart.

He walked slowly to the back side of the manor, intent on packing his bag and getting out before the party wound down. He did not expect the warmth of a hand on his wrist and he turned, hand raised to strike, only to find it was Thomas, his grip tight.

"Where are you going?"

"Up to my room. I'm not feeling well."

"Oh? To try to stab yourself again. I think not." Thomas scowled.

"I'm not going to try to hurt myself."

"Good, then let us go up together." His beautiful smile made Richard's heart ache.

"Thomas."

"I'm tired of the crowd and tired of Miss Dougherty's hands all over me as if she had just bought a fine stallion and has the right to inspect him as she wishes." Richard turned and faced him with a small smile. He was rather well endowed. "I wish to only be touched by hands that love me." Thomas said quietly, as he looked down at Richard's hand in his, and caressed his knuckles with his thumb. Richard saw his lip quivering.

"Fuck," he whispered, wanting to cry. "My dear and sweet Thomas. I fear I shall never be able to leave you." Thomas looked up quickly at him.

"I beg that you do not." His features shifted, desperate as if he was putting together the pieces.

"It is not safe for you."

"I am not afraid."

"I will not risk your life, for my love."

"Your love is all I truly have to live for," Thomas said, voice intense with the thickness in this throat as he pulled Richard to him and kissed him fervently, warm mouth and hard pressure. To possess, to take, to love, to cherish. To have and to hold. Until death.

"Unhand my son!" The cry in the quiet garden was a cold shock to the system and Richard felt his heart seize in his chest as they broke their kiss to look into the angry and approaching mob of Thomas's father and brothers.

"Father—"

"You beast, you vile and contemptuous animal!" The duke yelled, enraged. Thomas stood, his back to Richard in protection, at his full height as they approached, fists and jaws tight.

"This is a disgrace!"

"How dare you—"

"What devil has possessed—" Angry voices raised in hate came at them and Thomas and Richard found themselves cowed back to the walls of the garden.

"Stop!" Richard yelled suddenly and came to stand beside Thomas and then in front of him. "It is not his fault. I—"

"What are you doing?" Thomas broke in.

"I seduced him. When he was confused. I—I used my saving him to win his affections." Richard said desperately.

"You disgusting beast—"

"Hold your tongue!" Thomas said and lunged at his brother but Richard held him back.

"A duel!" Richard shouted suddenly and the trifecta of blind hatred stopped in their tracks. They sat back and listened. "I agree to a duel," Richard begged.

"Don't be an idiot!" Thomas hissed back at him.

"I will duel for your son's honor. If you kill me, the matter will be settled."

"Fine," Thomas's father agreed.

"What? Surely not! This is madness! What happens if he kills one of you?" Thomas yelled at both ridiculous sides, fighting for his honor as if he were a damsel in distress. "No harm has been done here!"

Thomas's father stepped forward and narrowed his eyes on his son. "He duels or you are to be sent to the institution where they will right your mind." Thomas sat back. Richard's heart broke in his chest. He'd read about the treatments of the day. Basic and barbaric lobotomies that would ruin Thomas's brilliant mind, leaving him a complacent idiot with no thought of his own.

Richard pushed Thomas back. "The fault is mine. I will be there. Tomorrow morning at dawn."

"And if you die the matter is settled, and he shall marry Miss

Dougherty without further complaint." Thomas's father arched a brow, with his command.

"No!" Richard argued, getting closer to him. "If I die, then the price of his freedom has been paid and you will leave your son to his position, with or without marriage."

"And if one of us should die?" James asked, eyes narrowing. Apparently, they hadn't decided who would be fighting for the fate of their brother. But James seemed the most likely candidate.

"I would not kill my beloved's family," Richard said, voice choked. "In the event neither is harmed … You shall let me go, back home to my family. And you will continue with your lives as you would have, should I never have darkened your door. Thomas will relinquish the line to James."

Either way Thomas would win the choice. The most likely thing would be that Richard would die. He was willing. From the minute he'd jumped through the portal he'd been willing to die to save his country and to save the only man he found honorable enough, passionate enough, to make such a sacrifice for.

"No! Absolutely not, I will not allow it!" Thomas yelled.

"You have no choice!" Richard yelled back. Quieter, he pulled Thomas's face close to his, held his forehead to his. He took a deep breath. "My love. This is the fork in the road. The split-second decision and I have made my choice. You will have your freedom. My blood spilled or not."

"I will not," Thomas cried, aching. "I will never be free without your heart near mine. Richard, please. Do not do this." Thomas clenched his teeth and shook his head against Richard's.

"All will be well, my rose," Richard whispered.

"Dawn is but a few hours away. You will return to your quarters and the servants will watch your door." Thomas's father said to Richard.

"Father—" Thomas came up from his delicate moment and stood proud, strong against his father's aging frailty. "I beg that you let me duel in his stead."

"Michael, you will keep your brother in his room. Until after the sun has well past risen," The duke said to the youngest brother who nodded in compliance. "Thomas, you will do well to listen to your father and your expectations. You will consider a proposal tomorrow to Miss Dougherty, before I even bury this man. Terms of this duel or not, this society will never accept this disgraceful and godless behavior."

Before either could protest, each of Thomas's brothers nodded to their father and James withdrew a pistol, aimed at Richard. Richard lifted both hands, his heart beating like a frightened rabbit in his chest.

"That is not necessary."

"I assure you it is." Michael said, judging Richard's size.

"My own brother?" Thomas leered at James who shrugged.

"I am next in line, brother. You know where my ambitions lie."

"Not even a fraction of the man your brother is," Richard sneered at him until James pressed the cold barrel into his chest. Richard inhaled sharply and stepped back.

"A duel has been called, to shoot me before would be most dishonorable indeed," he said, cold steel in his voice that he did not feel.

"To your quarters," James commanded. Richard looked at Thomas, whose face was unreadable. From moments before, he had since donned a mask. Was it acceptance? Unable to change the fate they were both resigned to now? Had his mind and his heart been changed by the simple thought of death? Richard's heart sank. He might as well die tomorrow. Then Thomas would go on living and maybe even be more resolute in his duties to change the world. For a better one. A one where love was more important than hate. Where education ruled over ignorance. Where libraries stood stronger than churches.

"Goodnight," Richard whispered to Thomas.

"Doctor Shaw. I shall see you in the morning," Thomas's

father said before shoving his son into the manor and up the stairs.

"The field … two miles east of here. To avoid the wedding guests." Richard said to their retreating backs. Thomas's father turned with a furrowed brow before nodding. Richard hoped it didn't seem too strange a request. But if he were going to be facing death, he at least wanted it to be close to a way home. He would not falter in the face of a bullet. But if he were shot, he might be able to stumble into a chance at surviving.

35

THE DUEL

The night was long and horrible for Thomas. He banged against his locked door. He paced. He threw himself on the bed. Rolled in the sheets and scents of their love until it drove him insane and he set to pacing again. What madness was in Richard's heart that he would even suggest a thing? He'd known of artists, people in polite society who had wives but kept lovers. He ached and pined and threw bottles and bowls and shaving instruments across the floor stopping to watch as the bowl, hair and water from Richard's long-awaited shave spread across the floor.

"His father," he whispered. The man who had scarred him, the man who had hated him. Thomas thought back to the talks, the discussions all of the ways that Richard had tried to tell him, the abuse he'd suffered for loving who his heart loved. For being a man with different preferences. Thomas sat at his desk and held his head in his hands. Richard had been everything a lover and a friend should be. Gentle, reassuring, thoughtful and cautious. He'd been accepting and willing to show his scars and vulnerability. He'd been everything that Thomas had ever wanted in a partner.

And he was going to die for it.

Thomas yelled out into the darkness of his room.

No gun, no pistol, no weak-of-mind-and-body brother, who had not fought on the battlefield of anything that wasn't a resigned gentleman's game, would stop him from getting to that duel. Caging the fire of his anger into his chest and mind, Thomas started to plan how to get out of the room and to the field, in only a few short hours.

Richard thought of trying to sleep. Knowing that the brain needed rest and quiet to process and think clearly. But sleep would not come. He was heartbroken that the last few moments he'd had with Thomas had been such a painful memory for them both. He did not expect to live past tomorrow at dawn. His poor Thomas. His rose. His love.

His poor mother. Where had she been in the skewed timeline he'd left? The woman who had so bravely stood up to his abusive father and had fought for him. The woman whose name he'd taken. Passed down from the undeniably clever housemistress that had helped reunite Lillian with Matthew. Oh, how he wished he could have met Miriam. Richard shook his head. He was grasping at nostalgia and day dreaminess. His library, his books, his life that he'd left behind. How they paled compared to the weeks he'd spent, finding Thomas. Courting him, falling in love with him in a million small and beautiful moments. How he would love to see his face, one last time. Touch his cheek. Watch those blue eyes sparkle and challenge.

Richard fell to his knees, held all of his most dear memories into his heart and into his brain. Replayed the story of his life in all of its tragedy and triumph. He had lived, hadn't he? He'd fought. He'd overcome. He'd learned and earned respect, he'd loved. He'd loved. Wasn't that all a human heart could hope for at the end of their days, facing their final dawn?

"What I wouldn't give to tell you one last time," he whispered, tears wetting his bare and scarred cheeks. "I love you, Thomas. I've loved you my whole life."

Richard fell to the cold stone floor and sobbed unabashed until his body was exhausted and he fell into fitful dreams. An old woman, stood before him in a high tower. She had sharp eyes and a face that felt older than the world. In the dream, she held out a silver tube, ornate and engraved with ancient markings. Inside was a scroll, the map. Just like the one he'd stolen.

"Time is yours now."

"I buggered it all up." Richard said and pushed the map back towards her.

"You have more to do."

"I'm going to die."

She only smiled at him, as though she held a secret not yet willing to tell and nodded to the door. When Richard turned back to it, map in his hands, it opened and the bright light of morning blinded him through the tower's window.

Richard opened his eyes. It was not the bright light of dawn, but an hour before. He rose from his crumpled state and went to the water pitcher. He splashed water on his bare face. He traced over the books that Thomas had given him and opened the poetry book … read aloud the words

Let me not to the marriage of true minds
  Admit impediments; love is not love
  Which alters when it alteration finds,
  Or bends with the remover to remove.
  O no, it is an ever-fixèd mark
  That looks on tempests and is never shaken;
  It is the star to every wand'ring bark
  Whose worth's unknown, although his height be taken.
  Love's not time's fool, though rosy lips and cheeks

Within his bending sickle's compass come.
Love alters not with his brief hours and weeks,
But bears it out even to the edge of doom:
If this be error and upon me proved,
I never writ, nor no man ever loved.

Richard's hands felt warm and strange, fingertips tingling. He held his breath and removed the bent map from his rumpled coat. It practically unfolded itself and the tiny glitter of a portal from the night before had ignited to a brilliant light.

Mere inches from the very field where he was set to die in a short breadth of an hour.

Lillian did not wish to be roused. She'd had too much champagne, and had made love to her husband most of the night. She smiled, despite the headache, into her pillow. How many times they'd loved one another last night? She'd lost count but she knew her husband was naked and sprawled sideways across the bed when the knock came on their door and pulled them both up from their exhaustion. Matthew fell from the bed, landing on his naked ass. Lillian sat up and laughed. Being the more dressed, she threw on a robe and went to answer while he quickly crawled beneath the covers. She wasn't prepared to see Natalie there, tears in her eyes and so upset she could barely breathe.

"My dear Natalie, what has happened! Was it the wedding night, are you all right?" Lillian gasped. Natalie shook her head.

"It is Richard." She burst into another round of crying.

"What's happened to Richard? Where is he? Is he hurt?" Questions volleyed from her mouth and she opened the door to let Natalie in while she donned her slippers.

Matthew had heard the crying and was already nearly dressed.

"You must stop them!"

"Who?" Matthew asked.

"Papa and my brothers," she answered and Lillian's heart plummeted into her feet. They knew. They knew about Richard and Thomas. They were going to kill them.

"Where are they?"

"Thomas is locked in his room. My father and James are meeting Richard to duel in a field, not far from here. Please. I didn't know where else to turn, we have to stop them." Natalie fell to the floor in tears. Lillian straightened her shoulders and pulled the girl up from her knees.

"You take Matthew, find the spot, beg your father to reconsider. The duel will end if you are in the field."

"What will you do?" Matthew asked, donning his jacket and taking up his medical bag from the foot of the bed.

Lillian took her robe off, adjusted the chemise nightgown and tied her hair up into a messy bun of sensual curls. "I'm going to go free Thomas." Matthew looked at her sideways.

"How?"

"A woman never divulges her secrets." She pecked him on the cheek and shooed them both down the hallway. She went the opposite direction. Towards the locked and guarded door of Richard's beloved.

When she arrived, the younger brother, Michael, was standing still and poised, listening without feeling or flinching to the man yelling and kicking the door from inside. Lillian saw the wood shake as she approached, biting her lip.

"What are you doing here? It is not proper for a married woman to—"

Lillian pressed her finger to his lips.

"Shhh ... I saw you and your brother watching me last night," she said softly and stared at his lips. Michael, not used to a scandalously dressed woman leaning in so close to him, wavered before he straightened his spine.

"You should not be here."

"Oh, I make it a habit to be wherever I want," she winked and the door shook again. "What is going on in there? He seems mad." Lillian looked over Michael's shoulder and pressed her full breast to his arm. Michael fumbled away from the door.

"Madam, please."

"You can call me Lillian, Michael, we're practically old friends now." She pressed closer and could feel the young man shake. His body heat rose, his eyes dilated, he stared down at her breasts. The moment of distraction was just enough for her to reach around his body and unlock the door, as she smiled up at him.

Thomas burst through the door, confused and looking at the situation. Michael fell backwards, and his pistol rattled across the floor. He was flushed and too confused to understand what had happened.

"My lady?" Thomas huffed with a nod. Lillian picked up the gun and pointed it at Michael who backed away, his hands held out. Thomas took his belt and tied Michael's hands together behind his back.

"Pity you never served, Michael. The skills you would have acquired could have kept this very thing from happening." Thomas tsked his tongue and pushed him back into the room, locking the door. Lillian waved the gun at him.

"Take the gun. We must go. We don't have much time," she told Thomas, straightened her robe back over her shoulders and looked back at the closed door.

"I must thank you for your—ample distraction," Thomas smiled as they ran down the hallway.

"It was not difficult. Some men are too easily swayed by a couple of handfuls of flesh. Idiots."

"Richard was right, you are an astounding woman." Thomas smiled over his shoulder at her and Lillian urged him on, hope driving her heart, that they would not be too late. They ran in earnest towards the field. Lillian hiked her skirts up to Thomas's great delight and made it nearly a competition.

"I did not know the lady could move so quickly."

"Four years all state," Lillian said, as if on cue but blushed and shut her mouth. "I am fond of running. Make haste, my lord, Natalie saw them leaving minutes before I could emancipate you."

They took off, across the field in the very earliest light, the sun not yet risen. The dew on the tall grass brushed against them and clung to their legs with a cold chill. Not as cold as the chill in Thomas's heart. Why would his legs not work faster? Why had he not escaped sooner? They could be across the county by now if he had only gotten out and taken Richard by horseback to some place far and distant. He would have hated that, Thomas thought with a smile. Escaping on the detestable back of a beast like that. They turned around the large grove of trees and made a mad dash towards the end of the grove where the distant figures of his brothers and Richard could be seen.

"We must be cautious my lord. If they see us, they may shoot him on sight," Lillian said.

"Certainly not."

"I know not the character of your family," Lillian admitted as they hunkered down and got closer. Thomas snuck after her, hiding along the tree line as they came nearer.

"You may have a point," he said lowly. After all, wouldn't a family who loved you show some degree of mercy? Not his. He nearly cried. What would they do once he saved Richard? Where could they possibly go where hate and condemnation would not follow them? He must keep Richard alive. At all costs. There was no purpose to his life, without him. When Lillian stopped him, behind a tall tree, she pressed her finger to her lips for silence. He heard Richard's soft voice, his favorite over every other sound on earth.

"He is my heart. If I cannot be with him, I would rather you put me in the ground." Richard had said.

Thomas made to show himself but Lillian held him back.

"It looks as though James's heart is turned. I see him faltering. He will not fire. When the shooting is done, we will claim him back," she reassured.

Thomas moved to intercede again, but she tugged him down into the tall grass. "If anything should happen to him, I will never forgive myself. But if you were somehow hurt, Richard would never forgive me."

"Kindly unhand me! I cannot take that risk!"

"Look!" Lillian pointed to where James was lifting his pistol to the air, just as Richard was, in the last instant when the shots were fired.

Thomas's heart swung from maddening happiness to despair at his father's next action. Having both shots wasted, he prepared one of his own. Thomas did not think. His feet carried his heart where it knew it needed to be. Next to Richard. If they were to kill his love, then he would be put in the ground next to him.

36

THE SHOT THAT RANG THROUGH TIME

Richard was led through the grounds and out to the field. Every chance he could, he looked for the portal. The map indicated it was close to a bend in a sizeable tributary, strong enough to be denoted by rough lines on the map. Just within the shade of a small grove of trees, he could hear the rush of it as they walked. He saw a short stone fence that seemed to follow the path to where he intended to either lose his life or escape to some new time, probably to be lost to the fate of the cosmos for the rest of his existence. James and Thomas's father escorted him.

"Should there not be a doctor with us?"

"If this were a proper duel," James said behind him. Richard detected a wavering, an uncertainty ... perhaps even coming to terms with an act that was indeed nefarious. This was not a proper duel. And a man of any honor would know that. Shivers rolled up Richard's back. They could very well kill him, unarmed, as soon as the place was reached. How had Thomas turned out so well and brave? He thought it must have more to do with his mother and sister, or possibly even his grandmother. He wished he knew more about Thomas, about his childhood, about what he would do if given another life. Richard wished he could see Thomas one last time.

He wished he could hold his face in his hands, run his fingers through his curls. Kiss him softly, assure him that he would be fine, that he would live, defiantly and spoiled, even without Richard in his life. The map felt hot against his heart. Pulling and leading against his skin. Richard looked up and saw a strange arched doorway in the fence, just beyond the tree line. It seemed to shimmer as he watched it on their way to the open space of the field beyond the grove. The steady sound of the rushing river grew louder.

"Here will do," The duke said and cleared his throat. Richard turned. Expecting pistols drawn already on him, expecting to hear the booming roar just before his life was cut short. But James merely studied him and opened the ornate wooden box his father had carried. Inside were two revolvers. Richard hadn't the slightest idea how to even load it. It didn't matter. He had no intention of killing James. Tyrannical brother, scheming to replace Thomas or not, he was still family and he would not have that on his hands. Richard took one and James took the other.

Watching carefully, Richard tried to emulate what James did with his, first the powder, then the cloth, then the ball … tamping it down. The duke inspected both. It was then that Richard saw a third revolver at the duke's belt. He stared at the gun, took in a deep breath, and nodded his head.

"Before we begin," he said, gun pointed down at the ground. "You must know that your son, Thomas, is a good and brave man. He is wise, and compassionate and will make the greatest leader this country has ever seen. You must know that whatever level of depravity you think me capable of, the truth is that I love him. I love your son. Wholeheartedly and purely."

"Stop!" The duke commanded.

"I will not. I love him to the depths my soul can reach. I love him in every quiet moment and through all the blood and loss of battle. He is my heart. And if I cannot be with him, I would rather you put me in the ground." Richard's eyes filled with tears. James hesitated, the gun faltering at his side. His eyes turned soft and he shook his head.

"Father, surely there is another—"

"Enough. Back-to-back you go," The duke growled, unable to look Richard in the eyes. As they paused before pacing, James spoke over his shoulder.

"I am sorry, Richard. I am sorry for this."

"I will not blame you, James. Please see that he is taken care of."

"I will."

"Begin!" The duke barked, and twenty paces were called. Richard counted each one. In each one he thought of the steps he'd taken to be here. He thought of his mother. His brothers. His own father. Dear Lillian and what it was to hold true love. The babies he hoped she and Matthew would have. He thought of Thomas most of all, in those last three steps.

"Let him be safe," he whispered. *Eighteen*. "Let him be loved." *Nineteen*. "Let him live." *Twenty*. Richard breathed the prayer, and the gateway of stone mere paces from where he now stood started to vibrate and glow.

"Turn!" The voice called. Richard turned, saw James across the field his shoulders less square, his countenance less severe. "Draw!"

Richard pointed his gun to the sky. James pointed at Richard's heart. The moment the duke barked "Fire!" Richard anticipated the searing pain in his already wounded chest. This time on mark. This time, the end. He fired the revolver into the sky, and it kicked brutally in his hand, almost making him think that was the hit of James' bullet. When he looked past the cloud of smoke, he saw that James' hand was also in the air. A small smile rested on his face.

"No! You buffoon!" The duke yelled and Richard turned to see him reaching for his pistol. Richard turned to run towards the portal and the gun shot rang out before he could reach it. But the bullet didn't hit him.

A body did. Startled and confused, all the air released in a whoosh from his lungs, Richard struggled beneath the familiar smell and weight of Thomas in his arms. Where had he come from?

"Thomas!" Richard cried.

"No!" The duke's surprised anger lifted up from the field and the world seemed to pause. Richard sat up, expecting Thomas to scramble to his feet.

But he did not move.

"Thomas?" Richard tried to lift him. "My love, Thomas, please you must get up." Richard rolled him over to find the bullet disappeared into his chest and a deep stain of red soaking through his white shirt. Fear ripped through Richard and his body filled with the sharp sting of adrenaline. "No!" he bellowed and rose from the ground to touch Thomas's face with his blood-smeared hand. "No!" His body convulsed with tears and heat, and suddenly Lillian and Matthew were beside him, Matthew checking his neck, his nose, for signs of life.

"It is weak, his heartbeat. And he still has breath, however, I cannot know if he will make it back to the house." Richard rose with fire in his veins. He would kill the man. He would bash his head in with his bare hands. He would die making sure the duke never saw the rest of history play out. He would—

"Richard—" with a weak protest and an outstretched hand, Thomas called him back. Richard knelt down and picked Thomas up in his arms. Matthew protested.

"Jesus Christ, you shouldn't move him!" Lillian gasped.

"See to it that we are not followed," Richard growled as the two men now approached them and Michael approached from farther away. All faces held expressions of horror as to where the bullet had landed.

"What are you going to do? Where will you go?" Lillian gasped. "Richard, he needs help!"

"I know," Richard looked down at Lillian. "I know." He kissed her forehead and bolted, strong legs pumping, body and muscles on fire as he ran, head long, into the gated portal. Not knowing if he would simply end up on the other side of the fence, or would accidentally launch them both, headlong into the river. Maybe fate would be kind. He heard Lillian calling his name but had nothing left behind him to live for. All he had was in his arms, dying.

He put his faith in the universe and jumped through.

Lillian watched them disappear straight into the portal, and not reemerge on the other side. She stared in horror and moved to follow but Matthew held her hand.

"Stop!" he said suddenly, one hand on his bag, one on her wrist. "We don't know where it has taken them."

"I can't just let him go through alone! What if they end up someplace without doctors? The dark ages? What if they are all alone? What if he dies?"

"I cannot lose you again!" Matthew yelled suddenly.

"Then come with me," she said softly and took his hand.

"Lillian we are safe here. We know where we are and we are together. We have to have faith that they are also where they need to be. The universe brought you back to me to right the wrong. We have to believe it has done the same for them."

"But, I don't want him to go!" Lillian said and started to cry. Natalie and the rest of his family came up behind them. They stared at the surging river beyond the gate.

"What's happened, where did he take my son?" the duke demanded.

"You shot Thomas!" Natalie yelled and pushed him, nearly

knocking the duke to the ground. "You shot my brother! Your own son!" The duke's look of horror was unparalleled, and both the brothers took steps away from him.

"For whatever wrong they might have done in your eyes, Richard held his pistol to the sky. He did not aim at you or James. He was honorable. You shot him, unarmed after the rules of the duel were laid out. You have dishonored our family!" Natalie said, eyes fierce and mouth set in defiance. The duke's anger drove him to recoil his hand in preparation to strike her. Matthew grabbed it midair, stopping him and Lillian stepped in between them, shielding the young woman.

"You would strike your daughter and kill your own son?" Lillian seethed. "You do not deserve your title sir. I suggest you take a look inside your soul. Or I will hold court with the King and tell him what you have done."

The color drained from the duke's face and he took his hand back to stumble away from the group. James and Michael went to the gate and walked through, only reaching the other side where the river ran steadily. They both stared after its murky and surging course. The severity of their actions, and the loss of their brother seemed to sit heavy on their shoulders.

"They were together," Michael said softly. James only nodded.

Lillian held on to Natalie as she poured her grief into tears and clung to her. Matthew held them both. The grove was dark and the world less light a place. Lillian wondered why anyone would even consider bringing a child into this place. A world so full of hate, so full of the haves and the have nots. A world that took centuries to change into something even remotely better.

"How do we ever build a world that does not take beautiful things?" Lillian said as she stared at the river and started to sob.

"We begin today," Natalie answered with strength in her voice. "We build it together. My brother's death," she paused to sniff, "dear Richard's death, will not be in vain." Natalie pulled herself from Lillian's arms and stood tall, following her brothers through the gate and standing before them.

"We have work to do. Work he will never complete. Every wish that Thomas had brought up, every paper he had written, every suggestion that he'd crafted to be set before parliament, we will bring forward." Both brothers looked at one another and back to her. That she, the smallest, the 'weakest' in society should be the one taking the reins and not allow the honor of their family or her brother's purpose die and be swept down a river, was a refreshing surprise.

James and Michael nodded. Matthew took Lillian's hand.

"I hope they made it through to somewhere safe," Matthew whispered.

"So do I," she said and sunk into his chest, feeling every sad and hopeful emotion overtake her. "Let's go home."

37

SERENDIPITY SHINES ON THE WORTHY

That Richard should have crossed over, into the parking garage of the Marlborough Provincial Hospital was more than he could have hoped for. That the head cardiologist was in attendance and bored in his office, having had a surgery canceled that very hour, was serendipitous. That the duke's bullet was lodged into the wall of Thomas's heart rather than torn through, because it had been slowed down by the angle he took when tackling Richard, was beyond lucky. That the year they came through was the same, and only three weeks later than the date Richard had left, was heartening. That the world appeared to be healed from its apocalyptic turn was a great relief.

The surgery had lasted three hours. Richard called his mother while he waited. Everything appeared to be normal, minus the small detail of him kidnapping a man from a different time. The police had questioned him and Richard had given them a story of a mugging gone wrong, on their way back from an event. When asked if he knew where the criminal had fled, Richard could only shake his head.

"I only know that he is long gone, sir."

When the doctor came out to a very dirty, very oddly dressed

Richard covered in his partner's blood and sobbing, he shook his head and handed over the plastic cup containing a lead bullet to the police. They stared at it just as disbelieving.

"I don't know what kind of antiquated firearm was used, but that slug is probably over a hundred years old."

Richard tried to feign disbelief, knowing it was closer to two hundred years old. The police thanked Richard for his time, handed him a card and left. The cardiologist waited until they were gone.

"And who is the young man? We were in such a rush to get him into surgery I wasn't told."

"Thomas, Thomas Alexander of Marl—" Richard had stopped mid-name. He looked at the hospital crest on the doctor's coat. "My um … my fiancé." The doctor nodded. "I believe his wallet was taken in the altercation." Richard said tiredly. He reached into the satchel but realized he had no wallet himself. "I have also lost my wallet, unfortunately, though if you allow me a call to my bank, I can—"

"No need to worry. He's a British citizen, this is an emergency. We're not like those barbarians across the pond." The doctor laughed. "He should be out of surgery and back into the recovery room as soon as we close him up. I don't know how long it will take him to regain consciousness. He lost a great deal of blood." The doctor stared at where the police had disappeared with the evidence. "That's a nasty and rather odd-looking bullet. Are you certain you didn't see the firearm?"

"It all happened so fast," Richard said and shook his head.

"Well, no matter. It's out now and will cause him no further trouble."

"Thank you, from the bottom of my heart. Thank you," Richard breathed. The doctor shook his hand and left. Richard stared at the bloodied cuffs of his shirt. His country was seemingly the same. No revolt when he'd mentioned that

Thomas was his intended. The system that cared even for a stranger out of time.

How he'd explain it all to Thomas, he wasn't sure. He had some time to think. But for now, he had a few calls to make. When they brought Thomas into the ICU, he was on oxygen and unresponsive. Richard remained by his bedside.

His mother came up from Bournemouth and kept vigil with him. Richard told her they'd met while he was on sabbatical in Wales. And had fallen in love nearly instantly, once he'd gotten over Thomas's spoiled ways. Even Richard's brothers had come to see him. Richard had the doctors look at his own stitches and they shook their heads at the poor and puckering scars. They asked to have an MRI of the wound, out of sheer curiosity. Richard obliged while his mother stayed with Thomas. The medical staff was in shock at how close to dying he'd come, not once but twice.

"You two are quite the pair."

"I think, at least I hope, our adventuring days are over," Richard smiled up at the doctor and put on a clean and pressed shirt. His mother was holding Thomas's hand when he'd returned. She was telling the comatose Thomas how special her son was and how she hoped that he was, indeed, the one he'd waited for. The one he deserved.

Richard's brothers had brought him clothes and, at his request, had brought some in Thomas's size as well. The style from when he'd left was unchanged. Perhaps this is what the universe had wanted after all. For him to bring Thomas back. He wondered if Lillian, or Matthew, or even Natalie had had anything to do with the way the world began working in harmony again. He'd have to do more research as soon as Thomas was well again.

He would get well again. Richard couldn't allow himself believe that Thomas would not recover. He would not survive if Thomas died. As he sat by his side, he answered emails and called the administration at the university to explain that his long absence was due to an in-depth study of the Regency era and a phenomenal paper was soon to be published. It wasn't a total lie. Perhaps Thomas would help him write it.

They agreed to approve his "sabbatical" for another month. Especially since they wanted him back. No one else ran the library quite like Doctor Shaw. He missed Lillian fiercely and vowed that as soon as Thomas was well, *please, God let him come out of this*, that he'd research the entire history of the timeline they'd escaped. He hoped he'd find lots of blushing babes in her family tree. All of the love and all of the light that they deserved.

Three days passed. Then four. Thomas was beginning to look gaunt. What he wouldn't give to bring him back to life. What he wouldn't give to ease him into this new and peculiar world. When he asked the doctors what more could be done, they said he needed something worth fighting for.

So Richard began to read to him. Every hour, every day. Until his beard had grown back and his mother had to return to work. In that time, the hospital was filled with well wishes from his coworkers and the nurses who had fallen in love with the devotion and attention with which Richard took care of Thomas. In fact, they all loved to pause, mid shift and sit outside of the hospital door to listen to the lion reading to his love.

Until one day, in the midst of Shakespeare's 14th sonnet, Thomas woke up.

A STRANGE AND BEAUTIFUL WORLD

The world was loud and bright.

And Thomas was confused. He heard so many sounds he didn't know which to focus on. He'd been hearing Richard's voice, reading to him. He'd thought they were in the carriage, rocking back and forth and they were on the road away from his father. But Richard's voice faded and the only sound Thomas could hear now was the incessant bleating and beeping as if a large bird was sitting beside his bed. His eyes were heavy and his body felt like weighted lead. Richard, poor Richard. Had he saved him in time? Where was he?

"Richard," he tried to say but his voice cracked and crumbled like dry leaves in the dead of winter. He opened one eye but the light was blinding. Were they in the field still? It must be midday. Unless—unless he'd died. "Richard," he cried softly aching in his chest, his arms, in every muscle.

"I'm here," the soft voice came like rain to a dry field, like soft snow on Christmas morning, like the trickle of a river over rocks. Of all of Thomas's favorite sounds, Richard's voice was paramount. "I'm here." Richard said again and Thomas felt his hand being taken. "Can we dim the lights please?" Richard asked and the daylight lessened, became a soft and gray glow. Leave it to this man to have such a power. Thomas heard music. Gentle beeping, ticking, the soft whoosh of air, like some giant breathing. He opened one eye. Everything was fuzzy.

Including Richard's face, when it came into focus, concerned and looking down at him, in strange glasses, concern in his golden-brown eyes.

"How did you grow it back so fast? I had such plans for those smooth cheeks," Thomas wheezed, as he reached a heavy arm out to touch him. Richard held his hand to the soft beard that was only now just growing in, and kissed his palm. "Why does every limb feel like a rock?"

"You've been asleep for many days."

"Asleep? Impossible. It was just this morning I found you in the field."

"Oh you found me, you did," Richard's brow furrowed and he leaned in. "You're a right idiot you know, jumping in front of that bullet. We had an agreement that you needed to live."

"What is my life if you are dead?" Thomas said.

"You shouldn't have."

"But I did. Because I love you. And I never wish to be parted from you. In life or death." Thomas whispered and Richard pressed his forehead to his. "Are we dead? Why does it feel so strange here?"

"I have so much to tell you."

It was not as difficult a conversation as Richard had thought it would be. In soft and low tones, with Thomas's hand in his own, and after calming him down to the new and strange world around him, Richard told him everything. From the moment he'd seen and met a young girl in his library who did not belong in that time, to the love story of the doctor and his Lillian, to the search they embarked on to get her back to Matthew. He told

Thomas of the strange and secret society of Timekeepers, what little he knew, and the map of portals he'd stolen. Richard let Thomas look it over.

He spoke very little but listened intensely. Especially when Richard confessed that he'd been a student of the history of Thomas's life. That he'd looked up to him for a long while.

"You'd read about me?"

"You were quite the amazing man. You shaped the country." Thomas blushed and looked down at the map, quiet and unlit. "When you'd decided to die, and the doctor was not there to save you, it changed everything. Our country was in ruins. There were no social systems. No compassion. Violence abounded."

"But I am a soldier. A man of violence."

Richard looked at him, lifted his hand to his lips. "You are a man of love, of good judgement, of poetry as well as those things."

"So you just intentionally threw yourself through time, risking death and the destruction of history, just to save me?"

Richard shrugged and lifted his eyebrows. "To not let lies exist between us, I came back in hopes of finding Matthew and dragging him to the battle where you were wounded." Thomas chuckled at this and they both laughed until Thomas grasped at his chest and Richard quieted, worried over him. Thomas shook his head.

"I am alright. Only mad that I'm attached more to machines than to you," he said softly, eyes brighter than they'd been. "So then—you—"

"Saw you on the battlefield and made rash and ridiculous decisions."

"*You must live.* That's what you'd said to me. I thought it so strange when I was so intent on killing myself."

"I would have taken a thousand spears," Richard said, eyes filling with tears as he gently caressed each knuckle on Thomas's hand and turned it over to kiss his palm. Thomas shivered and clenched his hand around Richard's. "I wish you had not taken a bullet for me," Richard shook his head and sobbed.

"Perhaps now you understand," Thomas said, and pulled Richard up from his chair. He scooted over in the small hospital bed and beckoned him to lay down. "What it was that my own heart went through when I saw you in that bloody room. What I felt when I saw you, gun pointed skyward." Richard nestled in, pressing Thomas's body close to his. The warmth and breath between them was a universe of longing and hesitant relief.

"My love," Richard said softly and kissed his forehead. "When you are healed, I long to show you a lifetime of how much I understand. I will forever work to earn your heart." Richard said and Thomas made a small, frustrated grunt, his hand holding on to Richard's thigh.

"We must be careful," he said and looked up at Richard, nuzzling under his chin.

"We need not be," Richard said softly and tilted his face up to catch his lips in a soft kiss. Thomas stared at him quizzically.

"But we are—"

"Free ... here we are free, Thomas. To love. To marry. To adopt children to ... live our lives far from fear. Well, farther from it."

Thomas pulled away to look at him, both of them misty in eyes. Thomas shook his head.

"How can this be?"

"Because someone, a long time ago, decided that love was the cornerstone of life. As it should be." Richard leaned down and softly kissed him. There was a small gasp and they both looked quickly to the door. One of the nurses blushed and brought in a huge bouquet of flowers.

"I'm so sorry to interrupt, I wanted to drop these off. Oh, my god, I'm so happy you're awake. He's missed you so! You're just— the most beautiful couple," she said and gently touched Thomas's shoulder.

"Thank you, Geraldine," Richard said and smiled.

"You are going to invite us to the wedding, right?" she said, a sassy tilt to her hips.

"Wedding?" Thomas looked at Richard and Geraldine smiled with a wink before leaving.

"As accepting as they are, they still require that you be in … some sort of committed relationship before you're allowed to visit someone in such a serious condition as you were, so I told them that you were my—fiancé."

"Fiancé?"

"Betrothed?" Richard shied away, unsure if Thomas was angry.

"You mean we are to be married? You—but you—You haven't even asked me properly!" he laughed and shoved Richard out of the bed. "Or is it that I that I am meant to ask you?"

"As you wish it, my lord."

"Let us ask each other," Thomas whispered. Richard left to find something in his jacket pocket before coming back to the bed. To his duke. His rose. He was giddy with joy and his heart pattered anxiously in his chest.

God, how he would love and worship this man. Feed him and care for him, and find him enjoyable employment, and warm his bed. How they would talk, and read, and argue, and pout, and make up for it all. He wished to find the world together, anew. Just outside their door, the entire staff of the cardiac unit waited, bated breath and listening. Richard climbed back into bed with Thomas, and opened the small box with his shaking hands.

"Thomas Alexander, past future Duke of Marlborough, Captain in his majesty's royal army, I know you have your choice of partners, being of fair looks and deliciously built."

"Oh, Doctor Shaw, please. Brevity," Thomas said, starting to kiss his neck tenderly and working up towards his jaw.

"Wilst thou make of me the happiest soul alive? And be my husband?" Richard said, his eyes closed to the tender and sweet touch, from a man who he would devote his life to keeping strong. Thomas took the box and looked at the silver ring, embossed with a beautiful rose and a sapphire in the center. Thomas gasped.

"You could not keep me from it. But only if, Doctor Richard Shaw, keeper of books and reader of poetry, man of many talents, brute with a club, and beast in the bedsheets—"

"Brevity!" Richard howled with laughter before kissing Thomas quiet and slipping the ring on his finger.

"Will you heal my heart in complete and say you'll be my beloved husband. Promise me adventure and poetry. Reading and quiet nights, until we two leave this world better than we found it."

Richard took in a deep breath, kissed Thomas's warm lips with his own, shaking in the tears of happiness. "I will. I will."

"I love you, Richard."

"You are my heart, Thomas."

The eruption of applause and joyous merriment from outside the room startled them and both heads turned to see a procession of nurses and doctors, flowers and balloons and even champagne come through to celebrate.

FOUR YEARS LATER ...

The Sunday morning sun was slow to rise, as if it wanted to give the lovers a few more moments before it woke the world. And by the world it meant the sweet sleeping baby nestled into the crib in their room.

Rolling over in his sleep, Richard snuggled and spooned Thomas into his arms with a tender growl. His body reacted, and Thomas moved seductively against the growing hardness between them.

"Morning, my lion," Thomas yawned and reached his hand back to caress Richard's stubble. He'd not been keeping a beard lately, and Thomas hoped it was on account of him finally accepting his past and all of the scars that came with it. Richard grumbled, slid his hard member between Thomas's legs and bit at his shoulder.

The sound from across the room caused them both to pause.

"The cub awakes," Thomas whispered and smiled over his shoulder to his husband before caressing his jaw. Richard faked a cry into Thomas's bare back.

"I cannot wait until nap time." He kissed Thomas sweetly and rose to check on the cherub girl, now cooing softly for her daddies.

"You love every minute with Natalie," Thomas also rose and put on a t-shirt, coming to stand beside the crib to watch as their beautiful baby girl kicked her legs and smiled up at her fathers. She threw out her tiny arms in a stretch and made happy gurgles, as she turned over to push herself up. Using the crib, she stood and held out her hands, making grabbing motions to be picked up.

"Oh my heart," Richard said and lifted her into his strong arms. He snuggled her close. "Miss Natalie Lillian Shaw, you are a charmer."

"She gets that from me, you know," Thomas smiled and kissed her cheek to her giggling delight before kissing Richard.

"I am a lucky man, indeed." Richard said softly and cupped Thomas's cheek. "How could I deserve such happiness?"

"Because you were brave enough to throw yourself into danger."

"For love," Richard whispered and kissed him sweetly.

"For love," Thomas said and embraced them both.

In the soft morning light, they began their day. Where a market, naps and reading on the couch, a lifetime of love, and school plays, and laughter spread out before them, each in the exact time and place it was destined to be. A place at peace in each other's arms. Trials and hardships not so hard as bayonets to the heart, or the thought of living even a moment without the other. Everything survivable. Everything attainable.

For love. Because love ...

Love is not love that alters when it alteration finds.
  Love does not bend with the remover to remove.
  It is an ever fixed mark, that looks on tempests and is never shaken.
  It is the star to every wandering soul, on earth, and through time.

THREE YEARS AFTER THAT ...

"This cannot be right," Richard said, sifting through the documents he'd brought home from work. They'd been on loan from a library in Cairo, and he'd been working the last five years to follow the scant trail of Lillian and Matthew Blackwell, that seemed to ebb and flow, until it disappeared somewhere in Egypt.

"What?" Thomas said, around a bite of toast and avocado that he was sharing with Natalie. She was spreading it meticulously across her tray table, in giant arcs. "She will be the next Rembrandt, of that I'm sure."

"Let us hope for Monet or Van Gogh."

"But with both of her lovely ears intact," Thomas smiled and gently tugged on one, causing Natalie to giggle, avocado now smeared in her hair. "What is it you've found?"

"It says here that Lillian—" Richard stopped, covered his mouth.

"What? What on earth has happened to her?"

"She—" Richard sobbed and Thomas dropped his toast to take him into his arms, kneeling at his side and taking both hands in his.

"Whatever it is—"

"She dies. At the hands of her husband, Matthew Blackwell."

"Impossible," Thomas breathed and sat up to take the copied files in his own hands and bringing them to the light of the kitchen window.

"I don't understand. How on earth can this be?"

"It can't. We can't allow it." Richard said and stood. Thomas shook his head.

"My lion, we must be calm and rational. There is very little we can—" But Richard was already moving towards the kitchen drawers, searching through them and stopping at the linen drawer, where beneath the baby burp rags and flour sack dish cloths, was a neatly folded piece of parchment.

"What are you doing with that? You told me you got rid of it!" Thomas said.

"I couldn't risk it falling into someone else's hands," Richard said indignantly.

"We are not taking our child through a portal!"

"I just want to see!"

"Richard—" Thomas's tone was warning.

"Daddy!" Natalie's tone matched Thomas's before she laughed uproariously.

"We cannot let Lillian die, and I cannot believe that Matthew would do such a thing. Please, my rose." Richard whispered. When those beautiful eyes asked Thomas for something, using his pet name, he could rarely refuse. When Richard's eyes filled with tears, his argument was over. They were going to have to do something about it.

"Fine, but we go together. All of us." Thomas said, a serious scowl.

RATE AND REVIEW

We hope you enjoyed *Courting the Lion* by S.E. Reichert. If you did, we would ask that you please rate and review this title. Every review helps our authors.

Rate and Review: Courting the Lion

MEET THE AUTHOR

S.E. Reichert (Sarah Reichert) is a hopeless romantic, novelist, poet, and wanderer. She has eight novels published with 5 Prince Publishing, and a few more on the way. She's been writing since she was eleven, and the illusion and folly of it has yet to fade. She is the Director of a small, struggling, but big-hearted writing group (Writing Heights Writers Association) whose sole purpose is to encourage, educate, and support writers of all levels in all genres throughout their journey. She is a mom, an introvert, a lover of solitude and the woods, and a poet forever at heart.

OTHER TITLES FROM

5 PRINCE PUBLISHING

www.5princebooks.com
Courting the Lion *S.E. Reichert*
Come to the Cape *Emi Hilton*
Time To Byrne *S.E. Reichert*
Bookish *Bernadette Marie*
Dare You to Choose Truth *Lauren Lipp*
Enlightenment *Nicole Kelley*
All the Little Moments *Savannah Reed*
The Rocking of the Ocean *Barbara Matteson*
New to Newport *Emi Hilton*
Trusting the Alpha *Courtney Davis*
Sweet Summertide *Sarah Dressler*
No Words After I Love You *S.E. Reichert*
Demons and Tea Leaves *Courtney Davis*
Shadow of the Throne *Russell Archey*
Shadow Among the Stars *Courtney Davis*
The Pack *E.C. Saulness*
Keeping Kama *Emi Hilton*
A Winter's Wedding *Sarah Dressler*
Trimutant *April Marcom*